When the Mountain Crumbled

A DAY TO REMEMBER

When the Mountain Crumbled

ANGELA K COUCH

BARBOUR
PUBLISHING

When the Mountain Crumbled © 2024 by Angela K Couch

Print ISBN 978-1-63609-922-4
Adobe Digital Edition (.epub) 978-1-63609-923-1

All scripture quotations, unless otherwise noted, are taken from the King James Version of the Bible.

This book is a work of fiction. Names, characters, places, and incidents are either products of the author's imagination or used fictitiously. Any similarity to actual people, organizations, and/or events is purely coincidental.

Published by Barbour Publishing, Inc., 1810 Barbour Drive, Uhrichsville, Ohio 44683, www.barbourbooks.com

Our mission is to inspire the world with the life-changing message of the Bible.

 Member of the
Evangelical Christian
Publishers Association

Printed in the United States of America

DEDICATION

To Jonathan – you are a mountain of strength in my life. Thank you for not faltering or crumbling under life's pressures.

ACKNOWLEDGEMENTS

I have been blessed with a wonderful family and community who have made this book possible. A huge thanks to my husband, who not only supported me in my writing and made sure I had time but was the brave soul who edited my rough draft! To my kids who put up with me when I'm on a deadline, including baby Evelyn who joined our family in the middle of writing this. To the Cardston Scribblers for talking shop and offering encouragement and advice. To my editors at Barbour who believed in me and helped bring this story to life. To God, who fills in where I lack and gave me the story to write.

Chapter 1

WESTERN CANADA
APRIL 28, 1903

Looming shadows stretched across the schoolroom, but the coldness seeping into Samantha Ingles' bones had nothing to do with the cool mountain air sweeping through the open window from the snow-crested peaks of Turtle Mountain and its confederates. No, it was the confrontation looming ahead—one impossible to avoid. . .only to delay. Samantha slid the window down with more force than intended, and the thin pane shuddered in its casing.

Yes, a delay was in order.

After pinning her hat in place—a small, pathetic thing, really, but she hardly cared—and buttoning her wool jacket, Samantha picked up the novel perched on the edge of her desk. With the book tucked under her arm, she shouldered her satchel filled with handwriting samples to be reviewed that evening and straightened desks and slates as she trekked to the door of the large schoolroom—*her* schoolroom. Satisfaction momentarily dispelled the stress of the day. She had come west on her own and was building a life here, one she could be proud of, one that would have a lasting impact on young lives.

Mother and Father would be proud. Wouldn't they?

Doubt tightened like a knot in her chest. Father, perhaps, would like that his daughter was industrious and not squandering his wealth. Mother... She wasn't here, so there was no point in dwelling on how she would feel about Samantha's age, marital status, or disregard for the latest fashions. There was nothing wrong with being a schoolteacher, and one on the frontier had little need for flounces.

Samantha pushed her spectacles higher on her nose and stooped to pick a scrap of paper from under one of the desks. Once she'd unfolded the crumpled sheet, a cartoonish image glared back at her with beady eyes and slanted eyebrows. The small nose was a sharply angled L in the middle of a long face with pointed chin. She had to admit Albert Clark was a gifted artist, even if she didn't appreciate his current depiction. Her chin wasn't that pointed.

Depositing the paper into the fireplace to be used as kindling the next morning, Samantha steeled herself against wondering how some people might see her. Boys were known for being cruel and not liking school, so the drawing could not be taken as a personal affront. Though she couldn't imagine the same being the case with the other schoolteacher, Miss Fredricks. She was too pretty and friendly and young. The girl was barely out of the schoolroom herself.

The building seemed so quiet after the hustle and noise of a school day, but Samantha peeked her head in the second schoolroom, where the younger children met. No sign of Miss Fredricks, so it was probably safe to lock the main doors for the night.

As a bustling mining town nestled in the Crowsnest Pass—the gate to the Canadian Rockies—Frank's streets were teeming with folks who had come to work the mines and to cater to those workers. A handful of hotels, a bank, shops and mercantile, liveries, and everything a body might need had sprung up over the past three years, so she'd been told. Samantha was a newer arrival, having been hired at the beginning of the year when the population of children had grown too large for one teacher to handle.

Even still, for a population of about six hundred, there was a decided lack of single women in this town. The simple walk to the boardinghouse had her face heating from the glances of the opposite sex. Though thankfully none lingered—another reason to keep her current fashion. The town was filled with unmarried men and more attention than Samantha had ever experienced in the east.

Oh, the relief to slip into McClurg's Boardinghouse—the kitchen, as the house itself catered to the ever-constant influx of miners. Samantha's student was easily sighted and saw her in return, eyes brightening.

"Miss Ingles!" Lillian Clark finished with the last of the plates, topping the large stack on the counter, and hurried across the busy room Mrs. McClurg was already prepping for the dinner hour. The room smelled like heaven, but eating at the boardinghouse was an extravagance she did not require. Not when it meant sharing a dining room filled with men.

Though...today it might be worth it to stave off confrontation a little while longer and perhaps some indigestion.

"I'm sorry I missed school again. I was asked to stay for an extra shift." Lillian's blue eyes widened with her apology.

"So your brother informed me this morning." Samantha couldn't keep the frustration from her tone. The girl was intelligent and craved learning. It was wrong for her education to be forfeited for a few extra dollars at the end of the month. Learning was worth the sacrifice. What future did the sixteen-year-old have if she slaved her days away serving in a boardinghouse? Other than marriage so she could continue to slave away for her husband and children.

"Is that for me?"

Samantha extended *Great Expectations*, which was eagerly snatched from her hands. "Of course."

"Thank you! I will take care of it and return it as soon as I am able." A smile stretched across Lillian's face. "I work late, so Mama insisted I spend the night here and not walk home after dark. This will make being away from home for the first time bearable."

"Lillian, it's time to set the tables," her employer called from the other side of the kitchen.

"Sorry," the girl whispered, tucking the book into her apron as she turned to leave. "And thank you!"

Samantha gave a polite nod to Mrs. McClurg and slipped out the back door. She strolled down the steps, and again onto the boardwalk. Her foot snagged, and she stumbled forward.

"Careful, there!" a man warned. Boots thundered in her direction, and a hand caught her arm.

Samantha jerked away while righting herself. "I'm fine, thank you." She glanced at the offending nail protruding from the edge of a board, before glancing into the clean-shaven face of a man probably a half decade younger than her. She stiffened away and attempted to sidestep him, but the motion did not have the desired effect, as he fell into step at her side.

"You didn't hurt yourself?"

"Not at all." Though her right boot made a flapping sound with each step. She glanced down to assess the damage. Her favorite boots were ruined. Yes, they were a few years old but the most comfortable she had ever owned. To replace them—

"That doesn't look good."

She sent a glare in his direction before she could correct herself. He was not responsible for her broken boot—just for being a single man inserting interest where it was not wanted.

He extended an arm. "I am aware of a shoe shop just past Manitoba Avenue. I'm sure they are still open."

"Yes, I am aware." She wouldn't mention the shop's proximity to the cottage where she was billeted. There wasn't much else on that edge of town but a livery and the homes of miners. Samantha started walking, but he caught her elbow. His mouth stretched into an easy smile. A handsome one at that.

"I'd hate for you to trip again. I'll accompany you, Miss. . ."

Samantha withdrew her arm. "As much as I appreciate your offer, as a schoolteacher I must guard my reputation."

He held up his hands as though surrendering. "Understood. But surely no one can fault us for walking in the same direction." The young man motioned her forward along the boardwalk. "I'm Robert Chestnut. My brother and I arrived only a week ago."

"Miss Ingles," Samantha relented and started forward, arms folded tightly across her stomach. She placed each step carefully to keep from further damaging the sole of her boot. She should be flattered by a man's attention, a new experience since arriving in a mining town. Years of boarding school and then a women's college left her woefully uncomfortable in a man's presence. Perhaps if Father had lived. . .

Samantha tightened her jaw and quickened her pace.

". . .dance on Friday."

Heat infused Samantha's chest. She could only imagine the man had extended an invitation. "I'm afraid—"

"I'm sure no one would think anything of it just because you're a teacher," he cut her off. "Folks in Frank are more understanding than in the big city, I imagine."

"That might be the case, but I still must decline." She gripped the ties of her reticule and barely managed not to stumble again as the sole of her boot folded under her foot. She wished she could unstrap the boot and carry it the final block or two, but years of decorum training forbid such an unseemly show. She was not some backcountry schoolgirl—she never had been. Nor had she been, nor ever would be, a giddy woman. "I mean no offense, Mr. Chestnut, but I have lessons to prepare, and am sure to be exhausted by the end of the school week. Though I am grateful for your kindness."

She dared not spare a glance at the man. Had her voice been too harsh? She was not known for dulcet tones after a day of keeping seventeen youth in line.

"I understand completely. Perhaps a quiet picnic after church would be more relaxing."

Or perhaps her tone had not been harsh enough. It made no sense that the man be so relentless when it came to her—unless the low population of single women in town was taken into account. Thankfully, they were approaching her destination, and she could end the conversation. She turned to the man, towering a head over her, broad through the shoulders, backdropped by the magnificence of the Rockies. What would it feel like to be cared for and cherished by a man?

Samantha shook the thought from her head. She was better off alone.

Love only brought loss. And if she were honest, he probably wanted nothing more than some entertainment and a stolen kiss or two—nothing permanent or lasting. Not with her.

"Thank you for your consideration, Mr. Chestnut—"

"Please, call me Rob."

"Thank you for your assistance, Mr. Chestnut, but I think it better if you set your sights elsewhere. I have one focus while in Frank, and that is the education of children."

"Children aren't the only ones needing educate'n," he replied easily but with a glint in his dark eyes. "Good day, Miss Ingles." He tipped his hat and headed back the way they had come.

She waited until he disappeared down the next block before starting down Manitoba Avenue toward the Stanford home. She cracked the door slowly, listening for any sounds of the family at home before removing her boots and walking quietly through the kitchen and upstairs to the small room—more of a closet—she'd called home for the past three months. The family must still be on whatever outing had kept the children from school.

Samantha dropped her satchel on the narrow cot masquerading as a bed and slipped on her only change of shoes before hurrying back out of the house with boots in hand. She needed to catch the cobbler before he closed his shop for the day.

Only a half block separated the Stanford home from the shoe shop, and a small bell rang over her head as she stepped inside. A dark-haired woman looked up from where she arranged a display of work boots in the window. "Good afternoon."

"To you as well. Is your husband available? I've had an unfortunate accident with one of my boots."

A laugh broke from the woman like the tinkling of the highest notes on a piano. "You mean my brother? I'm *Miss* Thornley. And just visiting, albeit for most of the winter." She motioned to the display. "Long enough to add a much-needed woman's touch to Lawrence's shop."

"Oh. . . Glad to meet you." Samantha managed a laugh as well, but one decidedly less musical. "Miss Ingles. One of Frank's schoolteachers. Is your brother in the shop?"

"Ah, yes, your boot's unfortunate accident?" Miss Thornley breezed from the room with a swish of long skirts, leaving Samantha to brush a hand down her own much plainer ones. Practical. Just like the tight bun she twisted her hair into every morning and the reading glasses usually perched on her nose. Only in a town overrun by bachelors like Frank would a man take notice of her instead of seeking a woman more like Miss Thornley.

The creak of a door pulled Samantha's attention to the man with a thick canvas apron and a smile to match his sister's. "Sorry to keep you waiting, Miss. What seems to be your problem?"

"The sole of my boot." She rushed to explain the damage and handed the footwear over to the cobbler.

"Shouldn't be too hard to have this as good as new by tomorrow afternoon. I'm afraid I can't get to it tonight as we'll be headed for dinner soon. I mean to treat my sister to an enjoyable evening at the hotel."

Miss Thornley brushed past him on her way back to the display. "I already told you, I came to visit, not be pampered."

"Months soaking in the sulfur springs doesn't constitute pampering?" he quipped in return.

She sent a glare in his direction, though a smile teased her mouth. "That was medicinal." The glance she sent Samantha held a grimace. "I have a touch of rheumatism that becomes quite uncomfortable in the winter months."

Lawrence Thornley juggled the boot to his other hand. "But she will be leaving tomorrow, so all the more reason to celebrate."

"Oh, you mean to celebrate my departure? Have I been so great a trial to you, brother dear?"

He answered with a laugh and the shake of his head. "Tell her—Miss Ingles, isn't it?—how talented the chefs at the Imperial Hotel truly are."

"I'm afraid I haven't had the pleasure." Samantha backed toward the door. She had no place in the middle of their banter or plans.

"Might as well get a room there was well. That much easier to catch the morning train."

"Oh, Lawrence." His sister groaned with a laugh.

"Well, the best to you in your travels home tomorrow, Miss Thornley."

And thank you, Mr. Thornley." Samantha ducked back into the street. Family interactions always left her more unsettled than they should.

Laughter at the front of the Stanfords' slowed her steps. Seven children flanked by father and mother, hand in hand, grins on faces, as though not a care in the world. "Ah, Miss Ingles, let me know when you would like some dinner, and I'll warm some soup," Mrs. Stanford called. "We ate while we were out."

"A picnic!" five-year-old Athol exclaimed, his blue eyes almost as wide as his grin.

"It's been the best day ever," his older sister Abby sang out. Her blond braids danced across her shoulders.

A picnic while they should have been at school. Samantha forced a tight smile. "I will fix a cup of tea and retire to my room, thank you. I have stories to grade." She pointed a narrowed gaze at the oldest girl. "I am disappointed not to have seen your entry, Mary. But feel free to bring it to me as soon as you have completed it tonight."

The girl's cheeks reddened, and her head ducked. Her mother stepped to her side, switching the baby to the other hip. "I am sure that is not necessary. We both know Mary writes beautifully."

"Her penmanship, yes. Her spelling and grammar, on the other hand, require work. Perhaps not a problem if she didn't miss school regularly."

"I do not believe she is so far behind."

"Yet you stifle her potential." Samantha gritted her teeth against further argument, though it brewed in her mind, pressuring up like boiling coffee ready to spew.

Mr. Stanford stepped past, momentarily breaking their locked gazes. "I must be off to the mine in the next hour," he said on his way into the house. "Come along, children."

The troops wandered past, and Samantha felt frustration build. Mary and her siblings should be in school and not gallivanting across the countryside every day their father had spare time to spend with them.

"I will bring your tea to your room, Miss Ingles." Mrs. Stanford bit out the words. "I am sure you have a busy evening before you." With that, she strode past.

Samantha followed slower, not saying a word as she bypassed the family and stole up to her room. Through the thin wall, girlish laughter echoed. Downstairs, children squealed, and then lower, upset voices rose through the floorboards. She hoped the school board would find her a new place to live as soon as possible, as obviously she was not welcome here.

Her tea arrived a few minutes later, but not a word was exchanged.

Samantha set the steaming cup aside and collapsed onto the bed. She pulled a quilt over her like a cocoon against the chill of the room. Indignation and frustration on behalf of the children were easier to recognize and deal with than the more uncomfortable sensation like a stone in her center.

She refused to dwell on what could never be.

Samantha closed her eyes against the burn of exhaustion and growing ache in her head. A folder of papers waited in her satchel, but maybe a few minutes of rest would clear her mind.

Just a few minutes...

Samantha jerked awake to black and a crack of thunder. No, not thunder. The ground shook like it wanted to cleave in two and swallow the whole house. A jolt slammed Samantha to the floor and overturned the bed over her. Pain spiked through her head, while the house spun. But it couldn't really spin, could it? The roof groaned above her. She choked on the air, now thick. She couldn't breathe. Couldn't move. Hail pelted on the roof.

She wanted to cry out for help and rescue, but who would hear her?

The beam above her gave way and crashed down.

"Oh, God..."

A flash of light—then all went dark.

Chapter 2

APRIL 29ᵀᴴ

A loud crack of thunder jerked Nathan Stanford from his sleep. The rumble came from the west, then stopped. He waited for a flash of lightning and listened for rain, but the night again settled into dark silence. A heaviness laid over him, adding to the weight of his wool blankets. He shoved them off and lit a candle so he could make out the thin hands on his pocket watch.

Almost a quarter after four in the morning.

Dawn was still a couple of hours away, but sleep had fled him along with the need for it. Nathan pushed to his feet and dressed, lastly pulling on the scarlet coat of his uniform. His flat-brimmed Stetson hung by the door. The wool of his coat was a blessing as the cold of the morning air brushed over him. Several inches of heavy snow covered the ground, and more floated down from the dark sky. No flashes of light. No more thunder. Still, the oppressive feeling remained.

Maybe it was just the case he was working on. They hadn't had much for whiskey runners in years, but yesterday a chief of a local Blackfoot tribe had sent word that the poison waters had been sold to several of his men, and someone had been seriously injured in a drunken brawl as a result.

Nathan blew out his breath and watched the cloud of moisture slowly dissipate in the air. Over the past decade, things had grown peaceful in this nook of the Northwest Territories. He had recently been assigned to Fort Macleod, one of the earliest forts built when the North-West Mounted Police had been sent west thirty years earlier. The west was no longer wild, but a booming civilization—with the crimes and problems associated with such.

"You're up early, Constable Stanford."

Nathan glanced behind him at his bunkmate, Constable David Burton. A blanket draped his shoulders. The young man was fresh from the academy and eager to go, but that didn't explain why he was awake either. Constable Burton seemed to read his mind. "Any thoughts on that crash?"

"I thought it was thunder." It was the time of year one would expect showers instead of blizzards, after all. Nathan looked to the west, picturing the distant mountains invisible in the darkness. "That doesn't seem so likely now." What else could have caused that noise? An explosion? A crash?

Why was the night so silent now?

The younger man nodded but made no comment. "You've been in the force for a few years now?"

"Twelve years." Nathan shook his head at the number and all that he'd experienced since donning this uniform. He'd joined the North-West Mounted Police when he'd been young like Constable Burton and anxious for adventure, distraction, and an escape. His family had farmed in Manitoba, but there was nothing there for him—or any of his brothers for that matter. The eldest brother had stayed on the farm, probably out of obligation more than anything else. The other three had spread out over the prairies, the youngest a ranch hand near Red Deer, one a blacksmith in Saskatoon, and another a miner just to the west, where the plains met the Rockies. Nathan's three sisters had found husbands, but they'd remained back in Manitoba near their parents. Nathan was the only one who hadn't married, but the life of a North-West Mounted Policeman hardly encouraged the keeping of a wife, and he had no desire to attempt that path again.

"Think you'll ever want something different?"

Nathan shook his head. He enjoyed his occupation. It gave him purpose. "Probably not. Not till I'm too old to saddle my horse and they try to stick me behind a desk."

They shared a chuckle.

"Definitely not a thunderstorm," Constable Burton mumbled after a couple of minutes, nudging the wet snow with his boot.

"Doesn't seem so." And yet Nathan couldn't get past the feeling that something was brewing over the Rockies.

———◆•◆———

Breathe.

An almost futile command accompanied the attempt to fill her lungs. But was it from a lack of oxygen or the pressure of the mattress against her back? Blackness crowded the room—or what was left of it. At least part of the roof had collapsed, but it was impossible to know the extent of the damage from her pinned position and the heavy darkness.

A child cried out—one of the girls in the room beside her. Cried out and then went quiet. The remainder of the house remained silent. Eerily so. Samantha tried to call to the girls, or anyone within earshot, but choked on the dust clinging to every breath. Panic again rose in her throat, threatening to suffocate her—she would die here, buried under the roof of the house. Helplessness fed every fear.

The child cried again, muffled and pained sobs. Abby.

Oh, the poor child! Was she hurt? Was her sister still beside her? What of the rest of the house? What had even happened? It was like an earthquake or an explosion or. . .

Her breath came in quick gulps only to be lost in a fit of coughing.

Focus.

Panic would not free her or save the girls. Samantha swallowed against the grit in her throat and began assessing her body's position. The main weight was over her torso, cushioned by the thin mattress and broken by the frame of the cot. One leg felt free, and she could wiggle her left foot, while the other was numb with pain. And immobile. Her chest pinned one hand, while the other stretched out in front of her.

"Mama!"

Abby's muffled cry from the other side of the wall spiked adrenaline through Samantha's core. She needed her second hand free. Emptying her lungs provided little space for movement, but enough to slide her hand against the floor. A sharp splinter bit her palm, but she ignored the stab of pain and continued pressing forward until her elbow snagged on the edge of the bed frame, forcing her to a halt in an even worse position. Her lungs constricted, unable to expand.

All she could do was push, while the need to scream pinched in her throat and burned her chest. Her body slid sideways, half rolling as the bed frame shifted the tiniest degree.

Frozen air filled her lungs with some relief. Both arms now free, she wiped one down her face, clearing away some of the grit and moisture. She clamped her eyes closed as words of prayers tumbled through her mind. Not prayers she'd ever spoken—she'd never made a practice of praying, had never given God much thought until now. Religion had never been of much importance, and church was a social event she was expected to attend as an integral member of a community.

She gritted her teeth against the realization of her sudden dependency on so distant and abstract a being—one she wasn't even sure existed. Still pinned, and with no sound from downstairs, the feeling settled deep through her that rescue would not be coming. Not soon. Probably not soon enough.

What good would the rote prayers she'd memorized in school be now?

Be still.

The words crept into her thoughts and Samantha forced her mind to calmy assess the situation. The dust. The sensation of the house spinning with the first roaring crash. The popping sound...what was that? Boulders tumbling down the mountain? Had there been an explosion at the mine? Had it brought the mountain down on them? Had anyone survived? Other than the girls in the next room who she could barely hear now.

Perhaps there would be no rescue.

Be still.

How? With so much unknown and doom hanging over her head. The thought of laying here in pain until she suffocated or starved to death. . .

"Be still."

She had no other choice but to wait for a rescue that might never come.

Chapter 3

High log walls cast long shadows over the core of the fort and its blanket of white, the morning sun still low on the horizon. Nathan tugged his flat-brimmed Stetson on his head while stifling a yawn. Maybe he should have tried to sleep longer, but he probably wouldn't have been successful anyway. His insides never had settled, nor had his mind. Something was wrong... He just couldn't say what.

The sight of a crowd gathered near the muster point of the fort sent a kick to his gut. Raised voices carried both orders and an edge of franticness. Nathan jogged across the soggy white ground and caught Constable Ryder's arm as he hurried past.

"What's happened?"

"Landslide in the night. Turtle Mountain covered Frank."

Nathan's mind stuttered while his chest collapsed. "What do you mean? The whole town?"

"We don't know. A detail is being sent to assess the situation and help in rescue efforts." The man pulled away and hurried toward the bunkhouse.

No, no, no... Images and faces flashed through Nathan's thoughts as he staggered in the opposite direction, toward their commanding officer. He had to focus on what needed to happen—not the thought of Rosemary and Peter buried under half a mountain. His breath came in short gasps and his head spun, but the words burst from him like gunfire. "I need to go too."

"I can't spare everyone, Stanford. I already have the detail assigned."

"My brother. My brother's a miner. His family. They live in Frank."

Silence sat heavy with meaning, but finally the officer nodded. "Very well. The train will be leaving within a quarter hour."

Thank you, sir. . . Nathan heard the words in his head but wasn't sure they made it out his mouth. He was already on his way to gather what he might need. A change of uniform and bedroll. His Bible stared up at him from where it had been buried in his trunk, and he shoved it into his pack. If what they said was true. . . No, there had to be a mistake. The town of Frank couldn't be buried. Surely God wouldn't allow. . .

Nathan clenched his jaw and hurried to collect Red Rover from the stables and lead him to the train. Nothing was certain. Not until he saw it with his own eyes.

The first one to the train, Nathan had little to keep his mind from every imagination, every worry, every fear of what he would find at Frank. All the while, a part of him wanted to flee in the opposite direction. The journey, though not much more than an hour, stretched out on every breath and thud of his heart. After doing his best to avoid Peter over the past decade, it seemed surreal to rush in his direction.

Please don't let it be too late.

Too late for what? After holding onto anger for so long, it wasn't as though he were ready to make peace with his brother or Rosemary.

"How are you holding up, Stanford?"

Nathan set his jaw before sparing a glance at Inspector Primrose, who had charge over this detail. No doubt he had been briefed as to Nathan's connection to the town of Frank. But what did the man expect him to say as they crawled toward any understanding of what had happened?

Instead of waiting for an answer, Primrose clasped his shoulder, nodded, and then continued to the front of the car. Not that anyone else followed his movement—no, all heads seemed turned toward Nathan, but thankfully whispers were drowned out by the rumble of the train's race down the track. If he'd been thinking, he would have ridden in the stock car with their horses. At least he could have distracted himself by keeping Rover company. As it was, guilt and worry pummeled Nathan in turn as miles passed painfully slowly under the small steel wheels of the train. Each minute an agony.

Then the train lurched, brakes squealing against the rails until jolting to a stop on the cusp of the Rocky Mountains, bare rolling hills reaching toward the jagged peaks. Nathan didn't bother trying to see out his window, instead hurrying down the aisle, shoving past the other officers toward the doorway. He jumped to the dry ground and raised his head toward the west—where huge boulders covered the tracks, the valley, everything for miles.

Someone swore beside him. Another threw a prayer heavenward. Nathan just stared, his chest squeezing painfully. He gasped a breath, but his lungs refused to expand. He'd never seen anything like the heaps and vales of limestone marring the landscape. It hardly registered in his mind that the snowstorm that had buried the prairies last night had not extended this far west.

"We're no good to anyone standing here," Constable Hardy muttered, starting toward the piles of rock. Nathan followed. Maybe from on top the boulders, he could get a better sense of the damage. Did any of the town remain?

Nathan tugged to loosen the top button of his coat and started his climb, sparing several glances at the mountain towering to his left where pale shale and rock marked where the miles of rubble originated from. A huge portion of the south peak had let go of the mountain and now covered the river, railway, roadways, and hundreds, if not thousands of acres of ranchland and who knew what else.

As he scaled over the limestone, all he could think about was the fate of Peter and Rosemary and their family. How deep was this stone piled? And the mine where Peter worked—had it collapsed or been buried? Had anyone survived?

Finally, Nathan balanced on a boulder the size of the train car and looked toward the west where the town of Frank stood. Buildings peeked over the gray and white stone landscape. Intact buildings. Some of the town had survived. Hope swelled within him, despite the unimaginable desolation. There was a chance Peter was alive, that his family was alive. Nathan clung to that hope.

———◆◆———

Warm arms embraced Samantha, along with the scent of rose water. Mother always smelled like blossoms, and her presence had the strength to chase away even the darkest, scariest moments. If only she could keep Mother close, keep her from leaving again.

"Chin up, child. It will only be a few months," Mother promised. "We will be back by summer to tell you all our adventures. One day, you will come with us."

That was what Samantha clung to. To not be left behind for once.

"Study hard." Father's look was stern, though his attention wasn't on her but the gold watch he'd pulled from his breast pocket. He snapped it closed and set a hand on Mama's arm. "We must be off."

Samantha's chin trembled, and tears welled in her eyes.

"None of that, young lady." Mother gave a look of censure as she pulled on her soft leather gloves. "Make us proud."

Don't go! *Her heart cried out to her parents as they turned away, their steps soft thuds echoing in her aching head.*

Thud.

Thud.

Samantha forced her eyes open and arched her neck to stare at the sliver of sunlight sending a ray through a crack in the roof.

Thud.

Her heart leapt as footsteps sounded across the roof.

"Help," Samantha squeaked. She coughed, trying to clear the grit from her throat. "Down here!"

Men's voices. Followed by a popping sound. Like rocks being tossed aside. Could the whole house be buried?

"Please, help me." Tears rolled from her eyes, clearing some of the grit while nails and boards groaned out their protest. They were coming. Finally, someone was coming.

Still, minutes dredged on, while her heart raced with renewed hope. Every breath hurt until light splashed across her face with warmth. Pebbles and more dust showered down as well, but she blinked against them and sought the face of her rescuer.

"I found someone! A woman."

More feet scrambled overhead, more dust. She turned her face away and buried a sneeze in her sleeve.

"We've got you, ma'am." The stranger's hand gripped her shoulder.

"We need a post or rail!" someone else shouted. "Something to lift this beam."

Samantha clamped her eyes closed against the pain in her foot and the need to be free. A sob tightened her chest. She was almost free, just a couple more minutes. She focused on the hand that never left her shoulder. She was no longer alone.

A long rail was produced and levered the beam from off the cot holding her in place. Two hands gripped her arms and attempted to drag her forward, but agony ripped through her right ankle. A scream scratched her throat.

"My foot," she gasped. "It's pinned."

Men set to work around her, digging deeper until pressure released and she was pulled loose. Strong arms lifted her into the brilliant morning sun overhead. She blinked, not at the brightness but at the miles of destruction laid over the valley and miners' cottages. Mud hung in every crevice and low spot, though she couldn't think of where it all came from with her mind struggling to clear and understand what surrounded her. Miles of rock buried not just the house she'd been rescued from but most of Manitoba Avenue, and everything east, from Turtle Mountain—which appeared to have had a huge chunk ripped from it—halfway up the foothills on the other side. Everything was gone. The shoe shop and her favorite boots. The livery. The rail line and Gold Creek. The mine. Ranches. How many people she had walked among and attended church with. . . How many children?

"Wait. The Stanford girls. Have you found the Stanfords?"

The man supporting her shook his head. One that she recognized as

Edgar Ash motioned to a show of splintered wood beyond the edge of the roof upon which they stood. "Not much left."

Samantha blinked with sickening understanding as she made out walls, some of them collapsing under the weight of rock. But how? The roof and attic where she had been trapped no longer resided over the remainder of the house. It had been ripped off and pushed aside. A shiver ran through her. How? And what of the Stanford family?

"You are the only one we've recovered," Mr. Ash said, wiping the back of his wrist across his sweaty brow.

"Except the baby," a youth offered, stepping near. "Mrs. Bansemer found her and took her in."

Samantha jerked around to find the Bansemers' home, tipped as though shifted from its foundation, but mostly intact—though piled about with rock and on the edge of a muddy pond that hadn't existed the night before.

The man took another step, and Samantha writhed from his hold. A spike of pain in her ankle stole her breath momentarily, but she managed to put weight on her foot. "I heard the girls. In the night. They have to be here somewhere." She dropped to her knees and began pushing aside the rock that had not yet been cleared away.

Mr. Ash came beside her. "Where would they be, Miss?"

Samantha paused to remember the layout of the attic. The doorway from the hall. The double bed the girls shared. "There." She moved to continue digging, but arms again directed her away, while a group of men already covered with mud and dirt took her place, removing rock, pulling away shingles and boards until, little by little, all was stripped away.

Let them be alive. Let them be alive.

She tried not to consider what they might find. Or who else was buried under all this stone. Faces and names skittered across her mind in tortuous detail. Allen, John, Wilfred, and Athol. Rosemary Stanford. She let her gaze wander to the other cottages—or where they had been. The Clark home was gone completely with Mrs. Clark and six children. . .no, five. Lillian said she was staying at the boardinghouse. She might still be safe. There was no way to know if her father had been home or at the mine. The Watkins cottage was gone as well, nothing but strewn debris, not likely to contain survivors, as was the Ennis home. What remained of the Ackroyds' home smoldered in ash. All she could think of was the children, several she had seen every day in her class. Had any survived?

"Oh, God. . ." She didn't know whether to curse Him or beg Him for help.

A cry, small but feminine, rose from within the attic, and a shout of surprise and haste from the rescuers. Minutes dragged on, until Abby, with dirty nightgown and face, was pulled from the broken house. Mary soon followed, and blankets were wrapped around their small frames. Some scrapes and probably bruises, but they were alive.

Samantha sank back, strength depleted. Shivers traveled up and down her body even as someone draped a woolen blanket over her shoulders. She wished she could close her eyes and imagine the devastation away. But she couldn't. She couldn't even look away from it all. It was too horrible.

"Get them to Dr. Malcolmson," Mr. Ash ordered, and Samantha felt herself being pulled back to her feet. She caught Abby's wide-eyed gaze as the child took in the wreckage of their home and community, as she realized that everything she loved had just been ripped from her. Like a knife to the abdomen given a hard twist, Samantha recognized the pain and that there was little a doctor could do for any of them.

Chapter 4

From a distance, most of Frank appeared as though it were any other Wednesday. People hurried about the streets like busy ants. It wasn't until Nathan stood among them that he saw the look of terror in their eyes. They hurried about looking for information about family, friends, or neighbors. One group huddled in blankets in front of the Imperial Hotel, staring to the southeast where the town vanished under gray limestone.

A red-clad constable appeared ahead, hurrying toward the troop of Mounted Police. His uniform was already stained with soot and mud. "I'm sure glad you've come."

Inspector Primrose dismounted. "Constable Laird?"

"Yes, sir." The man wasted no more time on introductions, instead turning to the landslide. "We've begun rescue efforts and have dug out a handful of survivors. Some bodies as well. A few boulders are still falling, but we're hoping the worst is over."

"What exactly happened?" the inspector questioned, following to where rock littered the street and mud formed puddles as though after a heavy rain, though most of the ground remained dry within town.

"The south peak broke away from the mountain just after four o'clock this morning. A hundred seconds, and it was pretty much over, everything in its path gone."

"The flooding?"

"The slide dammed some of Old Man River and Gold Creek. Most of this was probably pushed out of the creek when the rocks hit. Gold Creek has been rerouted." He swore under his breath. "Makes for quite the mess."

"What about the mine? What caused all this? Was there an explosion?"

Nathan dismounted and pressed forward, craving answers. He wanted to take his leave and seek out his family, but curiosity and duty held him in place.

"Impossible to say," Constable Laird reported. "The mine entrances are both blocked. We have a rescue party attempting to dig out the upper entrance in case there are any survivors, but who can say if there is anything or anyone to find? The whole shaft may have collapsed."

Nathan could no longer hold his tongue. "How many men were in the mine?"

"I was told twenty."

"Who would know their names?" Nathan tried to keep his voice even, but it came out clipped and not quite steady.

Inspector Primrose gave him a sidelong glance before again addressing Laird. "Take Constable Stanford to speak with the manager or foreman of the mine—whoever will have that information. The other men will assist with rescue efforts and getting the town organized."

The man nodded and Nathan handed Rover's reins to the man at his side before following. They only walked several paces before Laird looked over at him, eyes narrowed. "Constable Stanford. Peter Stanford is your brother?"

Nathan dug in his heels and grabbed the man's arm. "What do you know about my brother?"

"Peter was at the mine last night. I was informed as we were digging out his house. . .and what we could find of his family." Apology hung on his words.

"Rosemary— His wife?" Nathan swallowed hard, suddenly not sure he was ready for answers.

"Dead. And the four boys." He motioned ahead at the peaks of houses hardly visible above the rock. "Just found the last body."

Cold washed over Nathan while heat seared the back of his eyes. He swallowed hard. "His daughters?"

"At the hospital. The two oldest were somehow spared."

Nathan let out a small breath. "Are they. . ." He looked to the landslide, his chest tight. "Are they badly injured?"

"Hardly a scratch on either of them that we could see. Doctor Malcolmson will have more answers for you."

"Of course." His head spun as he tried to digest what had been said. Rosemary, once so full of life, was dead. And Peter—buried in the mine. Most of his family was dead. Just the two girls. . . What was he missing? He could hardly think, but something was missing.

"The baby—"

"The baby," Nathan repeated. Peter had mentioned Rosemary's pregnancy the last time he had tried to contact Nathan. He'd stopped at the fort to try to convince Nathan to visit his family for Christmas over a year ago. Peter never understood why Nathan had wanted nothing to do with him or his family.

"A miracle. . ." Nathan heard Laird say, though it was hard to focus on the words. "Thrown from the house. . .onto straw. . .alive."

"What?" Nathan couldn't quite comprehend everything said, but he clung to the last word. The baby was alive?

They stepped to the edge of the slide and the cottages in a broken line. Some had been buried almost entirely, while others ripped into shreds.

"That is your brother's home there." Constable Laird motioned to where a decrepit roof of a house peeked above a mountain of limestone and shale, pools of mud in every low spot. "It was actually torn in half, the remainder over there." He indicated where splintered beams and boards appeared among the heaps of limestone. A small group of laborers stood near in conversation.

How had anyone survived?

"I should help." Nathan cleared the gravel from his voice. "Where are the bodies?"

Laird looked at him, dark eyebrows brows pushed together. "We'll make sure they are all accounted for and prepared for burial. You should check on your nieces. The hospital is attached to Dr. Malcolmson's house a couple blocks that way." He waved to a young man trudging past. "John, can you show Constable Stanford to the hospital?"

"Stanford?" The lad tipped his hat back, looking between the two before nodding. "Of course."

"I'll send someone to find you as soon as we have word about your brother," Laird promised.

Nathan didn't bother with a thanks. He didn't have it in him. He fell in step behind the young man, feeling as though part of the mountain had landed squarely on him.

The "hospital" was no more than a small addition onto the doctor's home, set up with beds and cots. Some appeared made for the space, while other mattresses and cots had been squeezed into whatever space was available to make room for the injured. Most were already filled. Nathan looked around the room, but there was no one he recognized. There were a couple of mothers with children, and other sibling groups, but his nieces could be two feet away and he'd not recognize them for how much they had likely grown in the past few years.

"Excuse me," the young man pulled a nurse aside. "We are looking for the Stanford girls."

The middle-aged woman gave Nathan a quick glance and a sad nod, before motioning to the nearest corner where an unfamiliar woman reclined, foot propped up and bandaged, with a babe in arms. Two older girls sat close, pale faces somewhat familiar. He hadn't looked closely before, as he'd assumed the woman was their mother.

John turned to leave, and Nathan fought the urge to follow. He'd already garnered too much attention just standing here like a sore thumb in his scarlet coat—and he had no idea what to say to his nieces after what they'd endured. It would be easier to walk away and take his pain and frustration out on the mine entrance. At least that would bring him closer to answers.

It wasn't like he would be much use to the girls right now.

He was about to turn when the oldest girl looked his way. Her eyes widened as she studied him. She had to be twelve or thirteen, about the same age as her mother had been when Nathan first met Rosemary—and the girl was almost the spitting image of her mother. It was like stepping back in time.

"Uncle Nathan?" Her voice pulled him up short, and he felt himself nod.

"Yes." Though Nathan wasn't sure how she would know him. They had never met but once when she'd been much younger.

"Pa said you would come." She hurried around the beds between them and threw her arms around his torso.

He returned the embrace with more force than intended. "What do you mean, your pa said I would come? When?"

She looked up at him with eyes too much like Peter's. "He just said someday, someday you would come. He talked about you a lot."

Nathan's heart pinched in his chest. "How did you know who I am?"

Her brows arched. "You look like Pa." The girl gripped tighter. "They haven't found him yet. Just Mama's body," she mumbled against Nathan's coat. "And they say the boys are probably all dead too. But that can't be right, can it?" Her blue eyes were wet and pleading. As though he could reassure her. "Abby and me were all right. And they found Lucy thrown from the house, just fine. Maybe Allen or John are okay too?"

All he could manage was the shake of his head.

She clung tighter. "Pa's up in the mine, but they won't say anything about it."

"We'll figure it out. I'll go up there and look myself."

Her head cocked back so she looked up at him. "Will you?"

Nathan nodded, finding his throat too tight to speak. He wished he had more to offer.

"Thank you, thank you." She relaxed her hold and stared up at him with such a look of pain and hope. "You'll come back as soon as you know anything?" She glanced back at her two little sisters, and her shoulders slumped.

He felt her burden, but he was supposed to be the strong one. He squeezed her shoulder. "I'll be back. We'll figure this out. It's going to be okay."

She managed the tiniest nod at the lie.

"You three will be all right while I'm gone?"

Again, a slight nod.

"Who's the lady holding. . ." *Shoot.* He stopped cold as he realized that he didn't know which name was the baby's.

"Lucy? That's Miss Ingles. My schoolteacher."

"Good." A schoolteacher would be much better equipped to comfort the girls and see to their needs. They would be in good hands while he made his escape.

Chapter 5

Samantha had never been more at a loss for what to do. Lucy fussed in her arms, but Samantha wasn't sure how to do much more than hold the baby. She was trained for educating older children, not to be a nursemaid.

"Let me take her." Mary cuddled her sister to her shoulder. "She's probably hungry and misses Mama."

"Of course." And now was the perfect opportunity for escape. She would fetch the nurse or one of the volunteer women assisting in the hospital. Surely one of them was better suited to help the children. But even as she moved to put her feet under her, a painful process, Mrs. Matkin approached. Her husband was one of the missing miners, and she had spent the morning here, trying to stay busy though concern for her husband's fate deepened the creases around her eyes.

"Don't you be moving, Miss Ingles. Rest that foot until Dr. Malcolmson has a chance to make sure it's not broken."

"I'm sure it'll be fine," Samantha stated, though she settled back onto the bed. Considering the extent of others' injuries, hers were quite minor. "A room at one of the hotels is all I need. Just a place to rest." Somewhere quiet for the girls. Lucy was fussing again, likely ready for a nap after such a trying morning.

"Out of the way!" a man shouted from the door as it was shoved wide.

Samantha instinctively reached for Abby in case she needed shielding from whatever came next. A group pushed inside, a young man in their midst. Lester Johnson, a thirteen-year-old from her class. He wore nothing but a blanket by the look of it, and blood ran down his leg.

Samantha pulled Abby onto the bed beside her. This was no place for the girls.

"Do you think Lester's going to be all right?" Mary whispered, hugging Lucy.

"I'm sure Dr. Malcolmson will help him." But what of Lester's family? She'd seen their home, and it was amazing anyone had survived. He lived with his sister and her new husband only a couple of houses away from the Stanfords.

Samantha slid to the edge of the bed, this time making it to her feet—well, foot. She tucked the injured one under her and used Abby's shoulder for balance. "Mrs. Matkin, could I ask you to find the girls and me a ride to a hotel? Dr. Malcolmson can look at my foot when he has more time." In a day or two. If ever.

The woman looked from the party who had just arrived, to the three girls, and back to Samantha. "I supposed that might be for the best."

"I believe it will be." Samantha glanced at the middle girl. "Can you help me to the door, Abby?"

The girl's nod was so slight, Samantha almost didn't see it. And they began the arduous trek across the room, trying not to stumble over the blankets and low cots. A scream of pain erupted from the room where Lester had entered, and Samantha waved the girls out the door. Abby looked up at her with questioning in her eyes.

"He'll be fine." Samantha wished she felt half the assurance held in her voice.

Mrs. Matkin met them just outside, where a chill breeze was a blessed relief after the warmth of the hospital. "Jack will drive you to the Frank Hotel." She assisted Samantha to the back of the wagon, where the older man with a heavy beard waited to lift her up. Abby followed with Mary and baby behind.

"You'll tell our Uncle Nathan where we are?" Urgency edged Mary's voice.

"The Mountie?"

She nodded.

"I'll make sure he finds you."

The wagon rocked forward, each jostle a bite to Samantha's ankle. She didn't want to but couldn't help a glance toward Turtle Mountain, following the broken trail to the edge of town. The cold seeped deeper, settling into Samantha's bones, far more than the cool air alone could account for. Though most of Frank remained intact, how was the town to recover from this?

"Keep busy. Focus on what needs to be done."

Both girls looked at her, and she realized she'd spoken out loud.

"Is it possible to pause at the school, Mr. um...Jack?" Samantha called to the front. "Just for a couple of minutes so I can grab something."

The man grunted but nodded, and the wagon turned down the next street. Samantha began making a mental list of what would be needed. McGuffey Readers and maybe a novel for Mary. Paper and pencils for exercises to keep the girls busy.

As the wagon rolled to a stop, Samantha shifted to the edge.

"Perhaps it would be better if you told one of the girls what to grab for you, Miss Ingles." Mr. Jack eyed her crudely bandaged ankle. Both of her feet were bare, and she tucked them under the hem of her dress.

"I suppose you are correct." She quickly recited her list to Mary, along with locations. The key would be needed, as the school had not been opened today. Thankfully, she had not removed it from her pocket last night.

Lucy was again set on Samantha's lap, and the child immediately made her frustration known with a wail.

"I'll hurry." Mary took off at a jog and soon disappeared inside the large front door, barefoot and still in her nightgown with only a small blanket sheltering her shoulders. In all that had happened, Samantha had not considered the state of the girls after being rescued from their bed. At least she had fallen asleep fully clothed.

It seemed longer than it probably took for Mary to return with some of the requested items, which she quickly traded for her bawling sister.

"Thank you," was all that Samantha had to offer until they were settled at the hotel. The sun hurt her head, and the cool of the day was working its way through the sleeves of her linen blouse.

Upon arrival, Mr. Jack helped her down from the back of the wagon and then took her piles of supplies inside to deposit on the front desk. Samantha followed slower with the girls, barely making it through the front doors when a woman rushed to her, face wide with both shock and. . .was that relief?

"Oh, Miss Ingles, when my brother told me you were staying in one of the miner's cottages on Manitoba Avenue. . ." Miss Thornley shook her head while her eyes glistened. "And to think I kept fighting Lawrence about spending the night at the hotel! I haven't the nerves to go and see what remains of his shoe shop. He says there is nothing left. Not a splinter."

"Just a pile of rock," Samantha managed to murmur.

Miss Thornley threw arms around her. "Oh, you poor dear! I can only imagine what you have been through. It's a miracle any of us are alive."

Samantha didn't have the strength to pull away while the sentiment reverberated within her skull. A miracle? That the Thornleys had been at the hotel instead of the shoe shop? That the roof hadn't crushed her or the two girls standing nearby? A miracle that somehow baby Lucy had been thrown to safety?

"I should. . .I need to get the Stanford girls to a room so they can rest."

The focus changed, and Miss Thornley hastened to the front desk to arrange a room, lunch, and assistance to help Samantha manage the stairs. She followed and before leaving assured the girls that she would find them new dresses and shoes.

Abby curled up on the bed beside Samantha while Mary tried to get Lucy to take the bottle someone had brought for her. In the few moments of quiet, Samantha glanced over the piles of books Mary had brought from the school. Two McGuffey Readers, and *The Princess and the Goblin*—a children's novel by George MacDonald. Not the novel she had listed, but hopefully the fantasy would prove to be a useful distraction.

Chapter 6

"All we can do is keep digging and pray that the mine didn't completely collapse on the men."

Nathan looked past the foreman who had spoken, to the indent in the wall of loose rock where the mouth of the coal mine used to be. He hadn't stopped praying since he'd boarded that train this morning— for the little good it would do. God seemed quite distant right now. Nathan pulled at his buttons until he could throw his coat aside and reach for a spade. Others dragged or tossed heavier rocks aside, all to get to a mine entrance that might not even be there anymore. It was too early to tell whether he should be thankful his brother had been on shift at the mine and not home with his family. Who knew how many hours separated them from answers?

Despite the freezing temperatures last night, the sun beat on them now that they were hard at work. Sweat soon rolled down Nathan's face and between his shoulder blades, but he kept his focus on the image of Peter just a few feet away, within a prison of rock, oxygen diminishing. Peter had to be alive. All this couldn't be for naught.

The sun moved its way across the sky, but even when reprieve was offered, Nathan found he couldn't pause. Not for more than a couple of restless moments that couldn't be defined as rest.

A larger man, probably a miner who'd been off shift, took place and pace beside Nathan. "You're Peter Stanford's brother?"

"That's right."

"He's a good man. I've worked with him a lot over the past year. Happy to call him a friend."

Jealousy wormed through Nathan. Peter had tried to bridge the distance between them. As a boy they had been the closest of friends, but now. . .

"Heard two of his girls survived?"

"Three. They found the baby as well."

"Hallelujah."

Hallelujah? Rosemary was dead, as were their four boys. How could he praise God for that?

"What will happen to the girls if. . .you know."

Nathan gritted his teeth. Peter would be fine—he had to be. They would find him soon, alive and well, holed up deeper in the mine shaft.

And if not?

Nathan tried to push the nagging voice aside, but it refused to be silent. "I have other siblings." Someone would take the girls in if required. Even if Peter just needed time to get his feet back under him. "We'll figure something out." He didn't want to think about anything to do with the girls now. They had their schoolteacher to mind them and offer comfort. He wasn't ready to do either.

Nathan threw the uncertainty and fear into his efforts with the spade, ignoring the tumbling of yet another boulder down the mountainside. He'd stopped watching each one adding to the rubble at the base of Turtle Mountain.

"Who has the girls now?"

Nathan tightened his grip on the spade, not stopping his work. Why wouldn't the man leave him alone? "The schoolteacher."

"Which one?"

Nathan hadn't considered that the town was big enough for multiple teachers, but Frank was no longer a tiny village. Now it boasted over six hundred residents. Or, at least it used to. "I don't know." He hadn't even taken the time to note the color of her hair or anything about her, really. Hardly mattered, and why would it?

"I just feel bad for the girls if they're with Miss Ingles. She's a bit of a witch." The man mumbled the last as he finally moved away.

Nathan blew out his breath. Weren't most teachers a bit of a witch in the classroom? That had been his experience. But it would be different now with her role changed. Wouldn't it?

He tried not to think on the woman and his nieces as he continued throwing rock aside. His focus was Peter. Nothing else mattered until he found his brother.

The sun continued its trek overhead, and still their attempts felt feeble. Until his spade scraped against a thick piece of hewn wood. A beam. Shattered. At least part of the tunnel had collapsed.

A man cursed beside him.

"Might not be the whole mine. Might just be the entrance." Nathan spoke the words out loud as men gathered around to pull the beam from the rock. Over six inches thick, and it might as well have been kindling.

"It's no use," someone said from behind him. "The whole thing is probably the same."

"We don't know that."

"Sorry, Constable, but this mine has always been unstable. Just last week I was checking the supports, and we found a section broken like this. Snapped like twigs, and the roof eight inches lower."

"And the mine wasn't closed?" Nathan bit out a curse as he spun. "Men were still sent in there?"

The man, a wisp of gray at his temples despite his youthful face, backed away a step. "It's just the way it is sometimes with mines. Men know the risks."

Jaw aching from the pressure of his clench, Nathan twisted back to the mine entrance and yet another broken beam being unearthed. "I'm not giving up. Not yet." Not until they knew. Not so long as there was a chance that even one man was alive and trapped in there.

Another hour passed before someone laid a hand on Nathan's shoulder.

"Take a break, Constable. The others will keep working here."

Nathan turned to where Inspector Primrose stood, uniform still spotless. "I've had breaks." A few short ones at least.

"That's an order, Constable Stanford. Go back to town and get something to eat. Take an hour before you come back."

"With all due respect, sir," Nathan tried to keep his voice even, but exhaustion and growing hopelessness ate away at him, "I—"

"You'll be back. But you have your orders, and I expect you to follow them."

"Sir." Nathan tossed the spade aside and yanked his coat from the boulder he'd laid it over. He would obey, but that didn't mean he had to like it. He pulled out his watch. Four thirty. One hour from now he would be back on this mountain. Not a minute later.

He stalked back to town, a long enough walk, while skirting the worst of the flooded land and the largest of the boulders. Another group of men had already gone to work clearing the streambed to ease the rise of water. What a mess. All of it—him included.

Nathan considered stopping at the hospital to check on the girls, but he didn't have it in him. Neither did he have any answers for them about their father. He didn't have much of an appetite, but he felt the strain of the day wearing down his already low energy reserves. He'd not had the stomach for breakfast before they'd boarded the train, so he hadn't eaten in almost twenty-four hours. If he wanted to be of any use at the mine, he would need something.

Frank Hotel was the first place he came across that had a dining room, so he turned inside.

"Constable Stanford?" a man in a brown suit and a similar shade of mustache called to him.

"Yes." Nathan was at the disadvantage since he'd never seen the man before.

"We were asked to watch for you."

Nathan narrowed his eyes at the man.

"Miss Ingles said you would be coming for your nieces."

"My nieces? Are here?"

"Yes, Miss Ingles took a room for them. Number seven, on the second floor." The man motioned toward the stairs as though he expected Nathan to bound up them.

"I'll find them as soon as I've had something to eat."

"Oh." The man's eyes widened in surprise. "Of course." He led the way to a busy dining room with available seats here and there but no privacy, no peace and quiet, and already his uniform was garnering attention. The last thing he wanted was someone coming to him for information he didn't have.

"On second thought, is it possible to have something simple sent up to the room where my nieces are? They may be hungry as well."

"Of course, sir."

Nathan made it two steps before turning back. He'd heard the oldest girl rattle off their names only a couple of hours ago, but unfortunately, he had hardly heard her, and his thoughts were still in too much of a fog. "Do you by any chance know their names?"

The man's brow furrowed. "Whose names?"

Heat crawled up Nathan's neck, and he lowered his voice while glancing to make sure no one stood near enough to overhear. "The girls. My nieces."

The man gave a stuttering start before managing to say anything coherent. "I just caught the eldest girl's name. Mary."

"Thank you." As embarrassing as it was for Nathan to admit his folly to this stranger—better than confessing his neglect to the girl herself. Mary. He remembered something about her now. As the eldest, she had been named Rosemary after her mother. The shortened form of her name was probably to keep the two from being confused. For a moment he slipped back to the day he had heard of the child's birth—his brother's firstborn. He should have been happy for Peter, but instead he'd gotten drunk.

Nathan took his leave, away from the noise, away from the guilt of avoidance. He climbed the stairs slowly, his muscles stiffening with each step. Room seven was halfway down the hall, and silence hung in the dry air. He knocked on the door.

Footsteps scurried across the room and a moment later Mary's face appeared. Her mouth remained closed while her eyes widened and searched his for answers. Exactly what he didn't have.

"Nothing yet."

Her shoulders drooped, and she stepped out of the way, allowing him inside the small room hosting two narrow beds. One held the baby, fast asleep as though she hadn't a care in the world—lucky mite. The schoolmarm sat on the second bed, a book open on her lap. The middle girl sat at the small table with a sheet of paper before her, a McGuffey Reader at her side. She glanced at him, but her expression remained unchanged.

"What are you doing?" Nathan threw the question out to the room, though he knew who he wanted the answer from.

"Miss Ingles has us writing a report on a story we just read," Mary supplied from behind him.

"A report?" His workday was full of reports, and there was nothing he hated worse. To inflict that on children who had just borne such loss was incomprehensible. He fixed Miss Ingles with his sternest look—not difficult in the moment—and waved toward the door. "May I speak with you a moment, ma'am?" He ground out the words, anger rising as she didn't so much as move, her face remaining passive.

"If you have something to say, I must ask that you to say it here, but lower your voice as Lucy is sleeping."

"Excuse me, but what I have to say is not meant for younger ears." A few swears skittered across his mind, but his mother had taught him well enough to exclude them.

Her dark beady eyes narrowed though the lenses of her spectacles, and her lips pursed as though she were taking his measure. The man at the mine had been correct—if not a witch, she was a close relative. Though she couldn't be much past thirty, her mousy brown hair's tight bun gave her a severe look—like the rats back east. That was probably the best description for her. Even her voice was high-pitched and grated his nerves. "I'm afraid, Constable Stanford, that I am unable to comply at this time."

"Miss Ingles—"

"Constable." With the sharp authority with which she spoke, no doubt she was able to keep the children in her class in line, but he was long out of knee-pants and heeding anything hoity-toity females spouted at him.

"I won't take no for an answer."

"Then you will have to carry me."

"What?" Nathan stared at the woman. That was the last demand he had expected. "Excuse me?"

"I wish I could," she mumbled, still pinning him with those dark eyes of hers. "My foot was pinned under a roof during the slide and subsequently injured—to what extent I do not know. After what abuse it has already endured today, I have no desire to go anywhere." *Leastwise with you.* She didn't have to say it for her expression to communicate loud and clear. She was probably an effective teacher, and even as a boy he would have hated every moment under her scrutiny.

"Is it broken?"

"I don't know." Her shoulders seemed to slump a little from their rigid posture.

"What did the doctor say?" Why couldn't the woman just speak plainly?

"He didn't." She glanced at the girls. "He has been quite busy today, and a sore ankle is hardly consequential."

Nathan gave a low grunt and dropped his hat to the edge of the bed. "Let me take a look."

She gasped, almost giving him some pleasure. "That would be highly inappropriate."

He gave her a look of disbelief. "In my line of work, I've gained some training. As much as I would rather not, the longer a broken bone is left unattended, the more damage is done."

She scooted higher in the bed, as though she could somehow avoid him. "We don't know that it's broken," she squeaked. Perhaps she was more a mouse than a rat.

"That's the problem. And it's my duty to ascertain the damage." He sat on the bed and drew back the light blanket covering her wrapped foot. "Please don't think for a second that I will get any pleasure from this."

She seemed to shrink back even more, if that were possible, but her foot remained in place while he gently unwrapped the amateur bandaging obviously not done by the doctor or a nurse. He shook his head at the bloodied stocking that remained in place.

"Mary, can you run downstairs and ask for some towels and warm water? And fresh bandaging."

Mary made it as far as the door when a knock sounded. At the same time, the baby started to fuss. Nathan hollered for whoever it was to enter while Mary moved to comfort her sister. A woman with a tray and pitcher stepped into the room, her eyes widening at the scene.

"Ah, yes." His dinner. Which would be cold by the time he finished with Miss *Mouse*. He gave the schoolmarm the tight smile he usually reserved for those complaining while he locked them behind bars. This time, he was the one who felt trapped.

Chapter 7

Every muscle in Samantha's body stiffened at Constable Stanford's touch—as slight as that touch was. Completely professional. He was trained, after all. And yet, with his sleeves rolled up past his elbows and his hat and coat set aside, she could hardly ignore the warmth of his fingers or the concentrated furrow of his brow.

Silly girl.

She was just reacting to being touched by a man, a category of the species she had always been very conscious about keeping at arm's length. This had nothing to do with how attractive the man was.

Pain spiked up her leg, punishing her for woolgathering.

"That hurt?" he questioned.

"Yes."

He gave a noncommittal grunt, which seemed his most common form of communication. "How about this?" He tipped her foot to one side, and agony sliced through the joint.

She slapped a hand over the yelp that escaped her. Despite her reaction, he continued to poke and prod.

"Well, I don't think it's broken. Just sprained and swollen. We'll finish bandaging your ankle, and then I need to head back up to the coal mine."

Samantha's heart kicked in her chest. "Is that safe?" Not that her concern was for him, per se, but for the girls. They had already lost so much. And she couldn't quite shake the fear lingering in her soul.

He shook his head. Not with a *no*, but a *how is that even a consideration?*

"You should eat something," she suggested.

He took the roll of bandaging before glancing at the girls who picked away at the buttered bread and stew delivered earlier. Lucy seemed the only one with much of an appetite. "Maybe," was the only reply the man provided.

He spread a generous helping of green salve onto her open cuts and positioned the first layer of bandaging when a cry rose from the street below. He dropped the cloth and jumped from the edge of the bed. One leap had him to the window, which he shoved upward.

From her spot, Samantha couldn't hear what was being shouted, but the commotion grew outside. Her pulse raced with thoughts of what might be wrong. Then a cheer rose above the ruckus.

"What is it?"

Constable Stanford had already grabbed his coat and was halfway to the door. "The miners."

Mary and Abby raced after him, though still in their nightgowns, leaving Lucy on the floor and the door open.

The whole town seemed to come alive outside the window, but Samantha remained frozen in place, her foot half bandaged and a baby staring after her sisters. Lucy crawled toward the door.

"Wait here with me, Lucy." Samantha stretched forward and hurried to finish wrapping her foot, not caring how poor the result was. As soon as she'd tied off the end, she swung her feet over the side of the bed and beckoned again to Lucy—who continued on her path to the hallway. A woman bustled past but didn't so much as glance at the baby. Samantha had no choice but to brace herself up and hobble across the floor. Lucy was halfway to the stairs before Samantha managed to scoop her up and sag against the wall. Her foot throbbed painfully, but she still had to return to the room, now with her arms full.

Curse the man, even if she did understand what pulled him away.

Samantha took her time making her way to the window between the beds, but not without more abuse to her injured foot. She pulled a side table close and perched on the edge so she could look down on the street and the bustle below. Folks streamed from the hotel and other buildings. She caught sight of Constable Stanford's scarlet coat as he ran toward a group of men farther up the street. Even from here, she could make out their stained faces and dirty clothes. The miners. Over a dozen. Closer to twenty. . . They'd somehow survived.

A sob swelled in Samantha's throat at the sight, but she tried to blink back the tears. This was so unlike her. Never had her emotions sat so close to the surface. It had to be the exhaustion. She was so tired and so heartbroken for so many families—especially these three girls. Perhaps their loss was not so complete if their father was down there.

Samantha settled Lucy onto her lap to watch the celebration below. No, celebration wasn't quite right. The scar on the mountain looming over them cast a deep shadow over the town, darkening even the relief and reunions taking place on the street below. More than one of those miners had families affected by the slide—or killed. While Mary and Abby would be relieved to see their father, his heart would be broken to know his wife and all his boys were killed.

Tears slipped down Samantha's cheeks.

"They're dead."

The words tumbled through her brain, as clear as they had been said today—not almost two decades ago.

"They're dead."

Samantha let a wiggling Lucy back to the floor and tried to shake herself from the oppressive cloud draping itself over the entire room. She swatted at the tears and hobbled from the window to the small vanity with mirror perched above, and pitcher and basin waiting with cool water. She washed her face and cleared her eyes. No more tears. She had to focus on what others needed. She straightened the papers and pencils the girls had been using and marked their place in the McGuffey Reader. A piece of bread kept Lucy occupied, while Samantha helped herself to a couple of spoonfuls of the stew. She couldn't remember the last time she'd eaten. Yesterday felt like forever ago.

The room was tidy, and her foot ached something fierce by the time the door creaked open. Abby was tugged past the threshold by her sister, whose eyes were red and heavy with tears. Mary threw herself onto the bed and sobbed.

"No," Samantha looked for confirmation from the red-coated constable who stood like a shadow in the doorway, his jaw ticking. "Those weren't the miners?"

"Seventeen of the twenty miners were able to dig their way upward, instead of attempting to clear away the main shaft. Everyone inside the mine made it out alive."

Samantha felt the air flee her lungs.

"Three were on break and stepped outside for some fresh air."

Mary looked up, seeking Samantha. "Papa's dead," she whispered. "Just like Mama and the boys."

They're dead.

Constable Stanford pushed backward into the hall, his head shaking. "I can't believe it. . ."

Samantha sighed as she watched his retreat. Denial liked to linger at the beginning, threatening you with hope when there was none.

Chapter 8

Memories struck like rocks tumbling into him, hitting Nathan with growing force. Peter had been Nathan's closest friend and companion for the whole of their childhoods. Only two years older than Nathan, Peter had done everything with him. He had been Nathan's anchor in their large family, when no one else had really seen him. Until Rosemary had come between them.

Somehow that seemed inconsequential now.

Why had Nathan not tried harder to forgive his brother?

Unfortunately, the chance to make things right was buried under hundreds of tons of limestone.

Nathan shoved the blanket aside and swung his feet over the side of the bed. The world seemed silent, as though nothing had happened. And yet his insides felt torn apart.

He shoved his feet into his boots and pulled on his coat. He hadn't brought civilian clothes, so he had no choice but to wear his uniform into the cool night air. Under a streetlamp, he peered at his watch. Four thirty-six in the morning. Just over twenty-four hours from when the mountain summit had rushed down, destroying everything in its path. A livery with over fifty horses. Two ranches. A railway camp with who knew how many workers. Miners and families in their cottages.

Nathan squeezed his eyes closed against a swell of emotion that threatened to pour down his face as he pictured his brother joking with the other two men who had joined him for a quick midnight lunch outside the confines of the mine. They had no warning, nothing to save them from the boulders that had swept them into the eternities.

Rosemary and their four boys would have had less warning. Had they even had time for the roar to wake them, or had they opened their eyes to heaven?

Heaven.

Nathan clung to that. What other comfort was there?

He walked toward Manitoba Avenue until he reached the edge of the slide. The shuffle of soft footsteps turned him to the shadows. A small form stood draped in a patchwork quilt. They stared at each other for several minutes, though he couldn't see her face. Just that it was a child.

"What are you doing out here?" he finally questioned.

She sniffled—yes, a girl—and took another step toward him. "Followed you. I couldn't sleep."

"Mary?"

A couple more steps brought her under the glow of a streetlamp. "I can't stop being scared."

Nathan blew out his breath and crossed to her, opening his arms. Guilt stabbed him in the side. He should have stayed with the girls, offered them comfort. Not left them with the ice queen. He'd been so caught up in his own loss and the overwhelmingness of it all, he hadn't truly considered the depth of theirs.

"What's going to happen to us now?" her small voice whimpered.

The future? Was that truly more terrifying than the remains of the mountain hovering over them and the memory of being trapped under a roof? He tightened his hold. But what could he offer? They had plenty of other aunts and uncles, many with comfortable houses and cousins for them to grow up with. "Someone in the family will take you in and give you a home."

"But you're the only one we know."

"You never met me before today."

She kept her hold. "Pa talked about you the most."

Nathan shook his head. He was a single man with at least another two years in the force. And he knew nothing of raising children—especially girls for that matter. While he might be the only one Mary remembered, he was the least suited to be her guardian. "That will change. I'll write them and ask them to come."

She shivered in his arms, but he sensed it wasn't from the chill of night.

"Hey." He held her away from him so he could look into her eyes—too much like her father's even under the dim streetlamps. "I promise I will make sure you have a good home with a family who will love you and take care of you."

"And Abby and Lucy?"

"Yes, and Abby and Lucy. I swear it."

She leaned into him, her thin arms wrapping his torso. "I want *my* family." Sobs wracked her body, and all Nathan could do was hold her while his own tears tumbled free. He wanted his brother back too. . .he wanted a second chance.

———— ◆ ————

A wail rose like a siren through the night, dragging Samantha away from the pull of sleep. Not that she had slept at all—as much as she craved that relief, her mind refused to settle. And when it finally did, Lucy would begin to cry. Mary had been the most successful at calming her up to now, but the baby sounded inconsolable now.

Heaving herself to the side of the bed, Samantha felt her way to the apple crate they had turned into a crib for Lucy. Moonlight filtered through sheer curtains, assisting her efforts to find the child.

"Hush, hush." Samantha pulled the baby into her arms for the little good it did. She knew little about babies—so it was probably good she would never have her own. A glance at the bed where the older girls slept revealed one huddled form, tucked almost completely under the blankets.

Mary's place showed the quilt pushed back and the starkness of white sheets.

"Mary?" A pointless whisper, but desperation clawed at Samantha's chest. She was exhausted, and her hurt foot would not allow her to pace the floor with the child or offer more comfort than cuddling to her shoulder and the offer of a bottle. "Hush, hush."

Still poor Lucy bawled, probably wanting her mother, or something more than lukewarm cow milk. She wanted comfort, warmth, and love. What did Samantha know about any of that?

"Hush, hush." A pat on the back had little effect. Nor did rocking back and forth. Or forward and back. All that revealed was muscles Samantha hadn't realized were so sore.

Still the baby screamed.

What a nightmare.

Footsteps preceded the door cracking open and a slight form slipping inside.

"Mary, where were you?" Samantha's voice cut through the night like a knife. The exhaustion was too much, and the baby would have the whole hotel awake soon, if not already.

Instead of replying, Mary took her baby sister and danced across the floor with a rock to each step. She snatched the bottle from Samantha and pressed the nipple into the child's mouth. A few unsteady sobs and then the smack of lips against rubber. The room quieted, and some of the tension slipped from Samantha's shoulders. She glanced at the still open door and the form filling it. Her breath hitched. Now he came?

Yet the indomitable, and far too attractive, Mountie didn't move from his position in the doorway, his face shadowed but not so much that she couldn't make out the scowl there as he returned her stare. What, had she failed him because she hadn't been able to quiet the baby on her own? Did he dare judge her when the girls were his responsibility, not hers? She was a teacher, an educator of older children, not a nursemaid. She had no experience!

Anger spiked through her, but just as she opened her mouth he turned back into the hall and disappeared behind the door. Gone. Again.

Coward.

Here she'd thought Mounties were supposed to ride to the rescue. But no, they were men, and as a result undependable.

Samantha's shoulders slumped and her head tipped forward, pulling the tight muscles of her neck. The baby was quiet again, but how long would that last? Mary settled onto the edge of the second bed, rocking gently. The quilts shifted, making it clear that Abby hadn't remained asleep either. They had to all be as exhausted as she was, yet behind closed eyes lurked the fear of being trapped, the memory of a roof pinning them in place, the rumble of rocks filling the valley, thoughts of people. . .

Samantha hobbled the short distance to the closest edge of the second bed and laid a hand over Abby's still form. The child rolled away from the brief contact, leaving Samantha's hand lingering in space. Unwanted. Better to withdraw and let the child have her space. Hadn't that been what she had needed when she'd lost her parents?

Retreating to her bed, Samantha fought the desire to pull the quilt up over her own head and follow Abby's example. Instead, she squeezed her eyes closed and tried not to think. . .not to remember.

Chapter 9

Pounding, like rocks thundering upon the roof, shoved Samantha's heart to her throat and jerked her awake from her nightmares to. . .the door. The hotel room. The girls all fast asleep.

The knocking continued, and she pushed up from the bed, mindful of her foot as she hopped across the floor. She swung it open to a red brick wall.

Maybe not the most generous thought but she was exhausted, her foot throbbed, and he'd abandoned his nieces with her without any direction or notice of when he'd return. "You couldn't just walk in like you did yesterday?"

"I didn't want to. . ." Constable Stanford glanced down at the skirt and blouse she'd been wearing for the past two days. "Just in case you were not up and. . .ready for the day."

She sighed and hobbled to the nearest chair. "For your information, I was not yet *up*. It was a rough night." As he well knew. "But since this is the only outfit I have left, I had no choice but to remain fully clothed."

He seemed to consider her for a moment. "You were awake when. . .it happened?"

"I hadn't been." Samantha massaged her temples, her mind returning to the crack of thunder and the roar of the world crumbling down on her. She tried to shake herself from the too fresh memory. "I fell asleep when I should have been working." All those stories were gone now. And many of the children who had written them.

Her thoughts flashed to Lillian Clark who had written a beautiful piece about the beauty of the mountains in the winter. Had she stayed at the boardinghouse? Had any of her family survived? And Lester Johnson? Was he recovering from his injuries?

"Miss Ingles?"

Breathe. "What is it you want?" Her tone came out much harder than she intended, but she felt barely held together.

"Premier Haultain has arrived and ordered the evacuation of Frank. The immediate evacuation." He glanced across the room at the sleeping girls—well, Lucy still slept. The other two sat in bed watching. "If I can bother you long enough to have the girls ready, I will be back for them in a half hour." Constable Stanford stood like a statue, face passive as he waited for an answer.

"Of course." If only for the sake of the girls, though she felt sorry for them once they were fully under their uncle's care. He would be just as likely to hand them off on the next unsuspecting person he thought capable of caring for them.

She closed the door behind him, relief short-lived. Get the girls ready for the morning and to leave Frank. A spasm of pain up her leg was an all too clear reminder of her own situation—which she had mostly avoided considering until this moment. The girls at least had an uncle to sweep them away from this nightmare.

What did she have?

Nothing and no one. She should be used to it by now.

Heat burned behind her eyes, and she filled her lungs in an attempt to push down a wave of panic. Go to work. Focus outward. She'd get the girls ready and hand them over to their uncle before allowing for any thought of her own predicament. Maybe something would come up by then.

She startled at another knock and steeled herself before opening the door.

Miss Thornley stood with bundles in arms. She offered a quick smile and invited herself into the room. "So glad I caught you before you've left. The town will soon be nothing but a ghost town." She clamped her mouth shut and glanced at Mary and Abby's wide eyes. "Me and my tongue." Miss Thornley walked to the closest bed and lowered her bundles before offering the girls a smile. "I hope these fit."

Samantha hurried her awkward trek back across the floor. "What?"

"The clothes I found for the girls." She glanced back at Samantha and eyed her from head to toe. "And for you."

"You found a dress for me?" Samantha didn't dare ask where she'd gathered the clothes. She wasn't much on taking charity, but a change of clothes would be glorious—or at least had the potential to be.

"Yes, yes, yes, and I think it's the perfect color with your complexion." Miss Thornley emptied one bundle onto the foot of the bed and held up a sage green day dress. A simple dress, really, but with lace on the collar and cuffs, an extravagance Samantha generally avoided. But to be clean. . . "There are some undergarments as well that I picked up from the shop next door."

"Oh, I'll reimburse you. . ." Samantha quickly offered before remembering that her funds remained buried in the Stanford home along with her wardrobe. "As soon as I can." She would have to wire her solicitor in Toronto and have him send money, though she disliked digging into what her parents had left her.

"Tosh." Miss Thornley waved as though to dismiss the thought. "I will be back in Pincher Creek by the end of the day and don't want you worrying about it. It was a pleasure to help—something to add meaning to my life, make it more worthwhile." She lowered the dress and then herself to the edge of the bed. The feigned cheerfulness slipped away to reveal a look that better mirrored Samantha's deepest thoughts. "We're alive. For some reason God chose to save us, to prolong our lives. But for what? What reason? What have I to offer?"

Samantha opened her mouth with the thought of offering some insight or comfort. But there was nothing to say. Even though she wanted to argue, it was merely coincidence or luck that had saved them. But there was something in the woman's eyes that stayed Samantha's tongue, a spark of. . .

Samantha shook her head. Hope was not something she was familiar enough with to recognize. She had to be mistaken.

Miss Thornley continued speaking, though she wasn't looking at Samantha any longer. "I don't feel like I can go back to being the person I was two days ago. I've wasted so much time wishing for better health, and complaining about things. . .situations I didn't feel I could change. But what is stopping me?"

"What indeed?" Samantha cringed as she spoke the words. But what was she supposed to say? As far as she had seen, Miss Thornley had been a delightful and friendly woman. Even now she offered a smile.

"Exactly." She stood and handed Samantha the dress.

"Thank you for everything," Samanatha said. "And all the best on your journey home."

"You as well."

Home?

Another thing Samantha had little experience with. Uncertainty. Dependency on others. Standing on the outskirts of the community—*that* was where her expertise lay. So why feel so upset over the current upheaval and looming unknown?

———◆◆◆———

Nathan loaded the girls and their small bundle of clothes into the wagon before looking back at the woman who stood watching from the door of the hotel. The other guests had already fled the town, leaving the owners to shutter windows and empty the larder with little knowledge of whether there would be a return. The Canadian government was sending out a surveyor to take a closer look at the mountain and what had caused the slide, but a full report could take weeks, and if the mountain was found to be too unstable, there would be no rebuilding the town of Frank.

He gave Miss Ingles a short nod before moving toward the wagon seat. He needed to get his nieces set up in Blairmore, a small town a few miles west, so he could return to his duty here in Frank. His duty and arrangements for the burial of his sister-in-law and nephews. His steps grew heavier with each he took to the front of the wagon he'd been fortunate enough to borrow from a livery in Blairmore. With only an hour remaining before he'd agreed to have it returned, Nathan didn't have time to wallow.

He gripped the seat, ready to pull himself upward, but spared one last glance at the schoolteacher. She leaned heavily against the doorframe as she offered a small wave to Mary and Abby, who sat silent in the back of the wagon. Would the girls be all right on their own while he was away? Would there be someone in Blairmore willing or able to assist with their care?

Distaste soured his stomach, but what choice did he have? Nathan groaned but forced himself to turn. "What are your plans, Miss Ingles?"

"Um. . ." Her eyes widened like a frightened calf, almost making him laugh after the image of a cold-hearted spinster she had installed in his head yesterday. Suddenly she seemed a little more human. "I'm not certain."

"Well, evacuation orders are in place, so you might as well crawl in." It fell under his duty to see her as far as Blairmore, after all. And then, if he couldn't find someone with a little less starch and discipline, at least she would be nearby and maybe even feel in his debt.

Her dark eyes flashed, and her chin rose a degree. "*Crawl* in?"

All right, so maybe his invitation could have been better worded. He honestly didn't care what she thought of him in return. "You would prefer I carry you?"

"Honestly, at the moment, I'm not sure I wouldn't prefer to stand here and risk the mountain falling."

"Miss Ingles," Mary squeaked at the thought.

"Yes, Miss Ingles." Nathan started toward her. They didn't have time to dally. "Do be serious. If you have made no arrangements to leave Frank, I suggest you accompany us as far as Blairmore."

"Very well," she replied stiffly before disappearing inside. She hobbled out a moment later with a satchel in hand. She must have had it waiting for her in the lobby. Wincing with each step, Miss Ingles made her way to the edge of the boardwalk.

Nathan felt his head shaking. He didn't have time for this. "If you'll allow me, Miss Ingles." He bounded up the stairs and scooped her into his arms before she could protest. She yelped in surprise, then stiffened like a board. Thankfully, a moment later he was able to deposit the woman on the wagon seat and make his way to the other side.

"Miss Ingles!"

Nathan twisted in his seat to a young woman racing across the street toward them. Her blond braid whipped from side to side. A sigh of what sounded like relief slipped from the woman beside him. "Lillian."

Upon closer inspection, the young woman was still very much a girl, probably no older than fifteen or sixteen. She scampered up the side of the wagon like a raccoon and wrapped Miss Ingles in an embrace. "You're alive! I thought everyone on our street would be dead. Mama, Ellen, Gertrude, and the boys. They're all gone."

Miss Ingles tightened her hold on the girl—perhaps she did have a heart after all. "I'm so sorry. What about your father? Was he at the mine?"

Tear-filled eyes lifted and she nodded.

"Then he—"

Lillian shook her head. "He was on his break up at the tipple."

"Clark." Nathan nodded as understanding cinched around his chest, restricting his breath. "You're one of the Clark girls." Her father had stood with Peter during his final moments.

"The last one." Huge tears rolled down her flushed cheeks.

"But you are alive," Miss Ingles held her back just enough to meet her wet gaze. "Do something with that."

"Do you think God has some reason, some purpose for me?"

The woman beside him said nothing, but he felt himself nod. That had to be it. A lone survivor of a family. There had to be a reason, didn't there?

Lillian sniffled. "I don't have your book with me, but I'll find a way to get it back to you."

"No," Miss Ingles whispered. "Read it. It will help. It always helped."

Nathan wanted to groan out loud. This woman was something else. How would reading a book—other than perhaps the Bible—help soothe the pain this girl had? Somehow, he remained silent as goodbyes were said and the girl slipped away, despite every argument against the teacher's approach to grief. She'd obviously never felt so cutting a loss.

Chapter 10

A simple canvas tent. Three tan-colored walls and a flap for a door that allowed far too much of the spring breeze inside, but the few lodgings available in Blairmore had quickly been grabbed up by the first folks who had fled Frank. Given the circumstances, Samantha would try to be grateful for the roof over her head, even if canvas, and the lack of bugs and flies due to the earliness of the season.

"You might as well make yourself at home here today," Constable Stanford said from just outside.

Samantha managed a nod, not needing the reminder that the only reason she had a place in this tent was her usefulness. Not because she was welcome. No, the good constable had seemed a little disgruntled with the arrangement—and not just because he wouldn't have a place in the tent with them. The Northwest Mounted Police had already set up barracks closer to Frank that he planned to occupy, so obviously he simply wished for someone else to care for his nieces.

"Do you need anything else before I leave?"

Samantha stepped into the afternoon sun, mindful of her foot. Thankfully, the pain was not as acute as yesterday. "I imagine we will get along well enough once you're gone, Constable." She bit the tip of her tongue but didn't regret the barb. She was done with him looking over her shoulder at everything she did and finding her lacking.

Constable Stanford looked down at her while he snugged his flat-brimmed Stetson into place. "I don't know when I'll be back. Maybe not until tomorrow. But I'll check in when I can."

"Of course you will." Samantha managed a tight smile that probably didn't help her words land any softer.

He strode to his horse, already exchanged for the wagon that had brought them to what was quickly becoming a tent city. Samantha was about to turn inside when she heard her name. She turned to see none other than Robert Chestnut hurrying toward her.

He laughed out loud while shaking his head. "I thought for sure you hadn't survived the slide."

Something in his voice made her chest close in on itself. He was surprised, but there was no relief or even sincerity in his tone.

"You lived in one of the miner cottages on Manitoba Avenue, didn't you?"

"Yes, but as you see, here I am in one piece." She glanced at Constable Stanford who had not yet mounted, his attention instead on the newcomer. Made sense, him being who he was. His presence gave her no reason to remain a minute longer. "Excuse me while I see to my charges." Samantha ducked back inside the tent and pulled down the flap. Hopefully Mr. Chestnut would not be as persistent as the last time they'd met.

The conversation continued on without her, the men's voices loud and clear. "Rob" introduced himself to the constable only to be met with interrogation.

"How do you know Miss Ingles?" Constable Stanford questioned.

"We crossed paths a time or two in Frank."

Samantha could easily picture Mr. Chestnut's casual shrug that likely accompanied the pause.

"Don't tell me you have any interest there."

She glanced at Mary, who was thankfully distracted with Lucy and didn't seem aware of anything else. Samantha's own spine stiffened while her ribs constricted. The way Mr. Chestnut spoke didn't denote jealousy, but disbelief.

"Do you?" the constable replied coolly. Probably due to his protectiveness of his nieces and who associated with them.

A bark of a laugh was punctuated with a "No. She's been amusing to tease, as uptight and skittish as she is around men, but..." The man mercifully quit speaking, but Samantha could sense the cringe in his words. He had been toying with her. Of course, that made more sense than a man being actually attracted or interested in anything more than amusement at her expense. How grateful she was that she hadn't entertained his invitations! How she wished her vision would not sting or blur. She took a jagged breath but didn't dare move or draw attention to herself. The men resumed their conversation while headed away from the tent. Good riddance to the both of them!

Samantha swiped at a trickle of moisture on her cheek. A crack in her well-constructed dam. Another breath and she shifted away from the canvas and turned to the disarray which was to be her residence for the next day or so. Lucy sat on the floor playing with a couple of smooth sticks Mary had found for her. Abby huddled on the pallet they had made up for the older two girls. A blanket hid her face from the world. Silent and miserable.

Mary rose from Lucy's side to watch Samantha with her somber eyes. "Are you all right?"

"Of course." She tried for a nod. "Let's finish making up the pallets, and then perhaps we can do some writing today. You never did finish your story for me. Or we could read for a while. We have *The Princess and the Goblin*. I'm sure that would be very...diverting." Because right now that is what Samantha needed so very badly. A diversion from the turmoil and hurt she was desperately trying to ignore.

———◆◆———

Pity. That's what he felt, and Nathan hoped Miss Ingles hadn't overheard Mr. Chestnut—as unlikely as that was. It wasn't that he hadn't spoken the truth about the woman, but a man should be more considerate of a woman's feelings. Assuming the woman had any of those.

He shook off the unkind thought and encouraged Rover into a gallop. The sun sat in the western sky, reminding him that half the day was spent just getting the girls settled. No, *settled* wasn't the right word. Every single one of them was as unsettled and lost and miserable as he. Even Lucy, who probably had no concept of her loss and wouldn't for years, showed how much she missed her mother and home.

Nathan pushed Rover harder still, and the animal eagerly accepted the challenge, racing through the valley toward the scarred mountain. The wind snatched at his hat, so he tugged the brim lower and leaned over the horse's neck. His pulse raced with the pounding hooves, and he could almost feel the blood coursing through his veins. Life. Did Peter hear the rocks pounding down the mountain before they struck? Folks said the slide lasted less than two minutes. Was he killed immediately or. . .

Nathan shook the thought from his head and blinked the burn from behind his eyes. He didn't have time to contemplate such things. He had a duty to perform. Letters would need to be written to his parents and siblings explaining what had happened and asking for someone to provide a home for the girls. Of his three sisters and three remaining brothers, surely there would be options, cousins who would become like siblings, an aunt who could love the girls and help them grieve.

Miss Ingles in her tight bun and severe gaze flashed through his mind invoking a groan. Hopefully other arrangements could be made speedily.

Nathan slowed as he neared Frank, now almost completely empty but for the last few who lingered to close their shops and pack their stores. A large wagon sat in front of the bank, with two Mounties flanking it, likely to guard the mine's payroll and whatever else this town boasted for wealth. He nodded at his friends but kept riding toward Manitoba Avenue and what remained of his brother's home.

Behind Nathan, a train whistle blared, and he turned in his saddle. Sure enough, a train slowed as it rolled toward the heaps of rubble covering the tracks for several kilometers. He reined his horse in that direction, curious why they hadn't stopped at the Blairmore station.

The doors to the cars slid open, and men began disembarking before Nathan reached the platform. Laborers. Nearly a hundred of them if not more. How had they been gathered so quickly? Nathan guided Rover in their direction.

"Where are you all from?"

The middle-aged man squinted into the afternoon sun. "All over, but most recently Morrissey, British Columbia. We were held up there for an extra day." The man looked to the south, his features sagging and eyes widening as he took in the destruction in their path. "And to think we were raging about being forgotten."

"Forgotten?"

A younger man at his side took up the conversation. "We were supposed to be picked up from Morrissey on the twenty-eighth. We would have been in camp two days ago." He motioned down the tracks while his jaw tensed. His voice grew solemn. "But the train went past without us, leaving us stranded in these cars and steaming mad." The young man took a jagged breath and dragged the cap from his head. "We should have been buried under all that with our foreman."

"God be praised," the older fellow whispered, his gaze frozen on the ocean of limestone filling the valley before them.

Nathan glanced at the other men as they took in the same view and understanding widened their gazes. Many muttered prayers of thanks while others shook their heads with both horror and amazement that somehow they had escaped such a horrible fate.

Nathan started away from the train with only one more glance back. Over a hundred men spared because of a mistake. . . It couldn't have been a mistake.

He fished a leather notebook out of his coat pocket and stopped his horse on the edge of what was once Gold Creek. Some of the puddles had receded from yesterday, but the ground was still moist and sloppy. Bracing the book against the pommel of the saddle, Nathan took a pencil and scribbled down a few thoughts. About his nieces. About Mr. Chestnut and his brother. Lillian Clark. And over a hundred men.

"Constable Stanford?"

Nathan snapped the book closed and pushed it back into his pocket before looking up at the man hurrying over the rocks in his direction. A large mustache covered more than his upper lip, probably to make up for what lacked on the top of his graying head.

"Yes."

"You look a lot like your brother." The man wiped the perspiration from his brow and stuck his hanky in his pocket. "I'm sorry about him and his family. A tragedy."

Nathan nodded, though tragedy seemed an understatement, making him question the words he'd recorded moments before.

"We've taken Rosemary and the boys up to the church with some of the other bodies we've been able to recover. Anything in particular you want done?"

His teeth hurt from the pressure building in his jaw. This shouldn't be for him to decide. But what would Peter want? Nathan hated to admit it, but—"I don't know. We'll need something of a funeral for them. For the sake of the girls if nothing else. I'll need to see to their transport up to Blairmore and arrange a plot for them there." He'd already been told the Frank cemetery had been buried. Unusable, like most of the town now.

"I'll arrange for the transportation. I already talked with William Warrington. We'll be taking his wife and four young'uns to Blairmore as well once we've found everyone." The man's head dropped forward a degree and slowly shook.

"William Warrington." The name sounded familiar. "He was one of the miners, wasn't he. Hurt his leg?"

"That's him. Survived the mine just to come home and find his family gone. We dug out his brother-in-law a few minutes ago."

Nathan clenched his jaw against a swear. He should rip out the page he'd just written and burn it. God couldn't have a hand in this. It had to be coincidence that had spared anyone's life.

"Could use more hands digging out the rest of Warrington's house," the man continued. "It's grueling, heartbreaking work."

"Of course." Nathan dismounted and tied Rover in the shade of a willow, its lower trunk wearing scars from yesterday's events...but somehow still standing. Not like the several huge spruces chopped up like twigs and mangled along with everything else the rocks swept up with them.

Chapter 11

MAY 1ST

Samantha tied the bow on the back of Abby's dress and led her to the door. The child resisted every step, her feet dragging through the grass serving as a carpet in the tent. She understood the child well enough—who would want to attend the funeral of their parents and siblings? No time had been given for the adjustment from family picnics to tragedy.

A sigh slipped from Samantha. Maybe it had been good the Stanfords had allowed their children to skip school after all. There would always be another class, more sums to learn, and another book to read. But family once lost. . .

"Come along, Abby," Constable Stanford beckoned from where he stood with baby Lucy in his arms and Mary waiting at his side. A striking image in his scarlet uniform, with the brim of his hat cutting across his lowered brow.

Samantha shifted her gaze away. How insignificant she must seem to a man like him. She gave Abby a little push of encouragement and stepped back.

"You're not coming?" Stanford's question was more accusatory than inquisitive.

She forced herself to meet his eyes, trying hard to pretend indifference to the heavy emotion hanging on the morning air. "There will be enough mourners present. It's better that I am not in the way." She tried for a smile, but it slipped away with equal speed. "And this will give me time to tidy the beds and wash diapers." In the past twenty-four hours she had somehow become a maid as well as a nanny and schoolteacher, but it was only for a few days. She would go into Blairmore this afternoon or Monday and contact her solicitor and the school executives. Then plans could be made. Right now, she grasped her excuse to remain away from the funeral held for those who'd been killed in the slide. Already Samantha found herself on the edge of her emotions and fought not to plummet into the abyss.

By the look of stone in Constable Stanford's eyes, he either didn't buy her excuse or think they held any worth. But what did she care what he thought of her? She straightened her shoulders and relaxed her hands at her side. Control of one's emotions at all times—that was one of the lessons she'd learned over and over again throughout the years. No one cared what she felt, so why give feeling any power over her?

"Very well, then." Stanford turned stiffly and led the girls up the slope toward the Blairmore cemetery.

Mary slipped her hand into her uncle's while glancing back. Samantha offered a small wave. Perhaps she should go for the sake of the girls—or at least Mary. But she had her uncle and sisters. Samantha was really nothing to her. Just a schoolteacher, and teachers came and went like the seasons. Yes, they left lessons and understanding and a mark upon your life, but not in the same way, not with the same depth of connection.

Loneliness wrapped its cold fingers around Samantha's heart and gave a squeeze. Even escaping back into the tent did not help in prying her free of its hold. Instead, the ache increased at the sight of the book Mary had left open on her cot, the blanket Abby had clung to for the past day, and the smooth sticks Lucy had abandoned on the floor. Little things, so why did they make her sad?

Samantha turned back outside and looked down the valley. Turtle Mountain appeared unaffected from this angle. Blairmore provided a wide valley with the closest mountains green with forests reaching to the curved tops. No jagged cliffs or threat of the world crumbling down on them.

She blew out her breath, but her chest remained tight. A short walk up the side of the northern mountain sat a handful of graves—a number that would probably be doubled if not tripled today. Fathers, mothers, brothers, and sisters. People who had others who cared for and would miss them.

Hard not to consider what it would mean for the world if she had perished as well. No one would have cared when her body was recovered. Perhaps a letter would have been written to the school executives informing them of her demise and asking after her next of kin. The letter would be tucked away as there was no one to forward it to. No kin. No one who cared.

Samantha gritted her teeth. This train of thought wasn't getting her anywhere. She had her own letter to write to the executives, informing them of the recent events and asking for instruction. The school year would be over soon and with Frank evacuated, it wasn't as though she had a school in which to teach.

Honestly, she wasn't sure she would want to go back there if she could. The thought of Turtle Mountain looming overhead with its deep scar and piles of rock strewn for miles sent shivers through her. No, she would ask to be reassigned. Perhaps somewhere in the middle of the bald prairies.

———————

Nathan tried to keep his breathing even as he stared at the raw dirt, black and bare. Mr. Thornley, a friend and neighbor to Peter, had already etched the names into the hastily constructed crosses they had placed at the head of each grave, even including Peter's name beside Rosemary's. Despite it being a single grave. Despite his body being lost under heaps of limestone, an unmarked grave likely never to be found or disturbed.

If only he could take comfort in that. But instead, the thought left Nathan hollow inside. As did the thought of Rosemary's broken body buried only feet away from where he stood. For a moment he allowed his mind to wander from his brother to the woman who had come between them. She'd been a ray of sunshine with her blond hair and ready smile.

Being Nathan's age, they had shared a desk at school, and she had made class bearable. First because he had been able to distract himself with teasing her, though that had only gotten him in more trouble with the schoolmarm. Especially when she'd pulled them apart during a schoolyard skirmish.

Nathan almost chuckled at the memory. Rosemary had been able to hold her own against him. But she'd also forgiven him quickly, and before long they had become inseparable. Despite her dress, she'd kept up with him just fine, not hesitating to wade into mud to trap a frog or climb a tree to make a fort. Best friends. Her, Nathan, and Peter.

A hand slipped into Nathan's, and a head leaned against his arm. He added pressure to the hold. He was the adult here, the one looked upon for support and guidance. Not just because of the uniform he wore.

"I know the preacher said they are in a better place and will be happy in heaven," Mary sniffled. "But I miss them. I wish..." She buried her face in his sleeve which was already moist from her tears.

At least she was letting herself cry. Unlike Abby who stood behind them, silent as a stone, her face scowling.

Lucy sat in the new grass at their feet, letting the thin strands tickle her palm, unaware that her mother and brothers were buried feet away. Maybe that was a miracle.

"Constable Stanford?"

Nathan fortified himself before glancing to a man only a few years his senior but with gray at his temples and throughout his mustache. His homespun clothes and coal-stained jacket suggested he was a miner. "Yes."

"My name's Ennis. Sam Ennis. Just felt I should say how much we liked your brother and his family, both as a neighbor and to work alongside. Our house was right beside theirs." He nodded to the girls. "Our young'uns played together."

"I'm sorry." Nathan should be the one offering condolences. The man had likely been at the mine as well while his family... Nathan shook his head. "I'm so sorry." What could he offer more than that?

The man's eyes narrowed momentarily and then widened as though with sudden understanding. "My family survived."

Nathan rocked back on his heels. He'd seen Manitoba Avenue, seen the houses buried. "But you said. . ."

"I wasn't at the mine that night. I was home with my wife and young'uns. We were all asleep in our beds when the rocks fell. The house was partially buried yet somehow stayed intact just enough. A beam trapped my wife until help came and we were able to free her. We dug out our young'uns—at least the three of them. All except the youngest. There was so much mud, and she was thrown from where she'd been sleeping with us. Thought she was dead when we first found her, not breathing." The man drew his hat off his head and wiped his free hand across his glistening eyes. "But my wife was able to clear little Gladys' mouth and got her to breathing again."

Nathan stood staring mutely, not knowing what to say, wonder and something deeper taking root in his chest.

"But that's not what I came here to say, though I thank God for sparing them. And your nieces—God keeping them safe like He did. I know it may feel like He's turned His back on us allowing this to happen, but God is in the details. The slide could have easily taken out the whole town instead of just the edge. The fellows in the mine could have all been killed."

A part of Nathan wanted to argue, Mr. Ennis's view was skewed because his family had somehow survived the disaster. Other folks had not been so lucky.

Was it luck?

Nathan looked back at Rosemary's grave and the smaller ones where her four sons lay.

"They aren't really there," a voice whispered in his head.

It was something he already knew, but so easy to forget when faced with such tragedy.

"I need to be on my way, but we're also staying here in Blairmore, if you or the girls need anything." Sam Ennis touched the brim of his hat and started away.

"Thank you," Nathan managed to mumble. And he was grateful. Not just for the offer but for the reminder. He fished his notebook from his pocket to make another entry.

"What's that, Uncle Nathan?"

Nathan finished his scribbling before looking at Mary. He slapped the leather-bound book closed. "Nothing." And yet that seemed a horrid sort of denial. He tucked the notebook and pencil away and wrapped an arm around his niece. "Just trying to make sense of all this."

She didn't press for more, and he was grateful. He needed more time to untangle his thoughts from his emotions.

Chapter 12

Six telegrams sent. All reading the same stark words: *PETER AND WIFE DEAD ALONG WITH THE FOUR BOYS IN LANDSLIDE AT FRANK. THREE DAUGHTERS NEED HOMES. PLEASE REPLY.*

Nathan took more time writing out an explanation to his parents about the slide and Peter and his family's fate. The three girls were safe and sound, and Nathan would see to their needs until his siblings could step in.

Hopefully he'd hear back from someone in the next couple of days so he could again focus on his work.

As Nathan stepped outside, Mary jumped up from her seat on the bench leaning against the post office. A prickle of guilt settled uneasily into his gut. Mary had expressed more than once her wish that they could stay with him, but he was the single uncle with no wife and no prospects of one in the foreseeable future. He lived in the North-West Mounted Police barracks, rode after criminals, and went where he was told when he was told. There was no place in his life for three little girls.

Maybe there would never be.

The thought struck a deeper chord than it ever had before.

Nathan shook the sensation from him and lifted Lucy from where she sat on the bench, arms extended. Only then did he realize someone was missing. "Where's Abby?"

Mary huffed. "I told her to wait, but she wouldn't listen. Said she was going home."

"To the tent?" At least the girl had talked to someone. Nathan still hadn't heard so much as a word from her.

Mary lifted an uncertain shoulder.

"Come on." He wouldn't let himself worry yet. The camp was not far and easy enough to find from here. Barely a few feet down the boardwalk Nathan heard someone call his name. He turned to see Constable Hardy headed in his direction. Nathan braced himself for impact.

"Constable Stanford, I need to speak with you."

Nathan rooted himself in place, though his mind followed what path Abby was most likely to take. "About what?"

"Inspector Primrose gave me instructions before he left this morning. He suggested I dismiss you from your duties—"

"What?" The word broke free with little restraint. "Why would he do that?"

Hardy raised a blond eyebrow as though questioning Nathan's sanity.

"I'm fine. More than fit for duty."

Both brows reached for Hardy's Stetson. "Even with children hanging off your sleeves?"

Heat rushed to Nathan's face, and he opened his mouth with an argument. All he had was Miss Ingles. "I have made arrangements for the girls until one of my siblings are able to come for them."

Mary's fingers tightened around his.

Constable Hardy shook his head. "Take your time. You may continue to help with the rescue efforts, but you are no longer on active duty."

"But. . ." Nathan tensed his jaw against another argument, but there was no time. He had already misplaced one of his nieces. And being off active duty was only temporary. A few days or weeks would see everything set to rights.

With Peter and Rosemary gone and their girls orphaned? Would anything ever be right again?

"Constable Stanford?"

"Very well," Nathan managed, though the thought of it chafed. Like being stripped of his identity. What was left of him without the uniform? He was nothing. Had nothing.

Constable Hardy gave a few more instructions before taking his leave, abandoning Nathan to stare at the slats of wood beneath his feet.

Lucy wiggled to be let down.

"Not yet," Nathan grumbled, then cleared his voice. It wasn't her fault he was in a sour mood. "Let's get home first."

"The tent isn't really our home now, is it?" Mary asked as she fell into step beside him.

"No. Just a place to stay for now."

"I bet *you* have a nice home." She slipped her hand into his. "And even if you don't, maybe all it needs is a woman's touch. That's what Mama always said. I could help you make your home nicer. I'm a hard worker and would make sure the other two stay out of your way. I'll take care of them. We wouldn't be any trouble, I promise." Her words came faster and more panicked with each.

Nathan paused and pulled Mary to face him. "It's not that I don't want you, Mary. I don't have a house, no place for you to make nice and homey."

"Is it because you're running?" she asked quickly.

"What?" Nathan fought a sudden urge to laugh. "What would I be running from?"

"Papa wasn't sure, so I don't know. He just told Mama that was why you never came around, why you would never settle down—you were too busy running."

Nathan stared at the girl for a moment before gaining his wits enough to start walking again. And not because he was trying to "run" from her questions. Why would he have anything to run from?

"Don't you get tired sometimes? Always running?"

"Mary..." He glanced at her large blue eyes, so much like her father's, a brother who saw Nathan better than anyone else had. Except Rosemary. He had always felt seen by her too. Nathan huffed out a breath. Not a difficult thing. To the rest of the family, his parents especially, Nathan might as well have run away from home younger than he did. So busy with everything else in their lives, they wouldn't have noticed his absence.

Peter had been the only one who had really tried to stay in contact with Nathan. Why had he held back until it was too late?

"Let's go home." To a tent. The best he had to offer. One he didn't even sleep in due to Miss Ingles' presence. Nathan blew out a breath and started deeper into the valley where tents spread out like a field of canvas. Hopefully Abby had found the right one and was safe with Miss Ingles.

The walk was not long, but his arms burned from their burden. The tent's flaps were tied open to allow light and fresh air to move freely. Mary broke away and ran ahead, ducking into the tent though it stood a full two feet above her head. A mumble of voices, and then she reappeared.

Her wide eyes found his. "Abby isn't here."

"Not here?" Then where else could she be?

Miss Ingles appeared, glasses perched on her nose, glare in place. "Do you mean you lost Abigail?"

"I didn't lose her." She had walked away, though old enough to stay put as she'd been told. "But I mean to find her." He strode forward and deposited Lucy in Miss Ingles' arms. What had seemed a good idea fell apart as she stumbled back a step, gasped at the pressure of her sore foot on the ground and then staggered sideways. Nathan grabbed her arms and pulled her upright while muttering an apology. He took Lucy and set her just inside the tent before looking back to the woman clinging to the tent flap. Her brown eyes stared at him as he made his withdrawal.

"I'll be back when I've found her," he said for lack of anything better. Nathan squeezed Mary's hand and made his way to town and the livery where his horse was being kept. He would be able to cover more ground and have better vantage from a saddle. Strange thing was, he couldn't get Miss Ingles' startled look from his mind. All he'd done was help her right herself. Strange woman. Mr. Chestnut was right—she was mighty skittish around men.

———◆◆———

Constable Stanford was out of sight before Samantha's heart started to return to its normal rhythm. He had startled her, that was all. And Abby's disappearance didn't help matters. Poor child. Unfortunately, there was little Samantha could do, half-crippled and needing to remain with the other two girls. She could do nothing but worry and try to ignore the strange sensation Constable Stanford had evoked in her.

"Do you think she's all right?" Mary asked from just outside the tent, still staring after her uncle. "I should have never let her go. I should have sat on her if that's what it took."

"I'm sure she wouldn't have stood for that." Samantha lowered onto the single chair someone had donated to their living space. "Did she say anything?"

"Just that she was going home."

"Back to Frank?" Samantha withheld a shudder. Did she not realize there was nothing left for her there? She'd seen over half her family buried today. There was no home to go to.

This is your home now.

How well Samantha remembered the husky voice of the solicitor, and the raspy reply of the headmistress at the boarding school as they had informed her she had nowhere else to go. Her inheritance would keep her out of an orphanage or off the streets, but with no family to take her in, all she had were teachers who came and went like the seasons. Holidays were the worst of all. Even the teachers abandoned her, along with all her fellow students.

This is your home now.

Samantha glanced at the canvas walls filtering soft sunlight. What did *home* mean anyway? A place to live, to sleep? "Come in, Mary. I'm sure your uncle will find her soon."

The girl followed as directed, stepping around her sister. She met Samantha's gaze with pleading filling her own. "Will you pray with me? That he will find Abby and she'll be all right?"

"Pray?" Samantha shifted on the chair, though the discomfort came from within.

"I'm sure God can help."

Samantha had less confidence, but the pleading in Mary's eyes was impossible to ignore. And it wasn't as though she hadn't had any experience. With ritual prayers at least, those said at the school, in church, or over a meal. If the exercise made Mary feel better, what harm was there in whispering a few words heavenward? "Very well."

Mary grinned despite the tears shining in her gaze, and dropped to her knees. Samantha followed suit, albeit much slower. Her ankle protested the angle but would be fine if they hurried. She wasn't sure why sitting wasn't sufficient. She usually sat during dinner prayers or stood when ones were performed at the school. Did God really care that they soiled their knees? He likely wasn't paying any attention anyway.

A smaller hand gripped hers. "Can you pray?"

"Why don't you?" Personal prayers were new territory for her.

With a nod, Mary dipped her head forward. "Dear Father in heaven..." A pause drew out across the seconds, and Samantha's ankle cried in protest.

"Go on," she encouraged gently, trying to stifle a groan.

"Please help Abby find her way back here. Or that Uncle Nathan can find her. I...I don't want to lose anyone else, God."

Samantha echoed the *amen* when it was said, and gratefully returned to her seat. "Very good," she praised the girl, at a loss for anything else to say. It was unlike other prayers she was used to, ones more polished and practiced. This one was...real. As though the child believed God truly sat close enough to listen. As though she had confidence that God would indeed hear her.

Not a show.

Mary remained on her knees a few moments longer, her head bowed— like her world had just been ripped away and she didn't know how to hold onto it any longer.

"There is nothing else we can do to help, so let's keep busy while we wait, shall we?" Samantha shifted so she could reach the slate. "Come sit with me, and we can work on your multiplication. I know you have struggled with the larger numbers."

Mary moved to obey, double-checking Lucy's position on the ground and handing her a spoon and bowl to play with, before seating herself on the cot next to Samantha. She suppressed the urge to rub her hand down the girl's back. She was not the child's kin, but a teacher. She knew her role.

For the next half hour or so they drilled, forward and backward. Mary's mind was obviously wandering, what with her concern for her sister, but this was better than letting the poor girl mope without distraction.

The sounds of a horse clumping toward them jerked Mary upright. They both listened for a moment until a shadow stepped into the doorway of the tent. Mary dropped the slate and threw herself at her uncle.

"Did you find Abby?"

As though in answer, the girl in question slipped past and crawled onto her cot. She pulled a blanket over her head.

Samantha released a breath she hadn't realized she'd been holding. "Where did you find her?"

"Someone found her on the road north of here." His gaze flicked from her to the slate and then to Mary.

"But that is the opposite direction we thought." Samantha smoothed her skirts, not sure what reason she had to be suddenly self-conscious. "She wasn't headed to Frank?"

"Most likely she got turned around and wasn't sure what way was home." His voice grew tenser with each word. "May I have a word with you outside, Miss Ingles?" His voice was not inviting but carried a command.

"Very well." She moved forward in her chair. "Can you help me, Mary?"

Constable Stanford stepped forward. "Actually, I would like you to stay here, Mary, and watch the younger girls for a few minutes. I'll assist Miss Ingles."

He said her name like it was a curse, but Samantha had no choice but to slip her hand into his and be pulled upright. His grip on her arm allowed no argument as he led her outside. The sun met them with the brilliance of spring, but the chill in the air seeped through her dress.

"What is wrong with you?" he ground out between his teeth—almost a whisper if not for the anger giving each word strength. He kept walking, putting distance between them and the tent.

"I don't understand."

He laughed, of all things, though it was short and as cold as the snow hanging on the mountain peaks. "Of course you don't."

Samantha stumbled and pain spiked up her leg. She jerked her arm away from his grasp. "Would you care to explain your abuse?"

"My abuse? You are the one lecturing a child on sums the same day she buried her parents and brothers. While she's worried sick about her sister. Really? Arithmetic?"

"She seemed bored with reading, and she's always struggled with her numbers, so I don't see the problem. I was trying to help."

"No? You're not helping!" He roared, his head shaking. "This is not what they need."

Indignation seared up her spine. "And how do you know what they need? You're never here."

"Any person in their right mind would understand what they need."

"Are you saying I am not of my right mind?" She would have planted her fists on her hips were she not barely balanced. But the nerve of this man—

"I don't know. You *did* just have a roof fall on you. Maybe your foot isn't the only thing injured." He made a motion to her head.

"Excuse me?" Her hands fisted at her sides. "You self-righteous. . ." She struggled to find the perfect insult that wasn't too crude lest the children overhear. "My head is perfectly sound, thank you very much. Sound enough to know we are finished here. I have done my best for the girls, and if that is not good enough for you, then good riddance." She spun away from him, and another spike of pain made her gasp. Her balance wavered and she fell forward.

Chapter 13

Nathan bit back a curse as he grabbed for Miss Ingles. He gripped her arms and righted her, anxious to release her. Only, when he tried to do so she wavered, not quite balanced. Her face pinched with a look of pain.

He groaned and swept her into his arms. For the second time.

"Really," she huffed. "I am fine. Set me down."

"So you can fall over again and do yourself more harm?" While he had no affection for the woman, he had been raised to treat ladies better. He kept his hold and started back toward the tent.

By the set in her jaw, she apparently didn't like the situation any more than he, but at least she didn't argue further. Dark strands of hair had escaped her pins and fallen across her long neck. Everything about this woman was thin, like she didn't eat enough on a regular basis. She was awful pale as well, though that was understandable for a person who spent her time locked away in a schoolroom—especially for the duration of a Canadian winter. The pain in her foot might be a contributing factor to her pallor as well. As they neared the tent, she sent him a severe look, though something was different this time. Her eyes were clearer and unobscured by the small spectacles she often wore—the ones she'd had perched on her nose minutes before.

"Your spectacles."

Her brown eyes widened.

"I'll find them." He ducked into the tent and set her on the lone chair. "I'll be back."

"I'll pack my things."

He didn't bother replying, but he couldn't help the mirthless chuckle. What things? She'd lost most everything in the slide other than the schoolbooks and slate she'd taken to torturing the girls with.

His mind stayed on the woman as he searched the area for her thin wire spectacles. What did she have left? She probably had family somewhere but none close by—otherwise, why would she have agreed to stay with the girls? The hotel in Blairmore was already overfilled. Where would she go?

A glimmer of light off glass caught his eye, and he bent to pick up the twisted wire frame, one lens missing. He ran his fingers through the short grass and snagged the errant piece. She'd probably stomped on them when she'd started to fall. Or maybe he had when coming to her rescue. Either way, the frames were far too twisted to restore the lens.

His temper had cooled by the time he returned to the tent to find that Miss Ingles had moved to her cot. She sat with a pile of books on her lap, the corner of her bottom lip pinched between her teeth. Mary set the slate on the top of the books, and Miss Ingles offered a slight smile, though obviously forced.

"Do you have to go?" Mary glanced to where Nathan stood in the doorway. Her eyes pleaded with him. He wanted to question why she would want the uptight schoolteacher to remain but felt himself shake his head instead.

"No, she doesn't have to go." He stepped in far enough to set the mangled spectacles on top the slate. "If she would rather stay."

A small gasp escaped Miss Ingles.

"Probably my fault," he admitted.

She made no argument while her hands fiddled with the wire frames, trying to straighten them.

"I'm sure there is someone in town who can fix them for you. Why don't I go ask around." Nathan snatched the spectacles from her hands, not liking the pity again welling within him. He preferred simply disliking her. "I'll be back." He ducked out of the tent, confident she would mind the girls. It wasn't as though she were going anywhere without assistance. He needed a long ride to work out his thoughts.

Shoving the spectacles in his coat pocket to deal with later, he reined his horse toward Frank. He wanted to slump in the saddle, defeated, but the uniform pulled at his shoulders, keeping his posture. A uniform he had no right to wear right now. He was off duty. Indefinitely. But he was in no hurry to hunt out a change of clothes.

The two-mile ride to Frank passed quickly. Scarlet-clad guards stood on every corner, protecting the town from trespassers and looters, but otherwise Frank was deserted. He nodded to his fellows but continued down Dominion Avenue until he reached the overflow of Gold Creek. A group of men worked along the railway line, beginning the arduous job of clearing a new path for the train. Several others picked their way over the rocks, either exploring the damage or continuing rescue efforts.

Nathan tied Rover to the same scarred tree he had last time and climbed to the offset roof that had been ripped from Peter's home. Part of the roof had been pulled apart in an attempt to rescue Miss Ingles and the girls. He scaled the slope and then lowered himself into the attic where he was met by the soft scent of roses. A lantern would be helpful, but he would have to make do with what sunlight fell through the opening and plethora of cracks. Dust danced across thin beams of light as he crawled across to where a brass bed appeared to be holding up part of the ceiling. A deep blue patchwork quilt draped across the floor. A book peeked from under the side. A McGuffey Reader. Paper lay strewn across the floor, each decorated with cursive scribblings. He held one under the light to view the chicken scratching and misspelled words printed across the page.

Once a dog chased our chickens into the woods. . .

He lowered the page and glanced at the others. Stories by children. This is where Miss Ingles stayed. Nathan piled the papers and left them to continue to part of the room he could almost stand up in. Nothing was where it should be. Pictures shaken from the walls. A broken pitcher beside a tipped table. A jar of rose water with most of its contents spilled.

A puddle of broken glass drew his gaze to a picture frame in the midst. He picked up the frame and shook the final shards free. A man with a large mustache posed behind a petite lady with a feathered hat. At her knee stood a young girl, probably no older than seven or eight. Dark ringlets hung to her shoulders, and full cheeks betrayed a desire to smile, though her lips wore a more serious expression—probably by order of the photographer. He should have allowed the child to smile, as it no doubt would have lit her face.

He was about to set the photograph aside when he realized the identity of the girl. It had to be Miss Ingles as a child. He shook his head at the thought. Easier to believe she kept a photograph of a distant relation than that the pretty little girl with twinkling eyes had somehow become the tight-collared witch he'd become acquainted with.

Nathan left the photograph with the pile of children's stories and climbed back onto the roof of the house, this time making his way to where the main part of the house had been nearly demolished. The stairs into the heart of Peter's home had been ripped from their place, standing out a foot or so from where they should be attached. Rock that had ripped the lower wall apart speared to brace them up. He pushed on the top step with his boot and it didn't budge.

Most of the house was filled with limestone that had crashed through the windows and even most of one wall. Glass and wood splinters mingled with broken furniture and brick from the fireplace. Narrow paths had been cleared to the two bedrooms where Rosemary and his nephews had been uncovered. Crimson stained what remained of a bed.

Nathan sank to the stairs and wiped his hand down his face. Rosemary would have been safe with him. They wouldn't have been living in Frank, and she would still be alive if she had chosen him instead.

"I dare you to kiss me, Nate."

He could hear her voice like it had been yesterday, teasing, taunting. Her blond braids were wrapped together at the nape of her neck, making her appear older than her sixteen years. She had leaned near, her breath tickling his ear and smelling of the raspberries they had pillaged from her grandma's garden. Nathan never had discovered if she tasted as good. Peter had found them before he'd had the chance.

He shook the memory from his head and wiped at the sweat beading on his brow. Something had shifted between them after that day. Rosemary had slowly distanced herself from him, though he hadn't understood why until the next summer—when he had been the one to find Rosemary and Peter kissing out in the orchard.

"Come on, Nate, it's not that big of a deal. It doesn't change anything just because she loves me and I love her."

Peter had tried to pretend they could continue on as before. They'd all been friends, but she could only choose one of the brothers, and her choice had obviously been clear—as had Peter's. They had chosen each other and left Nathan in the dust. He'd lost both of them that day.

And now he'd lost them all over again. His two best friends.

His hands trembled as he pressed them over his eyes, as though that would dam the flow of tears. And if he could go back? What would he change? Would he have fought harder to keep her? Or would he have been quicker to forgive his brother?

Chapter 14

Nathan remained in place at the top of the stairs until his face dried, though his eyes remained sore and felt swollen. He couldn't remember the last time he'd allowed his soul to bleed. If only he felt some relief—instead of this horrible emptiness.

He sucked a breath into his aching lungs and pushed to his feet. Still, he stood in place, unresolved on what to do. Flee the scene of so much pain or seek answers? He searched the area with his eyes, taking in the carnage of what had no doubt been a home filled with boundless love and happiness—with Peter and Rosemary he could easily imagine what had once been. Somehow, Nathan found himself at the bottom of the stairs, nudging a rock the size of a loaf of bread with the toe of his boot. Broken china sparkled among the other rubbage. A patch of dark leather caught Nathan's eye, and he stooped to brushed away the dust and small rocks from the cover of a Bible.

"Why, God?" He couldn't help the question that had been plaguing him for the past two days. Why would God allow the mountain to fall and so many good people to die?

He thought he had no more tears to shed, but his vision blurred as he opened the Bible's cover to the date of Peter and Rosemary's wedding, followed by the names and birth dates of each of their children: Rosemary, Allen, John, Abigail, Wilfred, Athol, and Lucy.

"Why, God?"

Somehow the prayer shifted from question to plea, a need to find some understanding and way to accept what had happened. Yes, the world was fallen, and bad things happened to good people all the time, but in his line of work, Nathan was used to men being the main cause of tragedy. But man hadn't ripped down the mountain. This time, man was not responsible for so much death and pain.

"Why, God?"

Nathan gripped the Bible and started back up the broken steps to where the overwhelming expanse of the rockslide spread out before him. God couldn't be completely indifferent to His children's pain. There had to be some sign of His hand in all of this.

———— ◆◆ ————

Samantha looked up from the novel as Mary pushed into the tent, stick in hand. "How about this one?"

"Perhaps." Samantha set the children's novel with the other books and took the length of dead branch. A little taller than needed, coming past her waist, but it was stocky enough not to give way under her weight. It was the best of the options Mary's search had presented so far. "Yes. This will work. Thank you." Samantha lowered back to the cot and leaned the makeshift cane nearby.

"Are you leaving?" Mary asked for the tenth time since Samantha had started gathering her few belongings and packing them into her satchel.

"I don't know," she answered honestly. She wanted to leave. She hated the way Constable Stanford made her feel—plain and hard and distanced. His dislike for her was evident in every encounter, despite his need for her assistance with the girls.

Samantha settled onto a cot and propped her foot up off the grass floor, then watched as Lucy crawled in her direction. When she'd reached the edge of the cot, Lucy pulled herself into a standing position and banged her hands against the quilt as though applauding her own efforts. Samantha felt a tug at her heart as the child looked up with large, trusting eyes. Pudgy hands extended upward.

Part of Samantha wanted to ignore the child's request—a frightened part she didn't quite understand. But what harm could come from lifting a baby into her arms? Despite the logic, her heart beat heavily as she pulled the baby onto her lap. Lucy's head leaned against her chest while a hand patted Samantha's arm. Was the child trying to comfort her? Or was Lucy simply tired?

Light spilled deeper into the tent as the door flap opened wide, only to be blocked by a man's frame. Samantha stared for a moment, her brain not immediately recognizing the man in Levi's, a blue shirt, with plain brown jacket hanging open. Flat-brimmed Stetson was replaced by a relaxed slouch hat pulled low, but not enough to shade the blue eyes she recognized far too easily.

"You're. . ." Several thoughts flicked through her mind: you're back, you're staring. "You're not in uniform?"

A muscle twitched in his jaw, and he stepped farther in and dropped his pack and bedroll beside the chair. "I've been relieved of duty for the foreseeable future." The words almost hissed as they were pressed between his teeth.

"I'm sorry."

His lips pressed thin. "You had nothing to do with it."

"Of course not. I only meant. . ." that he seemed very unhappy about the arrangement, but he probably didn't need someone pointing that out. He seemed even more out of sorts than normal, and his eyes wore a red sheen. Samantha glanced at Lucy who watched her in return. "I suppose I will no longer be required here." Samantha tried for a quick smile before setting the child down. "I already have my things gathered."

"There is no reason for you to leave." His words came rather rushed.

"Oh?" From their exchange only a few hours earlier, it seemed almost imperative. And now that he was here with all his gear. . . "You are no longer staying at the Mounted Police barracks?"

"Like I said, I'm off duty." His hands fisted at his sides.

Samantha pushed to the edge of the cot and carefully lowered her foot to the ground. It still throbbed, but not as painfully as it had earlier that day. "Then my remaining here would be highly inappropriate." She reached for the stick Mary had found for her, craving a little independence and not to be looked down on any longer.

"I'll sleep outside," he mumbled. "I've bunked under the stars plenty of times."

What? Was he arguing she should stay? "What if it rains?"

"I have a tarp with my bedroll."

"Hardly a comfortable arrangement." She pushed to her feet, grateful that she had something to help her balance. The last thing she needed was him sweeping her into his arms again. Close contact with him did strange things to her insides that she would rather not experience again.

"I'm not concerned about comfort at the moment."

Obviously not, since being in each other's presence was decidedly uncomfortable.

"You need a place to stay, and I could still use some help with the girls until one of my siblings come."

"You have family coming?" That was news, but it made sense. He was good with the girls, but as an unmarried man, and a Mountie at that, it was not as though he could care for them indefinitely. He struggled caring for them now—which is why he still wanted her despite disagreeing with everything she did.

"That's the hope." He cast a glance at Mary's downcast look. "Why don't we step outside."

Samantha sighed. This conversation was better had away from the children, but their last hadn't gone well. It was better that she just left. If there was no place to stay in Blairmore, she'd find a ride to another town—perhaps Ellen Thornley and her brother had not yet left for Pincher Creek.

"Stop overthinking everything."

Her gaze jerked back to his. "I'm a teacher. Thinking is what I do."

"And you seem exceptional at it," Constable Stanford ground out. Though his tone carried no sarcasm, the flippant comment still sounded like an insult.

"I am." She started past him, grateful for the support of the walking stick. He was right, the girls didn't need to hear this.

He caught her arm, and leaned in close enough that his warm breath brushed her ear. "But what about feeling?"

Her feet faltered, and the makeshift cane almost fell from her grip. "Excuse me?"

He released her just as quickly and left her standing in the doorway. She bit down on the inside of her cheek, trying to keep at bay the sudden urge to cry. Though that would certainly disprove him quickly enough, Samantha knew better than to give in to emotion. Such sentimentality was a tap that once turned on would be almost impossible to shut off again. Emotion had no place beside rational thought—not when it only brought pain.

Samantha steeled herself, chin up, and started after Stanford. Thankfully he hadn't gone far—almost to the same place they had stood only hours earlier. A reminder that despite his protests, she needed to leave.

"Constable Stanford—" Or was she supposed to call him *constable* if he was not actively on duty? "What should I call you?"

He glanced over at her, eyes hooded. "Nathan. My name is Nathan."

"I am quite aware of that." But did he truly feel it appropriate to suddenly switch to Christian names. Just because he had no qualms about insulting her, that did not make them any more familiar than they had been that morning. "I mean—"

"I'm sorry." The apology came in a rush. "I shouldn't have said anything."

Samantha stared, trying not to be affected by an apology that didn't feel like an apology at all. He obviously hadn't changed his opinion—just regretted saying anything. What did it matter? He had no right to understand the hurt and pain she buried below the surface. They were strangers. Better for him to continue to think as he did. "It hardly matters either way. The fact remains I need to leave."

"And where will you go?"

She lifted her shoulder as though it didn't matter, though her insides twisted with uncertainty. "I am sure I can find a ride to Pincher Creek, or even Lethbridge." A bigger town where she could rent a room until the school executives gave her another teaching assignment.

"But why the rush?"

How dare he ask such a question after his boorish behavior? He was the one who wanted her gone though he fought the idea of being left alone with the girls. Samantha's teeth tightened against each other, but she somehow kept her hands relaxed. "You can move into your own tent and better care for your nieces." Had she made her voice too sweet? Could he sense the bitterness the words left on her tongue?

He fished something out of his pocket—a small picture frame—and studied the photograph encased within.

Samantha's heart stuttered along with her thoughts. "Where did you find that?"

His gaze rose, and he extended the photo. "In my brother's house. I assume it is yours?"

"Yes." A tremble fell through her as she looked down at the faces of her parents.

"The girl is you?"

"Yes." She said the word, but it hardly breached a whisper.

"I thought as much."

Samantha glanced at him but wasn't sure how to express her gratitude at its return. She was still so hurt and angry. Besides, if she spoke, he might hear the emotion coursing through her.

"Have you sent word to your parents? I am sure they will be anxious to see you safe."

"No."

"News of the slide has traveled across Canada. I'm sure they will be worried about their only child. If you like, I can send a telegram first thing in the morning."

"I assure you that is unnecessary." Samantha turned back toward the tent. The sun had already dipped below the western peaks, taking with it both warmth and light. Shadows stretched across the valley. Would she be able to find somewhere else to stay tonight?

"Even if you've had a falling-out with them, why wouldn't you want them to know you're alive and well?"

Would the man not stop digging? "Because they are dead." She refused to succumb to the urge to look into their faces, to allow the loneliness to consume her. She'd tidy the tent before she left. Yes. And make sure the girls had dinner. They'd be hungry.

"Dead?" The echo followed her.

"It happened a long time ago." Samantha glanced back. "Though thank you for your concern and for returning the photograph. Why don't I get the girls settled and then. . . I suppose at this point I will stay one more night and make other arrangements in the morning. My ankle is improving already, and I'm sure I will be able to get around more easily in no time. Once I figure out where I'm going, I will telegram the school executives." She was rambling but couldn't stop. "The girls will get on well enough now that you have more time for them." Samantha managed a small smile. She refused to be affected, or at least, to let him see how much she was. Better for him to believe her emotionless. Better for her to busy herself and not pause to consider anything deeper than her current needs—a place to stay far away from this valley and Turtle Mountain.

Chapter 15

"Knock, knock," Constable Stanford's voice sounded just outside the tent, and Samantha hurried to finish wrapping Lucy's diaper, made difficult by the baby's wiggles and kicks. The soft flannel shifted, necessitating a second. . .third. . .attempt at securing it in place. They would need to purchase more fabric for diapers as well—ones that fit better than the handful donated.

"Are you ready to go?" Constable Stanford—or *Nathan*—called through the canvas door. She might start thinking of him by his Christian name, but she'd refrain from referring to him so casually. Better to keep a professional distance between them for propriety's sake.

"Almost." Samantha glanced to see why the girls hadn't answered their uncle. Mary was still trying to coax Abby out from under her blankets, expounding on how fun it would be to go to the shops in Coleman, the nearby town that would hopefully have more selection than the tiny store Blairmore boasted.

Light and a cool breeze rushed into the tent along with Nathan. He wore a tight smile and the clothes he had the evening before. It still caught her off guard to see him out of uniform, and he looked no happier about it than he had last night, his hands absently brushing down his jacket, a scowl pinching the corners of his eyes. "The wagon is waiting."

The wagon likely had more patience than the man fidgeting in the doorway. Samantha passed him Lucy and took her makeshift cane to hand, then followed to the small wagon with a single horse hitched. The large red gelding seemed content to nibble grass while it waited.

"Here." Nathan set Lucy on the ground and assisted Samantha up onto the seat, his hands at her waist. She was becoming more accustomed to his touch, but her heart still sped and heat infused her face, though hopefully not enough to redden her cheeks. She had never been one to blush at a man's attention. Then again, she had never had much attention from the opposite sex.

Thankfully, her thoughts were diverted as Nathan handed Lucy into her arms and she settled onto the seat, fixing her attention on Abby who was barely visible from Samantha's perch. The child remained bundled in her blue patchwork quilt inside the tent. Mary gave a frustrated groan and threw a pleading look to Nathan who nodded and headed inside.

"Come on, Abby, we can't leave you behind."

The girl said nothing, instead ducking her head under the covers.

Nathan crouched. "Abby." He sighed. "Please come. We can buy a treat of some sort while we're there. Do you like cake? Pastries? Rock candy?"

No response.

"I'm sorry, Abby, but you need to come with us." He scooped her up, blanket and all, and deposited her in the back of the wagon.

"I'm worried about her," he mumbled when he joined Samantha on the wagon's seat.

Samantha glanced back at the tousled blond head that peeked out from under the blue quilt. "She just needs time. This trip will be good for her, help her think about something else for a little while." Distractions were the best cure for pain. Yet there was little to distract Samantha from thoughts of her own parents as they made the westward journey toward the nearest town. The view was no doubt lovely, but without her spectacles the world around remained a blur. The baby fell asleep in her arms, and only added to the heavy feelings dragging her soul downward. Lucy's pale lashes lay against her full cheeks, and her lips pursed like a small rosebud. What would it feel like to be a mother of such a precious child?

"I like your horse, Uncle Nathan," Mary said from behind, rescuing Samantha from her thoughts. "What's his name?"

"Rover." Nathan glanced back with a half-smile. "Red Rover."

Mary giggled. "Like the game?"

"I guess so. I wasn't the one who named him, but I guess it fits."

"I like it. Though I don't like the game. Allen isn't very gentle when he—" Mary's voice broke, and her breath hitched. Tears rolled free. Silence fell over the small group. Samantha struggled against the strangest urge to wrap the girl in an embrace, but for now all she could do was tighten her hold on Lucy and question what was wrong with her. She wasn't one for touchy-feely displays.

No one said much until they reached Coleman, and then even Abby peered around them at the small town, similar in many ways to Frank but with a little more size than Blairmore.

Nathan pulled the wagon to a stop in front of the post office and hitched Red Rover. "You said you have some business to take care of?" he asked, reaching for Lucy. Samantha shifted the baby as gently as she could into his arms. Lucy stirred but remained asleep, her fists stretching over her head as she nestled against her uncle. Samantha's heart throbbed in time with the pain in her foot, but she did her best to ignore it while she lowered herself to the ground. Nathan spared one hand to guide her.

"Thank you," she managed and hurried away—as quickly as one could hurry with a hobbling step. The post office was not busy, so she was able to send her telegrams and return to where the wagon waited in only a couple of minutes—but by then there was no sign of Nathan.

Samantha made her way to the back where Mary held Lucy and Abby huddled in her blanket. "Where—"

"Here you are," Nathan called as he strode toward them, the distance dissolving quickly with his long stride. He held a proper cane in his hand, carved and stained a dark walnut. Without an explanation, he took the stick from her hand and replaced it with the cane. "There you go."

She gaped after him while he deposited the stick in the back of the wagon and unloaded the girls. He lifted Lucy from Mary's hold and led them toward a mercantile. Samantha followed, the handle of the cane smooth in her grasp. "Thank you," she managed, though she wasn't sure he heard her for he never looked back.

Once inside the mercantile, Samantha made herself busy finding things the girls were in need of. Shoes that fit properly. Undergarments. Soap and toothbrushes. Diapers and washcloths. The list went on and on, incidentals important for clean and healthy children. She also gathered a few things for herself with the hope she could get credit with the store until her funds arrived.

Though tempted to pause and admire a selection of fabric, she decided against it. The store's proprietor, a burly man not much older than her, seemed to note her interest and moved her direction.

"I will give you a discount on any fabrics," he said with a hopeful smile.

"Thank you, but I have no use for fabric." She was not talented enough with needle and thread to attempt making clothes for either her or the girls. "But if you sell readymade clothes or know of a seamstress—"

"Of course," he boomed, cutting her off. "Miss Davis has a shop only two buildings down." He motioned to the south. "She can likely help you."

"Thank you." Samantha motioned to the pile Nathan had helped her collect on the counter and the man headed back that way, quickly sorting through their purchases. Samantha set her own items aside for when he was done, waving him away when he reached for them. "These will be separate."

The proprietor glanced from her to where Nathan stood with Lucy patting his cheek.

"Go ahead and add them to mine," Nathan ordered.

Samantha blocked the proprietor from taking them. "I can't impose."

"I have been imposing on your time for the past three or so days. I would say I owe you at this point." He spared her a glance, but his voice remained flat.

She withdrew her hands to avoid causing a scene but decided against further shopping today. She would make do with the two dresses she had until her funds arrived. Because contrary to Nathan's halfhearted insistence, she refused to be any more of a burden than she already was.

———◆●◆———

Miss Ingles was all bristles again, though he didn't understand it. She had been relaxed enough through most of their excursion, but by time they had left the mercantile, she'd bristled back up like a porcupine. Other than a few comments shared between him and Mary as they finished shopping and a pause at the single restaurant for lunch and pastries for the girls, silence reigned, causing unease to crawl up and down his spine until he was able to deposit the woman and children back at the tent. He readily excused himself to return the wagon to the livery, but even after the task was done, Nathan had no desire to go anywhere near Miss Ingles and her cold glower. No doubt she had mastered it to keep young boys in line, but he didn't care for it being aimed at him. He'd done nothing wrong—he reminded himself repeatedly while he rode toward Frank.

Not that the view of the town helped his mood. Especially as one of his colleagues leveled a rifle at him and called for him to stop. "No one is allowed in Frank without authorization."

Nathan groaned as he tried to remember the man's name. "Constable Hardy gave me the authorization, Constable Jenson."

The man's eyes widened. "Constable Stanford?"

Nathan nodded. Was the uniform the only thing recognizable or memorable about him?

"Sorry about that, Stanford." Jenson stepped back and motioned for him to continue.

BOOM.

Both men jerked around, then Jenson chuckled. "Can't help but be on edge in the valley. That's just the CPR laborers working to clear the railway. Been going all day."

Nathan pushed Rover in that direction. He needed a diversion, not to face Manitoba Avenue again. The rail line had run along the river, and Nathan followed what remained through the heaps of limestone cradling both sides. The Canadian Pacific Railway had made surprising progress, though a full mile of track remained covered.

What appeared to be the foreman saw him first and waved him back. "Got dynamite ready to go off down there," he hollered. "Who are you?"

Nathan dismounted and stepped closer. "I'm Constable Stanford, just checking your progress here." He held the man's studious gaze despite feeling out of place without his uniform, like he had to prove something to everyone he encountered. The feeling left his stomach sour and his nerves on edge.

Thankfully the man didn't ask where Nathan's uniform was, instead sweeping his hand over his large mustache and explaining what they had accomplished and that they hoped to have the rail through and repaired within the month—but hopefully less time.

"That would be good. A lot of people depend on the railway through here." He flinched as another explosion sent a spray of dust and rock into the air farther up the line.

The foreman hardly twitched. "We're doing our best. Right now, folks should just be happy they aren't buried under all this." He shook his head. "Just talking to Sid there about the Spokane Flyer."

"The Spokane Flyer?" That wasn't the train that had arrived with all the laborers. "What about it?"

Instead of answering, the man walked away, speaking with a younger man before continuing on to see what the dynamite had accomplished. The younger man started toward Nathan, his hands buried in his pockets. He withdrew one to extend it to Nathan. "I'm Sid Choquette. Mac said to tell you about the Flyer that was supposed to come through here Wednesday morning."

Nathan braced himself but nodded. "What happened?"

"Well, I might as well start at the beginning. I was up at the mine's tipple picking up coal cars with—"

"You were at the tipple before the slide?" Nathan gripped the man's sleeve. "You saw Peter Stanford? Was he up there at the time? How long before the slide was this?"

"Whoa, you know Stanford?"

"He's my brother. Was." Nathan choked out the last word.

Sid's face fell. "I'm sorry. And, yeah, he was up there along with Alex Clark and Fred Farrington. Chatted for a bit while we hitched the cars to haul back to Frank before the Spokane Flyer arrived."

"Spokane Flyer?"

"A passenger train on its way from Lethbridge. Due to that blizzard between Lethbridge and Fort MacLeod, it was running late, so we had some time for the load."

Nathan nodded, his mind fixating on the fact that this was one of the last men to see his brother alive. He wanted to ask how Peter had looked and what he'd said—everything about those final moments. "What happened?"

Chapter 16

MAY 3ᴿᴰ

Water fell against Nathan's cheek and ran into his ear. He raised his hand to wipe away the offending drop and felt moisture seep through the canvas and his sleeve in turn. The pitter-patter of rain surrounded him. The cool of the ground seeped through his bedroll. Two nights on the ground outside the tent housing the girls and Miss Ingles and he was left questioning his decision to let her stay.

He raised the canvas enough to see the sky—dim blue-gray, with morning not quite to the horizon. Would he last a few more hours under this spring downpour?

A whimper from inside the tent focused his mind. Maybe it hadn't been the rain that had roused him. A scream jerked him upright, and he pushed his bedroll aside. At least this gave him an excuse to slip inside to comfort the girl before she woke anyone else.

Canvas over his head, he ducked into the tent and shook off the rain and his cover. It was almost black within, so he followed the panicked breaths and whimper to the closest cot, his brain only partly registering that something wasn't quite right with the location. Was this Mary's bed?

Another panicked cry pushed aside Nathan's hesitation, and he laid a hand on the blanketed form and gave a shake and a whisper. "Wake up. It's all right."

The form twisted under his hand, her arms flailing. He caught one, while the other gripped his sleeve. She pressed her face against his chest while a shudder moved through her. Only it wasn't Mary's thin wrist he held. It wasn't Mary clinging to him.

"Miss Ingles?" Nathan's whisper came a little hoarse this time. He slid his hand to her shoulder, not sure if he should try to shake her or offer comfort. Or both?

"No, no, no," she murmured. "Not again."

"Miss Ingles," Nathan tried again. But she continued to cling to him, her body trembling. "Samantha." As he said her name, he mused that he'd learned it from an early report on survivors, not from her. To him, she was always Miss Ingles. And even though she had finally given up pushing schoolwork on the girls, she would always be the overly starched schoolmarm to him.

"Take me with you. Please don't leave me again." Her murmured plea into his coat was followed by a sob.

"Samantha, wake up."

She abruptly pushed away, jerking upright. Her breath came in jagged gasps.

"It's all right. Just a dream."

Her head shook, her eyes seeking his in the dark. "A dream?"

"Yeah." Nathan rocked back on his heels and reached for the chair to pull it closer. "Just a dream. Or a nightmare. That's probably more apt."

"A nightmare." She whispered the word as though coming to accept it. "Wasn't real."

"Are you all right now?"

She brought a hand up to brush the hair away from her face, and he realized his eyes were adjusting to the darkness. Enough to see her eyes widen. "What are you doing here?"

"Keeping you from waking up the rest of the camp, never mind the girls." He let out an awkward chuckle.

"What. . . What did I do?"

He shrugged and settled into the chair, ready to close his eyes and try for more sleep. "Cried out."

She gasped, her hands coming to her face. "I'm so sorry. I. . . I don't. . ."

"It's nothing to be embarrassed about. You had a bad dream."

"Still." Her hands remained on her face as she sank back to her pillow.

"It's all right to be human like the rest of us sometimes." He murmured, tipping his head forward to stretch his neck. He rotated it in a circle and then stretched his legs out and crossed his ankles. Would he be able to sleep in this chair? Or should he stretch out on the floor until the sun made it above the horizon?

"What are you doing?"

"Trying to get comfortable." The ground was probably the only option, but at least it was dry in here.

"You said you were going to stay outside."

"Yes, but it's pretty wet out there right now."

"You said your canvas would be enough."

"I might have been a little too optimistic." Yes, the ground was his only option. "Besides, it's morning. I just want to close my eyes a few more minutes before the girls wake."

"But they will find you in here."

"Is that really a problem? They're my nieces." Why wouldn't she just let him be for a few minutes. He hadn't slept well in days, and it was wearing on him.

"But I'm not."

"No, you are not. But you are awake now, and way up there." He lowered to the ground, wishing he hadn't left his bedroll out in the rain. Even damp, it would have offered some warmth.

"This is highly inappropriate." Her whisper squeaked, reminding him of his first assessment of her.

"No one cares but you." No one would even know except the girls, and how could they fault him for taking a few more minutes to rest?

"You don't even have a blanket?"

He stretched out on the open space between cots and tucked his hands under his head. Even the ground was warmer in here. "I'm very aware of that."

For a moment nothing was said, and a shiver ran through him. Then a pile of warmth fell across his chest. A smile pulled at the corner of his mouth. "Thanks," he mumbled, and let himself fully relax, enjoying the tatting of rain high above on the tent's roof. The quilt still held heat from its last occupant—so perhaps she wasn't quite the witch he'd once assumed, but a warm-blooded woman with fears and even pain like any other mortal.

"What were you dreaming about?" Probably something to do with the slide, he guessed.

She didn't answer right away, and he began to wonder if she'd fallen back asleep. Then she whispered. "The past."

He waited to see if she'd expound, but nothing was forthcoming. His own mind began to wander to his talk with Sid Choquette. The story he'd told kept pestering Nathan until he couldn't rest without fishing his notebook out of his nearby pack along with a pencil. Despite the dimly lit morning, dawn provided just enough light to write by.

Miss Ingles shifted on the cot above him, and she looked over. "What are you doing?"

"I met someone yesterday, someone who had been at the mine's tipple just before the slide."

She sat up. "He survived? How?"

"Sid was with a crew of three who had brought an engine to the mine for the coal cars. They had stopped and visited with my brother and the two miners who were with him eating lunch." Nathan released a shaky breath, but thankfully he kept his voice soft and even. "Ben Murgatroyd, the engineer, heard something above them and spooked. Yelled for his crew to get aboard and fired up the engine, racing the train down the tracks as the rocks began to tumble past them, keeping just ahead of the full force of the slide." For a moment he closed his eyes and saw his brother standing there with sandwich in hand, watching the engine race away without explanation, other than the popping sound of rocks bouncing down the slope, and then a sudden rush as the rest of the mountain broke away and crashed down on him. If there was only a way to go back and warn him to get on the train too or get back inside the mine. Why had he just stood there?

"And they made it." Miss Ingles' voice held a lilt of wonder. "Mr. Sid and Murgatroyd?"

"Yeah. They made it out of the way. But they knew about the passenger train coming from Lethbridge, the one due to pass through Frank any minute."

She inclined forward, her eyes wide as she waited for the rest of the story.

"Problem was they were on this side of Frank, and the Spokane Flyer was approaching from the other side."

"There was no way to warn them?"

"None, as the slide took out the telegraph wires and everything. But without a warning, the train would likely run headfirst into the rock and mangled track. A passenger train carrying who knew how many people."

"They would have died." She hugged herself and seemed to shiver, but he doubted it was from the chill of the morning air.

"So Sid and his friend took off over the rock on foot and in the dark with only a lantern to show the way. They ran almost two miles around and over boulders and heaps of limestone, while rocks continued to tumble from the mountain above. Sid made it to the far side of the slide just in time to wave down the train with his lantern."

———————◆•◆———————

Samantha kept her eyes closed tight until the burn of threatening tears subsided, all the while forcing her lungs to slow her breath. Even after her eyes dried, pain radiated from her heart. While Nathan had told his story, all she could think of was the train that had *not* been warned of a mudslide in British Columbia that had covered a length of track. Coming around the side of a mountain in the dark of night, the engineer had not been prepared to stop, and the train had derailed. Many of the passengers had been killed—including her parents.

She blinked back another prickle behind her eyelids and forced her brain away from the past. *Distraction*. Samantha rolled on her side and peered over the edge of her cot. The dawn lit the sky and provided enough light to see the contours of Nathan's face, the pinch between his brows and the hint of stubble on his jaw. She'd never studied a man so closely. She hadn't read many novels focused on romance or love stories, but the few she had returned with surprising clarity. What would it feel like to be loved by a man...or even just seen and appreciated by one?

She shook the thought from her head and forced her gaze upward and away. Better to stare at the dark canvas above than allow her train of thought down such a dangerous path...only staring at the darkness overhead took her back to her dream—or nightmare. The blackness. Trapped. Screams—were they hers? Or did someone else cry out for help? The girls were trapped too. But there was no longer a wall separating them. She could see them as rocks settled around them. No, that wasn't right. The girls were fine. Not crushed under the mountain that had crumbled down on them—not like the rest of their family.

An image from her nightmare flashed through her mind, and she quickly jerked her face back to where Nathan slept. Peaceful. Alive. No rocks. No mud. No death. Her heart gradually returned to its normal rhythm. She didn't want to think about the man—but just watching him rest was enough to chase the nightmares away. The steady rise and fall of his chest. The curve of his ear. The way his dark hair fell back, other than the several moist strands that clung to his forehead and neck.

What would it feel like to be in love? To have a marriage and family? Family...

A yearning welled within her—one she had easily pushed aside in the past. Family was a foreign idea to her. She'd never had siblings and her parents had left her—even before they had died. Nannies and then boarding schools. She'd craved her parents' attention. She'd tried to prove herself to them by studying hard and being the perfect little lady when they visited. But had she ever been enough—enough that they would want her with them?

She shifted her attention back to the man on the ground so close to her cot. The early light of a rainy dawn left much to her memory of his features, but it was more pleasant to study him than allow herself to succumb to the past.

Of course they wanted you.

She rehearsed what often felt like a lie. But they had promised she could join them when she was older and they had found a place in the west.

She almost laughed at the irony. Here she was, living in the west as her parents had promised, yet still alone. And that was her fate. Living and dying alone as a spinster schoolmarm whose mission and focus was her students and the betterment of their minds. Many had traveled this path before her—intelligent, brave women who had helped mold her for this life. They'd seemed content with their lives. They didn't need a man binding them into a role of housekeeping and childbirth. . .

Again, that pesky ache she had no desire to entertain. Because the truth was, she didn't know how to be a mother. Or a wife. And even if she did want such a thing, it wasn't as though a man would have any desire for her. Mr. Chestnut wasn't the first one to make such comments. She wasn't naive. Better to bury herself in a book or prepare lessons than entertain fantasies for romance and family.

Samantha turned away from Nathan and again stared upward, hating the tightness in her chest. Unfortunately, there was no escape from her thoughts this rainy morning. She was trapped in this tent with a man she was far too attracted to, and trapped with her thoughts. It was too dark to read, and a lamp would only awaken the girls. She sighed, the ache growing. The girls only highlighted what she lacked. She wasn't up to the task of comforting or mothering.

A whimper across the room made her cringe. Another restless night with Lucy. Poor Mary had gotten up with her at least three or four times, while Samantha stayed under her covers like a coward.

A whimpering breached a soft cry, and Samantha pushed herself upright. A twelve-year-old needed sleep. And Samantha had no excuse. Besides, dealing with a baby couldn't be worse than drowning in her own thoughts.

The ache in her foot was just that after the past couple of days of healing, so Samantha carefully stepped over the sleeping Mountie and maneuvered to the pallet where Lucy tried to kick free of the quilt she shared with Mary.

"Hush, baby," Samantha breathed as she pulled Lucy into her arms. The child instantly quieted, which was a relief. Samantha headed back the route she had come, careful with each step. She tried to give Nathan space as she stepped over his legs, but abruptly he shifted, rolling onto his side, his top leg bending. She tried to hop out of the way, but his foot snagged her leg and she fell forward, arms full of baby and unable to catch herself. All she could do was twist and drop.

Chapter 17

Nathan jolted upright as something heavy pinned his legs and a baby wailed. What on earth? He blinked his eyes open and stared at the woman tangled on the quilt covering him. "Miss Ingles?" he ground out in somewhat of a whisper. "What are you doing?"

"Nothing," came the terse reply. She sat on the ground, with her legs over his, nightgown up to her knees, baby squirming in her grasp. "You tripped me."

"I tripped you? I was asleep. *You* fell on *me*." He tried to pull his legs free while she struggled to do the same.

"You moved," she complained.

He didn't bother returning an answer, finally extracting himself enough to stand and offer a hand. Only, her hands were already full. He gripped her arms and pulled her upright. Her breath came in puffs that betrayed frustration and maybe a little embarrassment. For some reason he liked seeing her flustered, her stoic expression shattered. She appeared more human, more approachable.

"Are you all right?"

A shot of shame. Nathan should have been the one to ask that. Even if the accident had been her doing. "Are you?"

"Yes. Fine." Her focus flitted from him to the baby in arms whose wide eyes took in the two concerned faces looming nearby.

"Papa." With the cry, Lucy threw herself at him, arms reaching.

"Oh, sweetheart." What else could he say? It wasn't as though the child would understand an explanation that her father was dead and she would never see him again. Nathan knew he looked similar to Peter, and the dim light probably didn't help, but what could he do but hold her close and pretend to be her papa? She leaned into his shoulder, and he patted hers, feeling inept. He had younger siblings and even remembered the last two as infants, but he'd been too young to help care for them. He had no experience.

"Well done, *papa*." Miss Ingles' lip curved up with just enough amusement to show. He feigned a glare.

"When the sun gets higher, she'll see her mistake."

Miss Ingles shrugged. "You do look a lot like your brother. A little less gray at the temples. A few less wrinkles at the corners of your eyes. He smiled a lot."

"He had reason to." Nathan snapped back before he realized what he was saying and the irritation he felt. But it was true. Rosemary had chosen Peter and given him a family. His employment wasn't much, but he'd had a wife who loved him and seven healthy children. He didn't even have to deal with the loss of his family, or the orphaning of his girls. He was free now, probably happy among the angels above.

"What is stopping you?"

He looked at the woman questioning him. Dawn filtered through the clouds, adding a soft glow to the morning. "Stopping me from what?"

One of her brows cocked at him. "From being happy."

The nerve of the woman. Who was she to speak? She was about as miserable a soul as he'd ever met. "I just buried my brother and his family yesterday, for one. I don't have much to feel happy about at the moment."

"No of course not." Yet something in her voice seemed to mock. Before he could say anything more, she stepped past him toward the door and slipped on her shoes, then pulled a shawl over her head and shoulders. "I'll be back." She ducked out into the rain that thankfully seemed a softer patter now.

Nathan stood for a long moment, not wanting to consider her words but unable to stop. She was right to a degree. Maybe if he'd forgiven Rosemary and Peter, and opened himself to marriage and a family, he might have been happier. But he'd needed to prove himself first—to figure out who he was and what he was worth. Do something that would make him stand out from his brothers. Otherwise, he'd be forced to live in their shadows forever.

"Papa," Lucy crooned again, completely relaxed in his arms. She cocked her head up and patted his cheek.

"I'm sorry, Lucy girl." Nathan sank onto the chair, then bent down and snagged the quilt from the ground to pull over them. The air held a damp chill.

Across the tent, with a shuffle of blankets, Mary moved into a sitting position. She watched for a moment, before climbing out of her quilt and tiptoeing across the distance. He opened a spot for her on his other knee, and she slipped onto his lap, huddling in as though trying to make herself smaller, to fit better under the quilt. "I wish you could be our papa now," she mumbled against his shirt. "Then I wouldn't be so scared."

"Hey. Why are you scared?"

She snuggled deeper but didn't answer.

"I promised you will be looked after. You have other uncles—ones with kids for you to play with. You have aunts to spoil you like a mama. I know it will be scary at the beginning, but you'll have your sisters, and they will have you. Soon you will be surrounded by love and family."

She made no reply, but from the way she clung to him, she probably hadn't changed her mind yet. That was fine. She needed time—they all needed time—for the changes that would come. And time to recover from the pain and fear of loss. Time. They just needed time.

"But for now, I'm not going anywhere. I'm here. Whenever you need me."

He felt her nod. Good.

Then she started to tremble. Then sob. He wrapped his arm tighter around her and her sister as they huddled together. Lucy watched quietly while Mary cried. Nathan closed his eyes and tipped his chin against the top of Mary's head. She often seemed so grown, but at twelve she was still very much a young girl, one who had lost so much only a few days ago. He probably didn't fully comprehend the pain she felt right now. What could he say to it?

So Nathan simply held her and waited for her tears to subside.

Miss Ingles ducked back inside the tent, and he felt himself brace. She sent one glance his way as she pulled the shawl from her head. "Do you want me to take Lucy?" she asked, nudging her shoes off since the laces were already loose.

"She's all right."

Another slight nod as Miss Ingles glanced around the small tent as though seeking something to do or someplace to escape. She finally crossed back to her cot, the slightest hobble to her step, and slipped under the quilt, her back to them.

Nathan shook his head. If not for the few times he had flustered her or frustrated her, he would wonder if she had any emotion at all.

———◆◆◆———

Samantha lay still, trying to keep her breath silent and deep—as though she could pretend sleep when all she could think about was Mary and her sobs, an echo of her own so long ago.

Just once.

When word had first arrived of her parents' deaths, she had thrown herself onto the bed and cried every bit as hard as Mary did now. Cried so hard she could scarcely draw a breath. But the school's headmistress had followed her, watched for a moment, and then told her to stop such foolishness.

"Tears change nothing, but make you feel worse and make you look horrible."

The woman wasn't wrong. Her eyes hurt. Her head hurt. And it was hard to breathe. Samantha had taken the hanky offered and dried her cheeks. Tears wouldn't bring her parents back. She'd been whisked back to class where she had sat silent but with dry eyes. Days stretched into weeks and then years, and she had kept her eyes dry, focusing on everything she could control.

Why did she feel such a lack of that control now? Perhaps because she had nothing to do but lay here and try not to think or feel too deeply.

Minutes were counted in breaths, and the slow creep of the sun into the sky. It lit the world despite the gray skies. The rain eased to a soft drizzle. Mary's tears seemed to do the same, and finally she slipped back to her quilt for perhaps a few more minutes of rest despite her little sister babbling in Nathan's arms. Abby would be awake by now, and all the girls would be hungry soon. Hot porridge would be perfect on a chilly morning like this, but that would mean venturing back into the rain and managing to light a fire.

Coffee would be great as well. Perhaps the Mountie could be persuaded to light the fire and put the kettle on. Samantha rolled toward him and caught the pinch between his eyes as he watched his smallest niece play with the plain buttons on his coat. She obviously didn't care that they weren't brass like the ones on his uniform. But Constable Nathan Stanford cared. Whenever he straightened his jacket, a scowl crossed his face. The loss of his uniform chafed.

She well understood.

Not having the school to ground herself in each day. Not being able to bury herself in lesson preparation and tutoring—feeling as though a huge part of her identity was ripped away.

"What day is it?" Mary asked with a sniffle from across the tent.

A long pause made Samantha wonder if she needed to offer the answer.

"Sunday," Nathan finally spoke.

"Can we go to church today?"

"Church?" He sounded just as surprised as Samantha. And a little uncertain.

Samantha sat up, uncomfortable lounging any longer in a man's presence. She pulled a blanket over her shoulders to provide both protection from the chill in the air and the nearness of the man. "I don't know if Blairmore even has a church," she offered.

"I heard most folks traveled to Frank in the past." Nathan slanted a look in her direction. "But if the rain breaks, there is an outside meeting planned for early afternoon."

Why did it feel like he was offering a challenge? Did he think she avoided churches? Of course she attended—not because she believed or belonged or any such thing but because she had to keep up appearances in the community. She was more than capable of continuing the ruse. Samantha forced the corners of her lips upward. "Here's hoping the rain breaks."

As though God did exist and was eavesdropping, the light patter on the canvas eased to silence.

Samantha smiled as though she were actually happy with the shift in the weather. "I guess it's time we got a fire started and put some coffee and porridge on."

Something remained hooded in Nathan's eyes as he stood and placed Lucy on Samantha's lap. "I'll get started." He looked at her a moment longer as though trying to read her, so she forced her shoulders to relax and offered him what hopefully appeared to be a congenial smile.

"That would be wonderful. Wouldn't it, Lucy?" She looked to the child, a safer focus by far. "I only wish we could light that fire in here."

"Are you cold?"

Samantha waved him away. "I'm fine. The air is damp and chill, but at least we have someplace dry." She cuddled Lucy in under the blanket, adding a slight rock to her movement as she had seen Mrs. Stanford do in the past. "We're warm enough now, aren't we, Lucy?"

Much to Samantha's surprise, the baby cuddled against her chest, one small hand reaching up to pat her neck. A warning sounded in Samantha's brain to pull back, to keep the child at arm's length. . . But nature seemed to shout the opposite—*hold the baby tight, keep her warm and protected, let her inside your heart.*

Chapter 18

⁓

"You're alive!"

Samantha twisted at the exclamation, though mindful of her ankle. Before she had a chance to react, arms flew around her, engulfing her in an embrace. Amilia Fredricks, the other teacher from Frank, held tightly.

"No one I asked knew. Only that the house you were billeted in was in the path of the slide. But you look perfectly fine! Goodness, where have you been?"

"Just here." Samantha managed to pull back enough to motion to the children at her side. "I've been helping with the Stanford girls." Crowds swarmed around them, others offering welcomes and embraces as they met friends and neighbors. But despite the reunions, a solemnity...or perhaps *sorrow* was a better description...pressed heavily upon the entire group.

Miss Fredricks's pale blue eyes glistened as she glanced to Mary and Abby who had taken up residence in their uncle's shadow. "I heard about the boys," the younger woman lowered her voice to a whisper. "A tragedy. All of this. Understandably, the board has decided it best to discontinue classes for the season. At this point it's impossible to guess what will happen next. Will anyone ever return to Frank?"

"I don't understand how anyone would want to," Samantha inserted. She glanced at the gathering, recognizing some, not knowing most. There was no reason for her to remain in the area if school would not resume until autumn at the earliest. But what did that mean for her? Where would she go while she awaited a new assignment? Four months seemed an eternity before she could start teaching again, and uncertainty gnawed within her rib cage.

"Will you stay?" Miss Fredricks questioned.

Samantha felt her head shake as though answering them both. There was no place for her here. Or anywhere for that matter. "You?"

"I have family in Lethbridge." She shrugged. "I think I am done with mountains for the foreseeable future."

Samantha couldn't agree more but still held her tongue as Miss Fredricks gave her another embrace.

"All the best." She glanced over Samantha's shoulder at the Stanfords. "To all of you," she said before slipping away to greet another family with equal enthusiasm.

Constable Stanford stepped to her side. "Most people don't stiffen up like a board when a friend hugs them."

Samantha's jaw fell. "Amilia Fredricks and I are merely coworkers. Acquaintances."

He raised a brow. "You didn't look unpleased to see her."

"I wasn't. It's good to know she's safe." Samantha was merely not used to being so familiar with someone. She didn't remember the last time someone had held her like that—not including being carried around by the constable, of course. Friendship, though. . . Samantha wasn't sure she had anyone who fit that description. She hugged herself against a sudden chill.

"Uh-huh," Nathan hummed as though he saw right through her. As though he could count the years since she had allowed herself a friend. But what was the point of letting people into her confidence—much less her heart—if they simply went away? Her classmates had always moved on, as had her teachers, as did her students. Relationships were fleeting, shifting in time with the seasons.

"Is this close enough, Mary?" he asked, and Samantha forced her thoughts back to the grassy valley on the edge of Blairmore.

Mary took several paces closer to the slope, where it appeared the pastor had set up his makeshift podium. "Just a little closer."

Nathan followed dutifully, and Samantha did the same, until Mary waved to an open section that would hold the quilt they had brought to keep them off the moist grass. Though it had stopped raining hours ago, the sun had not breached the heavy gray clouds and little drying had taken place.

Nathan set Lucy on the quilt, then directed Abby to sit as well. The older girl hid her legs under her dress and kept her gaze on the patchwork of fabric. "I'll be right back," Nathan said before slipping into the crowd, weaving his way to where two constables stood talking.

Lucy started to crawl after him, but Samantha caught her and drew her onto her lap. "You wait here with us," Samantha chided. While they waited, she searched the faces surrounding them. Miss Fredricks had not wandered far and now visited with the Martin family who'd had children spanning both of their school classes. Samantha watched as the younger children hugged their teacher, who stooped and smiled at them.

Samantha averted her gaze, and it quickly snagged on Annie Bansemer. Her husband, Carl, stood at her side, arm wrapping her waist as though offering support.

Mary must have followed her gaze, because a cry of joy tore from her as she jolted to her feet. "Fransis! Rose!"

The eldest two Bansemer girls hurried to meet Mary halfway and threw their arms around her. Samantha's own heart raced a little faster. The Bansemers had lived with their nine children in one of the cottages next to the Stanfords on Manitoba Avenue. Had they all survived? Samantha looked around, not immediately seeing all. She pushed to her feet and started in that direction, Lucy in arms so she didn't lose her in the crowds.

"Miss Ingles." Mrs. Bansemer stepped in her direction, a smile spreading across her face. "I had heard you escaped with the Stanford girls, but it does my heart good to see you."

Samantha couldn't seem to find a reply. Why would the woman care? While Samantha had taught several of their older children, it wasn't as though the relationship extended beyond that.

"Oh, and to see Lucy so healthy, as though nothing happened." The woman shook her head, eyes taking on a shine. "I don't think I can express my fright at hearing her crying that night, not knowing where she was or how badly she was hurt." Mrs. Bansemer stepped near and cupped the side of the baby's face.

"You found her?"

She shook her head. "I was busy with my own children, but I heard her and sent a couple of the men in her direction. They were able to find her and bring her back to our house."

"Your house survived?" The thought seemed incredible. "I don't remember much from that morning."

Mrs. Bansemer nodded with understanding. "It was moved but remained mostly intact. Enough to preserve our lives." She closed her eyes as though offering a quick prayer. Probably of gratitude. "Carl and the oldest boys were away that morning, thankfully, but arrived back the same day."

"How wonderful," Samantha managed, not sure what else to say. It seemed more incredible than anything.

"A miracle," a deep voice rumbled behind her.

She glanced back into Nathan's solemn expression. She hadn't even heard his return.

"Very much so," Mrs. Bansemer agreed with a fervent nod.

Her husband came beside her. "Though you can understand we won't be testing the fates," he said, his gaze steadfast on his wife. "As soon as the road is clear, we will be on our way."

"Understandably," Nathan agreed.

Mrs. Bansemer placed a hand on his arm. "I am sorry for the loss of your family. How kind of Miss Ingles to stay on and help you with the girls."

"Yes. We are very grateful for her." Yet his tone didn't sound grateful.

"Oh, dear Miss Ingles," another woman entered the circle, but her voice was anything but kind. "I'm sure she is all heart when it comes to these girls and their unmarried uncle."

Heat crept up Samantha's neck. Out of the corner of her eye she could see Nathan stiffen—though she refused to actually look at him.

"I'm sure her concern is for the girls. She's been a wonderful teacher to our older children," Mrs. Bansemer graciously supplied.

"I've heard plenty about her teaching, and some would question its *wonderfulness*. She's far too strict and abrasive, I hear. My sister-in-law struggles to get her boy to the school because of how he's been treated by this woman."

Were they *actually* having this discussion with her standing right here? Yes, Samantha had been talked about plenty in the past, and her teaching criticized, but it was usually said in hushed tones when they didn't think she could hear. Samantha didn't know the woman personally, but she knew several boys who would struggle to come to school no matter who their teacher was!

"Looking at her now," Mrs. Bansemer again came to the rescue, "I see only a woman who cares for children and their well-being."

"Not their uncle's good opinion?" the other woman remarked snidely before stalking away. She cast a knowing glance over her shoulder, and Samantha wished she could shrink away.

"Don't mind her, dear," Mrs. Bansemer patted Samantha's arm. "Miss Harvy is the abrasive one. She should have never said such things."

Miss Harvy? That made more sense. Philip Harvy was a horrible bully to smaller children, and his antics were often met with disciplinary measures. Samantha tried to relax her expression, to pretend not to be affected by Miss Harvy's comments, but Nathan already backed away, as though he believed what was said.

Before Samantha could defend herself, the pastor stood and motioned for the congregation to quiet. Most of the crowd found seats on blankets or chairs that had been hauled outside for this purpose. Others stood around the edges of the gathering. There was no time to consider her options—at the moment, there was only one: pretend indifference and sit with the Stanfords on their quilt, keeping Lucy on her lap. The child gave her a reason, an excuse to be there. Otherwise, she didn't belong. Not in this congregation of believers. Not among the citizens of Frank and Blairmore. And most certainly not anywhere near Nathan Stanford. First thing Monday morning, it was time to leave.

Nathan tucked the notebook back into his pocket, hoping no one would think anything of him taking notes during the sermon—though that was not what was on his mind. He actually only caught bits here and there as the preacher droned on. His mind bounced back and forth between the conversation he had overheard, and on the woman across the quilt from him. What rumors were spreading about them? One would think that in the wake of a disaster there was enough else to worry about besides a local schoolteacher and her attempt to help a hurting family.

He wanted to laugh out loud at the accusation that she was trying to attach or ensnare him. Obviously, nothing could be further from the truth, and any fool with half an eye could see it. Miss Ingles was as approachable as a porcupine. Trying to gain his good opinion? The woman was spinster through and through, and the likelihood of that changing anytime soon—or any time at all—was questionable. Maybe if the man was a widower and had a passel of children who needed strict discipline and an education.

His lip twitched, but Nathan kept his chuckle at bay despite the severe glare from the woman herself. Of course, she had her moments. Like that morning with her hair loose while she brushed it in long tawny waves—only to pull it back up into a tight bun at the nape of her neck.

He shook the image from his head and again focused on the preacher on his knoll. He had shifted his theme to one of miracles, though the man seemed skeptical for a man of God. He acknowledged there was much to thank the Lord for, while still dwelling on the loss to the community. How did miracles play into tragedy? Wouldn't a true miracle have been the mountain staying together to begin with? Or missing the town completely? Though there were still ranches and camps that would have been destroyed. And the mine. . .

Maybe the town had brought this on themselves by mining in the first place. Had the tunnels weakened the structure of the mountain enough to be responsible for the slide? Would God have stepped in to save them from their own doing?

Were there miracles involved or simply coincidence?

Lucy crawled onto Nathan's lap, and he pulled her against his chest. Her body pressed against the notebook buried in his breast pocket as though God Himself sent the reminder. Lucy's survival could not be coincidence. Coincidence had not pushed a bale of hay almost a mile from the livery. Coincidence did not account for the child being thrown from the house as it was ripped apart by stones that could easily crush bone. Not one bone had been so much as bruised when she'd landed on the hay.

He had to stop fighting the notion of God's hand in all this and accept that the Lord above had different purposes.

But why would He allow so many people to die? Like Peter and Rosemary? The boys were still so young—too young to be taken. . .

Taken where?

Nathan sighed at the question. Because he knew the answer. Taken to a heavenly home.

What is death to God but bringing them home?

Is that what God did with the slide? Pick and choose who He wanted home?

Restlessness battled with a strange feeling of peace settling into Nathan's chest. Part of him didn't want to accept the answer. But deep down, he couldn't deny it either.

Chapter 19

Samantha again folded her spare dress into a sack, burying the funds her solicitor had sent to tide her over. As much as she had preferred to leave the trust her father had left her untouched, "desperate times" and all. This time, she would not be convinced to stay. People were already talking about her and the impropriety of the amount of time she spent in such proximity to a man. She could not risk her reputation or her career.

"Where will you go?" Mary asked, sitting beside her.

"Sparwood? Fernie, perhaps." With the railway tracks being cleared to the southeast, Samantha planned to travel into British Columbia—to the first town offering acceptable hotel or boardinghouse accommodations. She would wait there until she decided what to do next or received a new placement.

"I wish you would stay."

Samantha glanced at the girl, fighting the urge to wrap a reassuring arm around her shoulders. Or to push the loose strand of blond hair from her cheek. But no, that was not Samantha's place. "You have your uncle and your sisters. You will be fine without me." She moved to stand, but arms wrapped her waist, holding her in place.

"I'll miss you."

No, you won't, Samantha wanted to say. There was no reason the child should feel any attachment to her. Like any other student, she would soon move forward with her life and forget Samantha completely. Though why that thought tugged at her heart made no sense. Change was a part of life, as was goodbye.

So why did she not want to go?

Samantha pulled away from Mary and stood. She'd obviously lingered too long and was growing too attached. Such was not uncommon, with especially good students. Sometimes attachments were made—just not to last. The quicker Samantha left, the better for everyone involved. Mary had already lost enough. All the girls had.

Samantha stepped outside to the glare of the morning sun, and the image of Nathan—*Constable Stanford*—crouched to bank the morning fire. That was her biggest mistake. She should have never begun thinking of him on such familiar terms. He looked up at her, taking in the whole of her in one glance, from her head to the satchel clutched in her hands. "Are you sure your foot is up for the walk to the station?"

"It'll be fine. It hardly bothers me now." Not a complete lie. It ached with much walking but no longer bit with pain at every movement. She only had to make it as far as the station, and then she could rest it the remainder of the day.

Constable Stanford stood and stepped close enough that he veritably towered over her. "If Mary is up to watching the others for a few minutes, it wouldn't take long to give you a ride."

"I appreciate the offer." She was tempted to accept, but the longer she spent in his presence, the more twisted her insides became, and the more heat climbed her neck. Sweat moistened her hairline. Yes, she was attracted to the man—Samantha couldn't deny that. But she knew precisely what he thought of her and wished to distance herself from the shame of it. "You should stay with the girls."

Samantha took a breath and pulled her gaze away. Why was it already so hard to leave? Why did so much of her already cling to the idea of being needed—not just as a teacher, but as a . . . She shut the word from her mind before she had a chance to acknowledge it. She was a teacher. A teacher. A teacher. A spinster. Alone. "Goodbye."

"What?"

She glanced back at Nathan. Was he about to ask her to stay? He seemed surprised by something. Could it be he realized he didn't want her to leave? But he wasn't looking at her. His glare was fixed in place and aimed beyond where she stood. A pang of disappointment was better not to acknowledge either.

"Nate!" a voice boomed. A man of similar build, though thicker around the middle, raised a hand in greeting. He sat atop a small wagon with a petite, dark-haired woman at his side. Their clothes were fine, with satin in his waistcoat and lace ornamenting her deep blue gown.

"Charles." Nathan ground out between his teeth.

The wagon drew close and jostled to a stop. The man had the same dark hair as both Nathan and Peter, though Charles' hinted gray at his temples. The same blue eyes as well.

"Your brother?" Samantha whispered, with a glance at the man beside her as he straightened his jacket.

"Yes. Charles is the oldest."

Oh. But that did nothing to explain the tightness of Nathan's shoulders or the scowl pushing his brows together. Not that it mattered to her. She was leaving. And now that he had family here to help, there was no reason to look back.

Nathan knew he should step over and assist his sister-in-law from the wagon, but his feet refused to move. Why hadn't they sent a telegram to let him know they were coming? Not that Charles needed him for anything. He jumped down from the wagon and circled to help his wife. Maddie was the epitome of beauty and grace as always, despite having raised six children. She crossed to Nathan and offered a quick embrace.

"You look well, Nate."

"Course he does. He sits on a horse all day." Charles gave little more than a nod, his gaze already scanning the fire and the tent. Mary appeared in the doorway, and he gave a tight smile.

Sit on a horse all day? As though Nathan was little more than an average cowpoke?

"Where is your uniform?"

Nathan ran his palms down his ordinary brown jacket, wishing he could have been dressed in uniform. Charles never had seen him on duty. "I'm on leave to take care of the girls."

The sound from the back of his brother's throat was not quite positive. "Well, you can return to work soon enough. We won't keep you."

"Excuse me?" Nathan wanted to take Charles by the shoulders and force him to actually look at him instead of analyzing everything else and no doubt finding it lacking.

"Yes, we have discussed everything, so you needn't concern yourself anymore."

"Concern myself? With the girls? What do you mean you have discussed everything? With whom?"

"The rest of the family."

"But not me." Hot indignation shot through Nathan. How dare his siblings discount him so easily?

Charles laughed out loud. "We already know your stance on the matter."

"You're a confirmed bachelor, Nate," Maddie crooned. "We couldn't leave you to struggle with three young children for any longer than necessary. We came as soon as we could."

"The girls and I have been getting along just fine." Nathan crossed his arms and faced his brother, who still didn't look at him. "Just fine."

Charles finally glanced at him with a raised brow. "What do you know about children? Little girls for that matter."

"I know enough."

"But girls need a woman's touch. The poor dears."

"They haven't been without." Nathan glanced at Miss Ingles who stood silent, her expression a little too knowing. "Miss Ingles here is a schoolteacher and has graciously been assisting with the girls. So you can see, I have had everything quite in hand." He squared his shoulders, daring his brother to argue.

"I see," was all Charles said, giving Miss Ingles another cursory glance. His wife's head tipped to one side. "But not quite the same as family." She gave a tight smile. "No offense. I am sure, as a teacher, you are more than qualified to mind the girls."

Miss Ingles opened her mouth, but Nathan spoke first. "Family? The girls don't know you, have never met you. Miss Ingles provided someone known and trusted. She was boarding with Peter and Rosemary for the past few months, and I am sure is exactly what the girls need."

He ignored the twinge of shame for his lie, focusing instead on the look of shock on every other face—including the face of Miss Ingles. "In fact, I do not feel it wise to make any hasty changes. The girls have only just buried their parents and brothers. They need time to meet you and come to know you before you drag them back to Regina."

Charles faced him and crossed his arms. "We plan on staying the week to make sure everything is settled and await Brent and his wife's arrival. Wilfred and Laura should also be arriving soon."

"Why?" The funeral had already taken place. What was the point of coming now?

"Maddie decided that with our youngest now turning ten and the oldest two close to leaving home, she would enjoy taking on the youngest. Lucy, isn't it?"

Nathan managed a nod.

"Brent and Beth have children the middle girl's age and volunteered to house her."

Nathan tensed. Did they even know Abigail's name? Or care what she needed?

"And the oldest girl will be a wonder for Laura, who just had their third baby and could use help around the house and with the twins."

Nathan glanced back at Mary's wide eyes. "So you never thought to ask me my opinion? Even though I am the only one who knows the girls and have been caring for them?"

"Nate, it's hardly like you could. . .or *would*. . .even want to take them on yourself," his sister-in-law chirped in. "You are a confirmed bachelor."

"I never said that."

Maddie shook her head, her lips raised into a smug smile. "You're a Mounted Policeman. Hardly a career choice that welcomes a wife or children, or any other responsibilities for that matter."

"You're tired, Nate. As we all are. We'll take the girls and find suitable accommodations for them. That will free you up to get back into your uniform and to work. Nothing to worry about. We have this."

Nathan's hands tightened into fists, as though he could somehow grip everything slipping away. They were stripping him of any choice, any responsibility. But he had a responsibility to Mary and Abby and Lucy. He had promised. "No."

Charles had started to turn away but spun back. "Excuse me?"

"You are not taking the girls today. They are settled here."

"They're in a tent," Maddie complained.

"There are not many other options in Blairmore right now. No hotel rooms. No boardinghouses."

"Then why stay in Blairmore?" Charles inserted.

"Because this is where the girls belong for now. Miss Ingles will stay on and care for them while we wait for Brent and Will, and then we can discuss what homes the girls will join."

Charles eyed him, and Nathan felt his pulse take flight. He had never challenged his older brother. Not like this. "I already told you. Everything has already been decided."

"No. Things have been discussed, and you have expressed your opinions. I won't force the girls to go to a home they don't want. You will have to convince them of your plan." Nathan planted his heels in the firm soil and held his brother's gaze. So much like Peter's but with a hard edge now.

"Fine. Maddie and I will find a place to stay, and we can discuss things further." Charles leaned in close and lowered his voice. "But mark my words, little brother. You don't get the final say."

———◆◆———

Samantha remained in place. She preferred not to draw attention or the scrutiny of Nathan's family. She stayed outside while quick introductions were made to the girls. Maddie, the sister-in-law, gushed over Lucy, but even that seemed superficial and sounded like nails down a chalkboard to Samantha's nerves. She had to remind herself that this was what the girls needed. Family. . .

Only it wasn't fair that the poor things would have to be separated from the ones they loved the most and knew the best.

Thankfully, the brother and his wife didn't stay long. They wished to find accommodations as close to Blairmore as possible, but that would take them at least as far as Coleman, a village about five or six miles deeper into the mountains.

"Such a pleasure to meet you, Miss Ingles," Maddie said on their way to wagon, but as she looked Samantha up and down, pleasure was not to be seen in her expression. "Do take good care of dear little Lucy for us. We will be back for her soon."

A muscle worked in Nathan's jaw while he nodded at his brother's farewell. He watched silently until the wagon disappeared beyond the tent town and curve of the road. Air gushed from his lungs and his shoulders slumped.

"You don't seem happy that your brother has ridden to your rescue."

The scowl deepened between his eyes. "*My* job is to ride to the rescue, not his. I don't need saving."

And yet hadn't that been her role the past few days? She stepped closer and lowered her voice. "Perhaps it is the girls that need rescuing, then."

"From me?" he glanced at her, the question widening his eyes.

"That isn't what I meant. But they need a family."

"Yes. *A* family. Not to be divided out across the country to never see each other again." Another huff of breath. "But what do I know? I don't have children or even a wife. I'm the *single* brother and should just let them do as they want. They will anyway. They don't listen to *me*. Never have."

"I can only imagine."

He shook his head. "Let me guess. You're an oldest child, always in charge of everyone younger, the big boss."

"Not exactly."

He raised a brow. "You don't seem to be a younger child—relaxed on the rules and spoiled rotten."

A laugh tickled the back of her throat. "No, that does not sound like me, does it?"

"Not even a little."

Samantha tensed. "Where did you fit then?"

"Smack-dab in the center—four older and four younger."

Samantha couldn't imagine so much family. It seemed both wonderful and horrifying. "And what does it mean to be a middle child, exactly?"

Nathan fidgeted with the bottom of his jacket. "It means you get forgotten." He started to turn back to the tent, as though their conversation was at an end. The nerve of the man! Especially as the train's whistle sounded from deeper in the valley, announcing that her plans for that morning were in vain. She was stuck here. "And what exactly do you expect me to do now?"

He looked back. Understanding lit his blue eyes. "I'd sure appreciate it if you did stay on a few days more, so the girls have more time together."

Samantha sighed but nodded. It was about Lucy and Abby and Mary and what they needed. "Very well. A few days shouldn't hurt anything." But she wasn't so sure. A deep crevasse was forming in her resolve to stay detached. How much more could she take before she began to crumble?

Chapter 20

MAY 5TH

"What are you doing here, Constable Stanford?"

Nathan continued across the uneven rock, sidestepping boulders as he approached the group of men standing where splintered lumber suggested a building had once stood. "I came to help."

Constable Hardy eyed him. "I believe you are off duty for the foreseeable future."

"That doesn't mean there isn't a need for help out here. My nieces are. . .in good enough hands." Though it was strange that Miss Ingles' hands were suddenly preferable to Maddie's. It wasn't as though he had reason to dislike his sister-in-law, but just being in her presence chafed.

A pause, and then a nod. Constable Hardy motioned past the rubble toward the river. "Why don't you head down there. A couple of men are looking for the camp of an old trapper known to be in the area."

Nathan nodded and continued in the indicated direction, picking his way over the ocean of limestone. The popping sound of rock striking rock led him to the edge of the river where the heaps of stone sloped down, making parts of the shore visible with its spring foliage, as though the slide had somehow jumped the river here.

A *boom* made him flinch, and he looked upriver to where dust billowed over a rocky rise.

"Don't mind that," someone called from up ahead. "They're using dynamite to clear parts of the river and the rail line."

Nathan continued to where the man stood with two others, all three miners or laborers by the looks of them. One was probably in his forties, while the others couldn't be much older than half that. Nathan extended his hand to the first. "Constable Stanford."

The man's bushy brows shot upward, and his mustache twitched. "Where's the uniform? You fellows usually stand out a bit more."

Nathan offered a tight smile. "I'm off duty."

"So not one of the ones who've been keeping everyone out of Frank. Be easier to rob a bank than walk through town right now."

Nathan shrugged. "But there hasn't been one case of looting from what I've heard."

"There is that." The man nodded toward his companions. "I'm Matthew Kent, and these fellows are Larry and Trent. They arrived a couple days ago from British Columbia."

"Yes, I was there when the train pulled in." Nathan lunged over a crevasse in the rock and joined the men where they appeared to be tossing stones out of the way. "What did you find?"

"Nothing yet, but I knew Grissack. This was where he usually camped when in the area. He liked the way the river flowed around this outcropping. And the trees there"—he pointed to shattered stumps peeking from the top of the rock—"gave some extra protection from the weather."

Nathan came alongside and surveyed the area, trying to imagine what it had looked like a week earlier. While the others continued to shift rock, looking for any sign of a camp, Nathan stepped closer to the water's edge and studied the terrain. The heaps and mounds of limestone seemed to extend forever from this angle.

"How many do you figure there were out here beyond town?" Nathan asked.

"How many folks lived on the flats?"

"Yeah." He'd been so wrapped up with the loss of his own family and their neighbors on the edge of Frank, and the mine, he hadn't really considered camps down by the river or ranchers and their families.

"Too many," Kent murmured. "James Graham had a ranch over yonder, with his wife and boys. A couple of ranch hands were with them. Graham's brother's place is buried too. Williams. Locke. Mrs. Warrington and her young'uns. A bunch of miners from Lancaster, if I remember correctly, were set up in a cabin up over that way." The man released a heavy sigh. "At least fifty, if I had to guess. Men, women, and children. Buried under all of this."

A weight as heavy as the limestone surrounding Nathan seemed to press down upon him with renewed force.

"Maybe more," one of the younger fellows spoke up. "One old-timer I was talking to said a group of drifters, another fifty or so, came through last Tuesday and were thinking of setting up camp near here and looking for work. For all we know, they're all under this rock too."

Kent shook his head. "I doubt it. They likely moved on because there wasn't much here for them." He wiped a hand across his brow. "We'll probably never know for sure."

For the next while the men worked in silence, the solemnity of what they were doing heavier than the stones they moved. Nathan threw himself into the work, not wanting to consider what he had learned. It was too much loss and pain. Rock after rock, he tossed aside—until his fingers brushed thick fabric. He stilled and fell back a step.

"What did you find?" Kent came alongside, and then took his place with renewed energy. "Come on, boys!"

They all set to work, digging away the rock from the canvases, a tent, crushed, rolled, holding a man who, like Peter, had never stood a chance against the flow of limestone.

"Oh, Andy," Kent moaned as he cut aside a strip of canvas to reveal the body of his friend. Nathan stepped away, the tightness in his chest making it hard to breathe. Maybe it would have been better to allow the old trapper his rest under the rock, undisturbed, but they continued until they could lift the old man free.

"You know," Kent said as they wrapped the body back under his blanket, "Andy Grissack was one for the yarns. He sure could spin a good tale, making him a favorite of the children in town."

One of the younger men stumbled away several feet before he lost his last meal behind a rock. Nathan felt close to doing the same but managed to swallow back the bile. With the other men there assisting with the body, Nathan started over the rise to report their findings. He needed a few minutes. His stomach clenched and roiled as he made his way to where Constable Hardy oversaw another search. Nathan made his report and then turned back to where they had found Grissack.

"Wait, Stanford. There is something you should know. Someone else was found. Yesterday."

Nathan rotated on his heel.

"He was identified as one of the miners from the top of the mine's tipple."

"My—"

"Not your brother." Hardy interjected. "One of the men with him. Fred Farrington. Found his body a quarter mile from the mine, on the western side of the slide."

Nathan managed an acknowledgment before returning to assist the men in hauling the body of Andy Grissack back to Frank for a proper burial. But how many would be left under the rock in unmarked graves?

Nathan worked for the remainder of the afternoon, the warmth of the sun mingling with the physical labor of digging through rock. Sweat rolled from his brow and down his back, but there was something freeing in the work—much better than just watching on. Yet the whole time, he couldn't push his mind past the image of the old trapper's broken body and the thought of Peter, somewhere, buried in the miles of rock. With every stone Nathan tossed aside, he imagined finding his body. . .or what remained of it. He couldn't say what would be better. The closure of the discovery, or the memory of how his brother was.

The torn lumber of the livery marked where another body had been found among the remains of horses. So many horses. The stench was only bearable when the breeze swept through the valley with enough strength to drag it away.

Finally, exhaustion won over, and Nathan scaled back down the limestone, past the miners' cottages, and into Frank—a ghost town if not for the presence of men in scarlet. He should be here as well, in uniform, doing his job. Instead, Nathan mounted his horse and reined back toward Blairmore. The sun was hugging the peaks of the western ridges by the time his feet hit the ground again. He unsaddled his horse, curried him well, and tied him where he could graze before starting toward the tent to check on the girls. Charles said he wouldn't be back until Wednesday so at least that gave Nathan a quiet evening with the girls. And Miss Ingles.

The mumble of voices slowed his steps as he neared the tent. Miss Ingles encouraging. Mary hesitant. "I don't know if I'm ready to share," she spoke softly.

"Sharing your work is an important part of creation."

Nathan tensed. Had they begun studies again? Hadn't he made himself clear to Miss Ingles that her nagging was the last thing the girls needed?

"Very well." Mary cleared her voice, and Nathan stepped to the edge of the tent. Her voice was quiet, and he leaned in to listen.

> *"A loud crack of thunder,*
> *A groan, a scream, a roar,*
> *As everything I knew before,*
> *Was lost under the ground."*

His heart thudded and squeezed. A poem?

> *"Brothers who teased and taunted,*
> *But whose laughter brought delight.*
> *A mother whose gentle love*
> *Had the power to make things right."*

She'd lost so much. Could he truly allow any more to be taken from her? She loved her sisters—it would be wrong to separate them.

Her voice continued, so soft he almost couldn't make out the words.

> *"My father stood atop the mine,*
> *To breathe the cool night air.*
> *But the mountain crumbled down*
> *It's more than I can bear."*

His eyes watered, as again the image of Peter flashed through his mind. The loss. *His* loss. It ate away at him. Regret. Loneliness.

> *"To lose so much—to be left alone,*
> *And yet somehow, I survive.*
> *Now how to live when all is gone,*
> *I don't know how to try."*

Nathan pressed the heels of his palms into his eyes as he struggled with the need to sink to the ground and allow his tears to fall.

"Very good," Miss Ingles' voice filtered through the canvas, tight and terse. "Only the end of the first stanza requires adjustment as the rhyme is not quite right."

"What?" Nathan straightened, heat rushing through him. How dare she say anything about that poem, one written from the heart and a place of so much pain. He pushed into the tent, flinging the flap out of the way. "What do you think you are doing?"

Miss Ingles spun, eyes wide. "Excuse me?"

"Get out. You are done here."

Her jaw dropped, then tensed. "You are the one who demanded I stay."

"Well, I was wrong. Do you have any concept of loss? Or hurt? Do you have any concept of what it feels like to have someone you love ripped away? Do you even have a heart?"

The woman stared at him for a moment, and he caught the slightest glistening in her eyes before she pushed past him and fled the tent.

Good riddance.

Chapter 21

Samantha made it to the edge of the forest before the first tears fell. They rolled down her face and tickled her neck. No, no, no. Not now. She had to keep it together. . . But that poem. That horrible, horrible poem that had ripped down the last of her defenses and tore open wounds she had thought healed.

No. Not healed. If they were healed, she wouldn't feel like her eleven-year-old self when the news had first arrived.

Samantha leaned into the rough trunk of a lodgepole pine, the coarse bark biting her palm. The physical discomfort was almost a relief from the agony wrapping her heart. She leaned her forehead against the tree as well, as tears continued to sear her cheeks.

> *"To lose so much—to be left alone,*
> *And yet somehow, I survive."*

The final stanza played over and over in her head, Mary's voice merging with her own.

> *"Now how to live when all is gone,*
> *I don't know how to try."*

A sob swelled in Samantha's throat, but she tried to swallow it back. She had to regain control of herself. That was the only way to survive. To keep breathing and lock away the pain so deep it had no power over her. She'd done it before as a child. Why was it so difficult now?

She sank to the ground, turning so her back leaned into the pine. She was deep enough in the forest to not be able to see the tent where she had left the youngest two girls wide-eyed, Mary crying, and Nathan irate. She couldn't blame him for his anger. She shouldn't have corrected Mary's poem. It was too personal. Too raw.

But it had also been too real. Too sharp.

To lose so much—to be left alone. . .

Even now she couldn't push away the foggy images of her mother pressing a kiss to her head. *"Don't be afraid, darling. This is a wonderful school. You will be much happier with friends your own age and so much to do every day."*

Samantha had stared at her mother through her seven- or eight-year-old eyes. Happier? When all she wanted was to be with her parents? To travel with them. To live with them. It wasn't as though they hadn't left her in the past, but at least she had the familiarity of a home she knew and the care of Nan. Now they were pushing her away. Leaving her with strangers.

Tears blurred the world from her view.

"Be strong. Tears don't fix anything." Samantha didn't remember much about the woman who had led her to her room, other than these words. *"They just give you a headache."*

She did remember the headache. And had promised herself not to cry anymore.

But every night for weeks, she had broken that promise.

And yet somehow, I survive.

She had survived. She had. She had learned to hide her loneliness. Hide her disappointment when her parents didn't always return for holidays or summers when other girls rejoined their families.

Now how to live when all is gone. . .

Until her parents had died, along with the promise of being together again buried in her heart. She'd clung to it for years, and then it had been ripped away with them.

I don't know how to try...

Be strong. Tears don't fix anything.

And yet they continued to fall. And she hated herself for them. "What is wrong with you?" she chided. "You're a grown woman. Not a schoolgirl." Her parents had been gone for almost two decades. It was too late to cry for them. Too late to relive the moment as though she was losing them all over again.

"Miss Ingles?"

Nathan's voice came far too close. She pressed her palms to her face, trying to wipe away evidence of her tears even as more continued to fall. Better he not find her. The thought of discovery sank her deeper into the ground, the bark of the tree scraping her spine. If she stayed quiet, he might not see her.

No such luck. But wasn't that the way it was with Mounties? He probably tracked her or had a sixth sense for finding his prey. He stepped fully into sight and came to a stop. Samantha kept her eyes averted and pushed to her feet.

"Listen," he started, exasperation seemingly the foremost tone. "I'm sorry for what I said. I'm sure you are a kind enough person and simply have no concept what it feels like to lose someone you love."

She felt her head shake, and she bit down on her tongue. She should say nothing. Simply walk away and never face him again. "You know nothing about me or my life."

He blew out his breath. "No, I don't." And by the sound of it, he had no desire to. Which was exactly how she wanted it. The last thing she needed was to rehash a past that felt so fresh and raw.

"I should have left days ago. We've both known since the beginning that I am not what those girls need. I don't know how to..." To what? To walk them through their grief? To grieve herself? She closed her eyes, and a tear trickled down her cheek. Better to keep her gaze down and walk past him. She might be able to dry her face enough to grab her things and make a getaway.

He caught her arm as she tried to step past him. "I'm sorry. Maybe I overreacted."

"No, you didn't." And she didn't believe he really thought so either. Mary needed a shoulder to cry on and arms wrapped around her. Not a lecture or arithmetic lessons. Samantha couldn't even begin to understand what Abby needed. And Lucy needed a mother. She was not suited for any of that. She was a schoolteacher, raised by teachers to keep emotion at arm's length. She didn't know how to smile and comfort and. . .*mother*. She and everyone else would be better off if she didn't try.

"There is nothing wrong with living a sheltered life, of not having to deal with loss. You have been invaluable in helping with the girls. They just need someone who. . ."

"Who knows what it feels like to have both parents ripped away from you in a tragedy? To be left in the care of women who feel the best thing for you is to focus on your studies and forget your loss. Tears have no use." And yet new ones poured down her cheeks. Stupid, stupid tears! Why wouldn't they stop?

"What?"

She pulled away and started walking but turned deeper into the woods. She needed to escape notice a little while longer. With each step, she was losing the battle. All the resolve to stay unaffected crumbled inside her, burying her under a landslide of emotions she didn't know how to deal with or process. She felt helpless under their power. Her shoulders shook as she tucked herself behind another tree. If only she could find someplace alone, without the heavy tread of boots that followed her.

———•••———

"What?" Nathan stared after the woman for a moment, unsure if he should retreat and give her time or follow. He had never seen a grown woman in such distress. Well, maybe that lady whose husband he'd arrested for murder a year back. But this was different, and his role was different somehow.

He didn't have to go far before the woman stopped behind a tree, almost doubling over as though someone had kneed her in the stomach. Guilt smacked him upside the head. Confusion was its companion. How was *this* the witch of a schoolteacher who forever remained emotionless and aloof? Had he been so mistaken about her? Was she simply that good at wearing a mask?

He stepped near, not knowing how to proceed. Maybe he should have walked away.

"I don't know how to do this," she whispered between sobs.

"What?" She didn't know how to comfort the girls? Continue her ruse?

"Feel."

"What?" He really should stop repeating that word, but Nathan had never been more confused.

She shook her head and swiped at her wet cheeks. "No. I can do this. I just need a distraction. I'll get my things and find somewhere else to stay. I'll work on lesson plans for the fall. I have time, but it will give me something else to focus on. I just need to get away from this place, away from Mary and Abby."

The last comment stopped Nathan's attempt to quietly follow what she was saying and what she meant. "Why do you need to get away from the girls?"

She glanced at him, and tears spilled from her dark lashes. Flecks of gold glistened in the tears filling her eyes. Strange, he hadn't noticed the tones of color in her eyes before. "I was once them," she whispered.

Understanding trickled through his consciousness. "Your parents?"

"Killed in a train wreck. I was not quite Mary's age."

His mouth opened, but what could he say to that? "What about your siblings?"

More tears. He really should just keep his mouth shut. "No one else. Just me."

He couldn't even imagine. Of course he had wished for less siblings now and again, but maybe he'd been mistaken.

"I was raised in boarding schools and finishing schools and then a teacher's college. I was fine. I pushed past the pain. . .or thought I had. I don't understand how it can hurt so much now." She wavered on her feet, and he stepped in to steady her, a hand on each arm.

She closed her eyes and tipped her head forward. He dutifully stepped closer, and she fell against his shoulder. The motion was accompanied by a soul-wrenching sob. Her body spasmed as floodgates opened wide. He had thought she was crying hard before, but her earlier tears were nothing compared to the rivers pouring against his shoulder. What could he do but slide his arms around her and offer support as she sagged against him? Her hands slipped around his torso as well and clung to the back of his jacket as though clinging to the side of a crumbling mountain.

They stood in place for a long time. Her weeping rose and fell as waves breaking across a shore before slipping away. His legs grew tired, but what could he do but remain in place? He was trained to come to the rescue—just not in a situation like this. He was a defender, a protector, even an *avenger* if needed. . .not a comforter. He had no idea what to do. Words escaped him as well. All he could do was hold her. And that was problematic on its own. She fit against his shoulder far too well, her hair smelled of lemons and pine. . .and she needed him.

Chapter 22

Even as her tears dried, Samantha couldn't pull away. No one had ever held her like this, not in all her memories, not standing so patiently while she cried. She pressed her sore eyes closed, unsure of how to proceed. Nathan had been kind enough to hold her while she cried, but this would mean nothing to him—he cared nothing for her. So how to draw back? How embarrassing to have come so completely undone in his presence, never mind in his arms. And now to face him with her red puffy face, a wet shoulder in her wake.

Nathan seemed to sense her indecision and eased back a step, his arms bracing her up. He didn't say a thing as he peered down at her. Samantha stole a glance at his face and turned away. His hands withdrew their support, and she felt their loss. But this was for the best. Distance was for the best.

"I'm fine now." She managed to speak, though her voice came out barely a whisper. She cleared her throat.

"Are you?"

How dare he question her when she was barely holding herself together? Maybe she wasn't completely fine, but well enough that he could make his escape. "I just need a few more minutes. Alone."

He nodded but still didn't move. Instead, he watched her far too closely.

Samantha swiped the last of the wetness from her cheeks and chin. And neck. "I'm sure I look a mess."

He was wise and didn't say a thing. Just watched her with the strangest expression on his face. She knew better than to look at him. She turned completely away and filled her lungs with as much air as they would take. Even they ached. More proof that crying did no good. She still felt just as raw as before. Only now she had embarrassed herself, and her head and eyes hurt.

"Here."

She felt his wrist against her arm and glanced to the clean white handkerchief between his fingers. "Thank you." Samantha dabbed her eyes with the offering, though they were mostly dry by now. "I will come down and gather my things in a moment."

"You still think you should leave?"

She wanted to laugh out loud. "You don't?"

"Not anymore. I think the girls need you."

The way he left off, pushed another thought through her head. *And I think you need them.* She shook her head. "We both know better. Nothing has changed from when you told me to leave. I haven't changed. Not really. I still don't know how to help them get through their loss." She threw her hand up. "Obviously." She didn't even know how to get through her own.

"I think you're wrong." There was a sigh in his voice. "I think you just need to put off the act."

Samantha stiffened and turned. "What act?" Had he thought her faking all this?

"Stop pretending to be so tough."

"Tough?" Not what she had expected him to say.

"The girls need someone who can feel with them, cry with them, hurt with them."

Samantha immediately shook her head. "I can't—"

"Why not?"

Because she didn't want to feel or cry or hurt anymore. She wanted to shove that pain down deep again and forget it.

When she didn't answer, he gave a tight smile. "Please stay. They need someone who cares for them, and I know you do. They need someone who they know and who knows them and what they are going through. I was wrong before. That *is* you." He turned and started walking away before she could find her tongue.

Not that she had a reply.

Samantha gave herself a few more minutes, and made sure her face was dry before following to the edge of the forest. She watched Nathan's tall figure as he weaved between the tents and then disappeared. Would Mary question him why he'd been gone so long? Perhaps she wondered if Samantha was returning. What would he answer?

I hope so.

She could almost hear his voice, with that same look of expectancy he had thrown her way before leaving. He'd issued a challenge in that moment...but she wasn't sure she was strong enough to rise to it. Besides, what was the point? Another week or so and then the rest of his family would descend upon them, and the girls would be swept off to their new homes. What good could she do in so short of time? Especially when she had no idea *what* to do.

"Mary?"

Samantha's head jerked up as Nathan emerged from the tent, a franticness in his movements as he scanned the area. He called again, before glancing up toward Samantha. Even across the distance, their eyes locked, and Samantha felt panic skitter through her. She lifted her hem and jogged down to meet him, her ankle protesting at the extra impact.

She was out of breath by the time she reached him. "What's wrong?"

His teeth ground together, and his nostrils flared. "The girls are gone."

"Gone? What do you mean, gone?" Where would they go? "Did Mary take the girls to come find us, perhaps?"

"No, their things are gone. Clothes. Everything." He raked his fingers though his hair. "This is my fault."

"No, it's mine. You should have been here with them, not. . ." Heat climbed into her cheeks at the thought of him holding her.

"It's my brother."

Understanding lit her mind. "Charles? You think he took them?" It was the best-case scenario. The girls were with family.

"I'm almost certain of it. And I plan to get them back." He spun on his heel and headed toward his horse.

"But isn't this what you wanted? Isn't it for the best?" Even though the ache in her heart grew a little more keen at the thought of not seeing them again.

"He has no right to ride in here and snatch them away without even speaking with, me. They were my responsibility, but no, he has to do everything his way without even asking me my opinion." Nathan almost growled each word then mounted and glanced back at her. "Stay here?"

Samantha nodded. It wasn't as though she had anywhere else to go or the wherewith to get there. She would sit tight and see if Nathan brought the girls back. If they did remain with the brother, there would be no reason for her to stay after today. She would be on her own again—a strangely unpleasant thought that sank deep and soured in the pit of her stomach.

———◆◆◆———

Nathan steeled himself before reaching for the door latch. The last two and a half hours of riding to Coleman and searching for his brother had done nothing to dampen the flame of rage burning in his chest. If anything, he was more frustrated now at the end of the hunt. At least this better not be another wild goose chase.

He knocked hard and pushed into the two-story boardinghouse. The building had been built with hosting in mind, with a large lobby and open dining room to the right. With the evening meal past, the room was empty but for a young woman wiping tables.

The blond looked up and brushed a strand of hair from her cheek. "Sorry, sir, dinner is already gone, and we have no available rooms."

"I require neither." Though his stomach pinched in protest. "I'm Constable Stanford."

Her eyes widened as she glanced down at his lack of uniform.

Nathan straightened his jacket. "I'm looking for my brother, Charles

Stanford. I was told he is staying here with his wife and, as of today, three young girls?"

Her mouth formed an O, and Nathan breathed relief. Finally. "Yes, they are on the second floor. We were not told about the girls, so we've been scrambling to come up with cots and bedding for everyone."

"That's my brother," Nathan grumbled. "Not very considerate of informing others of his plans. Can you point me toward their room?"

"Of course, sir—Constable." She dropped the rag on the table and weaved between chairs until she was free of the maze. "Follow me." She slanted a coy look his direction and smiled far too sweetly.

"Thank you. I apologize for interrupting your work."

"It is no matter. It's not going anywhere."

Nathan managed a chuckle. Duty was like that, lurking over your head until satisfied. He followed, though suddenly unsure of how to approach Charles. Nathan wanted to storm into the room and demand the girls return with him, but would that do any good other than turning Charles against him and frightening the girls?

Nathan drew a breath. He had to get control of his temper. He wasn't the ten-year-old little brother going against someone twice his age—in fact the gap between them seemed to grow smaller with each passing year. Nathan was now a grown man and an officer of the law. He had tracked and arrested hardened criminals. How difficult could this be?

He thanked the woman, then stepped to the door she'd indicated and laid his knuckles to the stained wood. Voices. Footsteps. And then the door cracked open to Charles' face. His eyes narrowed. "So now you show up?"

Nathan opened his mouth with a retort, but before more than two syllables escaped, Mary pushed through the door and threw her arms around his waist. "You came!"

Defenses falling, he wrapped her in a hug and pressed a kiss to her hair. "Of course. I just wish your Uncle Charles would have waited to talk to me before stealing you away."

In one motion, Charles pulled Mary away and stepped into the hall. "Back inside, Mary, while your Uncle Nate and I talk." He closed the door and dragged Nathan a few feet farther away. "What do you think you are doing?"

"Exactly what I wanted to ask you."

Charles gave him a shove. "Providing a safe, warm place for the girls to stay."

"They had that."

"Ha! A tent? And where were you? Or your pretty schoolteacher for that matter? You abandoned them."

"Mary is more than capable of watching her sisters for a few minutes. I was..." How to explain where or what he had been doing at the time? "I was just inside the woods, seeing to some business." He wanted to cringe. That didn't sound great either.

His brother raised a brow. "We waited for almost a half hour. You think I wanted to snatch them away without allowing them to say goodbye?"

Nathan wouldn't put it past him. "You should have waited longer or come back another day. I am in charge of the girls."

Again, Charles' haughty laugh. "And who put you in charge? Just because you were here first? I find it hard to believe Peter would have entrusted his children to you of all people."

"What do you mean 'of all people'?"

"I think Maddie laid it out clear enough the other day. You are a bachelor, and a Mountie at that."

"You say *Mountie* like it's a bad thing."

"Well, it's not making you any more married or ready to shoulder any responsibility for anyone other than your own skin."

Nathan tightened his hands into fists as the muscles throughout his whole body tensed. "I have had responsibility over whole communities— men, women, and children who have looked to me for protection and guidance. You know nothing about my life."

Charles shook his head and glanced away as though to roll his eyes. "The life you constantly risk? You have a long way to go, little brother, before you understand real responsibility—the kind needed to take a wife and raise children."

How dare he... Nathan felt his arm cock, and then the door opened and Maddie stepped out, a whimpering Lucy on her hip. "Ah, Nate. I wanted to ask you something."

Nathan forced his hands back to his sides as he focused past his brother.

"Mary speaks highly of Miss. . ." She glanced back at Mary in the doorway. "Miss Ingles?"

Mary nodded, but her wide eyes were fixed on Nathan, as though pleading with him to do something to intercede.

"Yes, the schoolteacher. I would like to hire her as a nanny for the girls until the others arrive." Maddie added an extra sway to her movement, weariness evident in her expression.

"I don't get it. You raised how many children? I would think you would have this perfectly in hand." He couldn't help the edge to his voice.

"Nate," Charles warned.

Maddie gave a tight smile. "Don't be so rustic, Nate. We have always employed a nanny for our children. We have a simply wonderful woman living with us now. How else would we have been able to leave our children behind for weeks?"

Nate glanced from Mary to Lucy. Was it so rustic to think that these girls needed a woman who would love them as a mother would, not fob their care off on hired help? But that wasn't the fate for either of them now.

"I think we should look elsewhere for help, darling," Charles inserted. "I question the moral standing of Nate's Miss Ingles."

Nathan jerked. "You what?"

Again that patronizing look.

"Miss Ingles is an upstanding Christian woman. How dare you suggest—"

"That she was staying in your tent for most of the past week?"

"She was staying with the girls. I was at the barracks for most of that time."

"*Most* of the time?" Charles shook his head. "Mary said you have been staying with them for several days now. What upstanding Christian woman would allow herself into such a compromising situation?"

"She wanted to leave." He bit back his protest, realizing how it might sound. "I needed her to remain for the sake of the girls. I never slept inside the tent. Mary can testify to that."

Everyone glanced back at the girl, whose wide eyes blinked twice, while her mouth remained closed.

"Except for when it rains?" Charles chided. He shooed Mary back inside the room and pulled the door closed. "Really, Nate, this is hardly a discussion to be had in front of a child. And, yes, I question the appropriateness of your behavior."

He was not the one who'd slandered Samantha in Mary's presence. "There has been nothing wrong with my behavior in front of the girls."

"Then that explains why you followed Miss Ingles into the forest just before we arrived." Charles leaned in close and lowered his voice. "Exactly what business were you seeing to?"

Chapter 23

Nathan grabbed his brother's collar and shoved him against the wall, while Maddie's yelp and Lucy's cry broke through his consciousness. "How dare you slander her good name," Nathan growled at his brother, trying hard to fight the urge to plant a fist in his face. Though it was somewhat satisfying to recognize that he was both stronger and at least an inch taller than his older brother.

"Both of you, stop this instant!" Maddie protested. "Nate, let him go. And Charles, you know better than to tease your brother."

Teasing? Is that what this was, because it felt a whole lot more serious and ill-intentioned than the jests pulled on him as a boy. Still, Nathan forced himself to relax his grip as Maddie continued.

"Both of you are being ridiculous. Why would Nate even be interested in Miss Ingles? She's hardly his type. Fully a spinster and as plain as a house mouse." She laughed as though she'd said something incredibly clever.

Nathan stepped back but found it hard to ease the tension from his fists. Hadn't that been his own assessment of Samantha not a week ago? Why did it seem so wrong now, so cruel and untrue.

Maddie gave a knowing smile. "If I remember correctly, Nate is more into blond beauties with a better sense of fashion."

Heat infused his face at the thought of Rosemary. He hadn't thought anyone else had seen his interest in her. They had all been friends after all, and she had chosen Peter. Besides, just because the first woman he'd fallen for was blond, didn't mean he didn't find darker hair attractive. He could easily appreciate Samantha's long waves falling across her shoulders, the morning light bringing out deep tones and hints of warmth. . .

Nathan mentally shook the thought from his head. He wasn't attracted to Miss Ingles. But he had grown to appreciate her, and to understand her a lot better in the past few hours.

"I know a perfect nanny when I see one," Maddie continued, "and I am still convinced Miss Ingles is what the girls need. Who better to help them adjust since she had been with them since before the slide?"

Nathan looked at his sister-in-law and the baby on her hip, resignation sinking through him. He wouldn't be able to take the girls with him, and maybe it was for the best. Here, they would have real beds and four walls to keep them from the cool spring air. But if they could still have Samantha, that might make this whole transition much easier.

"I think you're right." Nathan glanced at Charles to see his surprise. "I will see if I can talk Miss Ingles into coming to Coleman for the next week to help with the girls."

"Thank you, Nate." Maddie's singsong tone grated as did his shortened name. No one called him that but his family, and he'd learned long ago that there was no point in trying to correct them.

"But I want you to send Mary out here before I leave."

Charles stiffened and opened his mouth with what was sure to be a protest, but Maddie patted him on the shoulder and feigned a smile. "Of course. We'll leave you for a minute." She eyed her husband. "Come along, Charles."

Charles shook his head but followed his wife back into their room. A moment later, Mary burst from the doorway and again threw herself into his arms. "Please don't leave me here."

Nathan returned the hug, then crouched enough to meet her eyes. "Hey, it'll just be for a little while. Besides, your Uncle Charles isn't so bad, is he? Besides, they have agreed to hire Miss Ingles to help mind Abby and Lucy. Will that help?"

Mary nodded. "I like Miss Ingles. I wish you hadn't made her cry."

Nathan opened his mouth to argue, but he had his own regrets in that regard. And yet, he did not regret their conversation in the woods, to understand even a little what had made her the woman she was. The question was, would she bury her feelings back behind her walls of emotionless candor, or allow herself to heal and help the girls in the process. No one could understand what they were going through better than she, but he didn't want them to bury their pain as she had—as Abby was already doing. Nathan wanted to blow out his breath in frustration, but Mary watched him too closely. He forced a tight smile. "I tried to make it up to her, and I think she is feeling better now."

Mary visibly relaxed. "Did you kiss her?"

"What?" Where had that question come from? "Why would I kiss her?"

"Because Uncle Charles asked if you had, and I didn't know. Besides, it's all right to kiss someone you care about."

Nathan managed to chuckle. "First of all, you can tell your Uncle Charles that I have never kissed Miss Ingles. And second of all, I have no plans to. Miss Ingles is a very nice woman and has been kind to help us, but I don't care about her." Something in that statement felt off so he remedied it with a "Not like that."

Mary seemed to consider his words, and Nathan tried to distract her with another hug. "I *do* need to go find her, though, and talk to her about coming back here tomorrow. You be good for your aunt and uncle." *For now,* he wanted to add. The thought of any permanency sat far too heavy in his gut. But what could he do about it? As much as he didn't like Charles being the one to name all his deficiencies, Nathan wasn't father material. Maybe he never would be.

As he said his goodbyes and issued Mary back into the room, the feeling of being pummeled didn't subside, adding to the weight of the day. His feet dragged the final few paces to his horse, and he drew himself into the saddle—only to sit there for several long moments, images from the morning throbbing with each pulse of blood through his veins. Dead bodies. The stench of rotting horses. And then there was Miss Samantha Ingles, weeping into his shoulder, body trembling in his arms.

Did you kiss her?

The thought hadn't even crossed his mind until now. Besides, Maddie was right that Samantha wasn't the kind of woman that would attract him. She was too. . .

Nathan groaned. When the only image that came to mind was her tear-filled eyes peering up at him, loose strands of hair escaped to her cheeks, he was in no frame of mind to pick apart why she wouldn't suit. He was simply too exhausted tonight. And disheartened. Tragedy seemed the theme of the day—and life in general. An old man losing his life to a pile of rock, Samantha losing her parents and trying to keep those feelings buried for years, and three little girls about to lose each other.

Nathan guided Red Rover toward the road leading back to Blairmore. He couldn't do anything for the old trapper or any of the others who had lost their lives under heaps of rock. He had done what he could for Samantha. Why did he feel he could make any difference for the girls? Like Charles said, Nathan was hardly in a position to control their fates.

———◆◆◆———

Samantha dragged the chair outside and faced it toward the west, then sat and watched as the sun sank behind the mountain ridges and a chill slipped into the air. She fetched a blanket from the quiet tent and again settled in to wait. Vibrant pinks and golds lit the sky as the sun dropped away. Slowly the colors faded to soft hues of blue which grew darker and darker until only blackness remained. Blackness and silence.

Samantha closed her eyes but remained in place. Would Nathan find the girls? Would he try to return them? The latter seemed unlikely. And if not, then what next? She had been planning to leave anyway. Now she had no reason to stay. Though the thought of not saying goodbye, of not apologizing to Mary, of not telling her how truly amazing and real and. . .*raw* her poem was. . .

A tear trickled down Samantha's cheek. Now that the dam had been broken, was there any chance of shoring it back up? Or was this her fate now—that of a constant watering pot?

She swiped at her moist cheeks and straightened in the chair. No, she had to get ahold of her emotions. And the quicker and farther she got away from Mary and Abby and Lucy, the easier that would be. She'd retire for the night and then be on her way tomorrow while trying not to consider how much she wished she could see them again.

Or their uncle.

The clomp of an approaching horse pulled Samantha's gaze upward, and she peered through the dimming light with sudden hope of Nathan's return. She waited, barely breathing. . .as the horse and rider continued past. When had she become so silly? She turned into the tent but didn't bother lighting a lamp. Her stomach gave a small reminder that she had not paused for dinner, but she had no energy or desire to prepare something for only herself.

Strange, she hadn't had that problem in the past. Everything before had been about her because there'd been no one else to consider. Had one week ruined her so completely to being alone?

"No," she whispered to herself. Just another adjustment. In a day or two she would be back to herself.

Samantha sank onto the edge of the cot she had been calling her own. While other chatter and sounds, including a crying baby, penetrated the canvas walls of the tent from her neighbors, the tent itself was awfully quiet—like the schoolhouse after the last child had gone home.

So why did it bother her now?

It's always bothered you.

Samantha groaned and dropped back. Now she was even talking to herself.

The approach of another horse. Her breathing stilled while she listened. The horse stopped, and boots hit the ground not far from the tent. Should she hurry outside and see what Nathan had to report? Had he brought the girls back? No, she couldn't hear the girls, and he wouldn't be able to bring them all that way on his horse. He'd be alone. Standing there. Waiting.

She lay frozen in place, her heart pounding. She wanted him to call to her, to beckon her out. To break the silence.

Go to him.

She couldn't. Mostly, because she wanted it too badly. And more. She wanted to see him. She wanted his arms around her offering comfort once more. How could she trust herself near him? She'd never craved anything like this before—or at least not for a long, long time.

Footsteps faded, leading away from the tent. If that was Nathan, she would now have to wait until morning to know if he had found the girls. She would have to wait until morning to see his face and know if the awkwardness between them had increased. The hours between seemed an eternity.

Chapter 24

Nathan rode to the NWMP barracks, or at least the tents set up nearby. The barracks themselves had been transformed into a temporary hospital to meet the needs of those who were still recovering from injuries sustained during the slide. He could only hope there was a cot available for him in the barracks, but either way he had nowhere else to go. He'd get some sleep and report for duty in the morning.

His thoughts would clear once he was back in uniform.

"Stanford, is that you?"

Nathan dismounted and turned to Constable Hardy. Just the man he wanted to see. "Yes, I'm ready to get back to work."

"What about your nieces?"

Nathan tried to ignore the unsettled sensation in his gut. Or the feeling that things were far from settled. "One of my brothers has. . ." *Confiscated them? Taken them from me because he thinks me inept?* "A brother has stepped in." And railroaded him. Nathan fought to keep his jaw and fists from clenching.

"Oh." Constable Hardy eyed him. "Are you sure you wouldn't like more time? I know the past week hasn't been easy."

Understatement. Peter and his family's deaths still loomed over every-thing. All the more reason to cling to the familiar—and a distraction. He needed purpose in his life.

Mary's pleading face flashed through his mind.

But she was no longer his.

"It's too soon, Stanford. I can see it on your face."

"No. I'll be fine. I need something." Now he sounded like he was pleading. "I mean, I want to be useful. I don't need to stand on the sidelines anymore."

"You've hardly been on the sidelines of this disaster, Stanford. You have been in the heart of it." Constable Hardy's mouth tightened, but he finally nodded. "Very well, but not back to full duty. We'll give you a few things to do, enough to provide a distraction, but I think you still have some things to work through, maybe with your family. Maybe with yourself. We have the manpower. You can still take the time you need."

Nathan gripped Rover's reins, grateful he still had something to hold onto while he managed a "Thank you, sir," he didn't feel. The man was placating him and nothing more. Nathan took his leave and saw to Rover while trying to not think about—about anything, really. By the time he found an empty cot and fell into it, he'd managed to narrow his thoughts down to the memory of Samantha sitting against an overgrown pine, tears wet on her cheeks, hair escaping its pins. Despite the red in her eyes and her flushed face, she had been rather. . .pretty.

Nathan wiped a hand down his face and tried to rid himself of the image. He would speak to her tomorrow to inquire if she would consider continuing helping with the children. For their sakes. He, of course, would keep his distance. The last thing he needed was to fall for the schoolteacher, or harbor regrets about losing the girls.

Yet, as he closed his eyes to sleep, Nathan couldn't push aside the fact that he was failing on both accounts.

Despite a restless night, Nathan awoke with the sun and dressed in his uniform. He didn't care if Hardy put him to work this morning or not. He craved the familiar and longed for the feeling of control and confidence. As he fastened the final button and straightened the scarlet coat, a surge of that feeling returned. He was a North-West Mounted Police constable. He had a purpose and a duty. This was his life. His nieces didn't need him anymore. They would adjust to their new homes and families, given time.

He pushed past an unsettled feeling he didn't quite recognize and started out the door. The glow of dawn painted the sky with hues of gold, laced with dainty pink clouds. He breathed deeply of cool air and set his resolve. No more being swept away by emotion. Peter was dead, and nothing could change that. He had done his duty to the girls, and they now were out of his hands. Samantha. . .

He needed to speak with her on behalf of the girls, but there was no need to include any emotion in that.

After a quick discussion with Constable Hardy and being told to take whatever time he needed before reporting back for an assignment, Nathan readied his horse and started toward Blairmore. He wasn't sure why his pulse seemed quicker than usual as he neared the tent city and wound his way to the campsite he had set for Samantha and the girls. Probably just the exertion of the morning ride as he'd been going a decent clip.

Nathan swung from his horse and approached the tent. All seemed far too quiet without Lucy's babbling coming from within, or the shuffle of feet, or Samantha's voice. Maybe he had come too early, and he was doomed to stand as he had last night, undecided whether to call out or ride away.

"Constable Stanford."

He jerked around to see Samantha approaching from the direction of the creek. Her face looked bright and freshly washed, though red still tinged her eyes. From fresh tears, perhaps? It was still unsettling to see her so fragile. Yes, that seemed the word for it. Even now, her mouth opened a crack as though there were something she wanted to say, and her large eyes held just enough moisture to make them shine. Her dark hair hung loose about her shoulders, and she brushed at the strands clinging to her damp face.

"Are you well?" he managed.

Her whole body straightened. "Yes. Of course." Her chin dipped at the words, and he found himself appreciating the delicate slope where it met her neck. "Thank you for returning. Are the girls well?"

He lifted a shoulder. "They will be."

Her mouth formed an O without a sound exiting. "I've been straightening the tent for you. I found a few things the girls will want, and the rest"—she shrugged—"you can do with as you see fit. I'm glad the girls have family to watch over them. They need that." The last was said emphatically. As though from experience. Except Samantha hadn't had family.

Did you kiss her?

Mary's question sprang from nowhere, and he quickly shoved it aside. He had come with a purpose. "Um, I'm sure there are families who can use the tent and any of the extra blankets." Though more folks were leaving the area each day. "I'll be staying at the police barracks for now."

She waved at his uniform. "I figured as much."

He tugged on the hem of his coat, though it already sat perfectly. "It's your plans we need to discuss."

"Oh." Her cheeks pinked. "I will be fine. The train will be headed west in a couple of hours. I figured Sparwood or Cranbrook will have more accommodations while I decide what to do next. I don't imagine I will be teaching again until autumn, and then who can guess where they will place me?"

The thought of her leaving shouldn't bother him so much. But it did. Of course it did—he was here on behalf of the girls. "If you aren't in a hurry, then another week won't make a difference." For the girls. Nothing more.

"A week? Is there a reason I should wait? The Frank school is closed indefinitely, and Blairmore is overcrowded."

"I was thinking Coleman."

Samantha's eyes narrowed. "Why Coleman?"

He was obviously doing a horrible job of explaining himself. Better to get all the information out in a full report. "Maddie and Charles, though mostly Maddie, wanted me to ask you to help with the girls for a week or so—just until my other brothers and their wives arrive."

"So you are going to let them be separated?" There was an edge to her tone, and he could sense her withdrawal as much as he could see it.

"I have no choice in the matter."

"How is that possible?"

He ground his teeth. It was bad enough to have his own conscience to contend against. "Let's see, I'm unmarried and an officer of the law. Children don't fit very well into that equation."

"Understandable. But couldn't you convince at least one of your siblings to take all three? They are sweet girls, and not that much of a burden." Samantha's head cocked to one side. "Why does your sister-in-law require assistance for the short week they will be here?"

"I wondered the same myself, but I think it's better this way. You have been here the whole time for the girls, a sense of the familiar."

Her head dipped forward. "That isn't how you felt yesterday, and for good reason. I honestly don't know how to help them heal. How could I, when I haven't come to grips with my own past?" It wasn't a question. She turned away completely now, and her body stiffened.

Nathan stood in place, despite the strangest urge to place his hands on her shoulders or pull her into an embrace like he had yesterday. How had his feelings changed so quickly? He'd been so frustrated with her, so convinced that she was heartless and cold. Now he wanted to protect her and offer comfort. "Healing takes time."

She huffed. "I've had almost two decades to figure it out."

"But you were at it alone." Like the girls soon would be... Hopefully his sisters-in-law would be attentive and affectionate as they walked Mary and Abby through their healing.

"I'd rather not speak of it anymore." She shrunk back, the familiar mask of indifference again in place. "I'm tired of feeling."

As was he, honestly. He offered a nod. "Understandable. But will you consider coming to Coleman and being with the girls? Shouldn't be more than a week."

"A week." Despite the lack of expression on her face, he could see the battle waged in her eyes. He touched his coat pocket, remembering the pair of glasses he had failed to have fixed. Though she looked much more approachable without them, he would see to it today. He owed her that much, even if she didn't agree to his request.

"Very well. One week." She met his gaze. One week, and then good-bye. One week and his life would settle back into some form of normalcy. Nathan wasn't sure why he suddenly dreaded that.

Chapter 25

MAY 6TH

The door opened to a scowl Samantha recognized well—one Charles Stanford apparently shared with his younger brother who currently stood behind her. She raised her chin and relaxed her hands at her sides, forcing herself to give him the look she gave to all disgruntled parents. "Were you not expecting me?"

"At last!" Maddie Stanford exclaimed from behind her husband. "Come in, come in!"

Frown still in place, Charles stepped out of the way, and Samantha entered the room. The area was not horribly small but seemed so because of how many beds and cots had been squeezed into the space. Samantha tucked her own small bag against the wall and straightened to face the disaster before her. She would worry about her own accommodations in due time.

Maddie was already to her, thrusting the baby into her arms. "Take Lucy so I can have a minute."

"Of course." For once, Samantha didn't hesitate to open her arms. She had missed the baby over the past day. To her surprise, Lucy extended

163

her arms and readily clasped them around Samantha's neck. "Why hello, sweet pea," she said without thinking. Until she caught Mary's wide eyes peering up at her. She'd almost forgotten it was their mother's pet name for her girls. She opened an arm to Mary, a small offering to rectify her blunder. "And how have you been?"

"Better now," she whispered into Samantha's sleeve, catching her off guard. Why the child would want anything to do with her, Samantha wasn't sure, but it triggered something deep within—a sense of belonging.

"Well then," Maddie said, her expression not quite as welcoming as moments ago. "Seems it is good you joined us. We won't be able to pay you much, understand, what with the expense of travel and maintaining our nanny back at home." She raked her eyes over Samantha's simple skirt and blouse, just like she'd done at their first meeting. "But I am sure we can come to an arrangement. Did Nate explain it will only be for the remainder of the week? Perhaps a little longer." She glanced at Nathan, a fine brow rising.

"I did," he replied from where he remained in the open doorway, hat tucked under his arm, red coat tight across his chest. How right the uniform looked on him. How dangerous it was to let her gaze linger.

"Perfect." Maddie's singsong voice was off pitch. "You may leave us then, and we'll get settled here. I spoke with the proprietor of the board-inghouse, and while they don't have a free room, there is a spare bed in a room to share with another lady. I'm sure that will be satisfactory and will keep you close for when I require your assistance with the children. Abigail especially has been quite ornery. Perhaps you will have more success with her." Maddie's chin tipped upward with the challenge.

"I think Abby needs time to adjust and come to terms with the changes," Nathan bit out. He didn't appear any more impressed by his sister-in-law than Samantha did.

Thankfully, Samantha was not required to share her opinion on what was to be done with Abby—all the better since Samantha wasn't sure what was best. Her brain and emotions had become such a tangled mess, it was hard to know what was up and what was down, never mind what she should expect from the girls. Or herself.

"It's a beautiful morning," Nathan's booming voice captured everyone's attention. "Why don't I take the girls for an outing in the fresh air? Miss Ingles is welcome to join us if her foot is up for the walk."

Samantha looked at him. She was exhausted after not sleeping well last night and had little interest in traipsing about on her sore ankle. But the ache was bearable and no longer required her to limp, and Mary looked at her uncle with such hope.

"How kind of you, Nate," Maddie said the words but did not seem at all assured of them.

"It will allow you to rest." He flashed a tight smile. "I'm sure you are exhausted after having to care for the girls all by yourself for most of a day."

His sister-in-law returned the smile, though strung even thinner. "So thoughtful."

"Come along then, Mary." He waved the girl to him and extended his arms for Lucy. Samantha allowed her to launch into his arms. "Why don't you bring Abby?" He nodded in the direction of the middle girl who sat in the corner, blanket wrapping her shoulders, eyes watching but with little expression.

"Of course." Samantha moved across the room, while trying to ignore the growled questions from Nathan's older brother. Their relationship and disagreements were none of her business or concern. She paused in front of Abby and waited until the girl's gaze met hers. Instead of saying anything—which hadn't done any good in the past—Samantha extended a hand.

Abby looked from her outstretched hand to her aunt, who had become involved in the hushed discussion with her uncles, and back to the offered hand. Samantha's breath hitched as small fingers slipped into hers and gripped.

"Come on," Samantha whispered and pulled the girl to her feet. Abby continued to cling to the blanket around her shoulders, but it was small enough not to drag on the ground, so Samantha didn't pull it away. Let Abby have that small comfort.

An image settled into her memory. The dark of a quilt draped over her head, while a cascade of color glowed from the light passing through the thin fabric. Reds and oranges and yellows. Until it was ripped away.

"Come along, child." Samantha couldn't remember who the woman was, only the frustration in her tone as the quilt, a shield from reality, had been tossed aside. *"The headmistress wishes to speak with you about your future."* Speak *at* and *over* her, more like. All the decisions had already been made on her behalf.

"We won't be gone long." Nathan took Lucy as Samantha passed by with Abby, and then motioned for Mary to follow. The older girl needed no encouragement and rushed out the door, which he promptly closed behind them. "Well, that went well." Sarcasm dripped from his words as he briefly met Samantha's gaze. "I apologize for putting you in the middle of all this."

"Dare I ask what 'all of this' is?"

Instead of answering, he glanced at the girls and indicated that they should follow him down the hall to the stairwell. It was probably for the best that he did not answer in front of the girls. It really was none of Samantha's business anyway. She was being hired to mind the girls, nothing more. The family would probably appreciate her keeping any opinions and such to herself.

A brisk breeze met them on the street. It swept through the mountain valley with more strength than when they had arrived a few minutes ago. Abby tightened her hold on her quilt, and Mary looked expectantly at her uncle. Samantha couldn't help but wish for a quilt of her own to snuggle into to escape the wind.

"Follow me." He turned back inside the boardinghouse, but instead of returning upstairs, he directed them into the dining room which was currently empty. The usual lull between breakfast and lunch. "Pick a table," he directed before disappearing with Lucy into the kitchen at the back.

Samantha raised her brows at the older girls. Abby remained quiet at her side while Mary walked deeper into the room, weaving between the tables until settling on a small square one near the window. Four chairs fit nicely.

By the time they were seated—Mary with the sun warming her back, Abby beside her, and Samantha enjoying the full view of the empty street and mountains beyond—Nathan returned. He held Lucy in one arm and balanced a full pie in the other hand. Samantha considered asking about her spectacles—it would be nice to appreciate the view—but decided against it. They were probably twisted beyond repair and would have to wait until she reached a city where they could be replaced.

"Who likes apple?" Nathan asked.

"Apple pie?" Samantha wasn't sure if she should point out that it was barely ten in the morning and the pie might spoil the girls' appetites for lunch.

"I think everyone here deserves a treat." He set the pie in the center of the table, and the girls leaned forward—all the girls. Even Samantha felt the draw, even just to breathe in the heavenly aroma of freshly baked apples dressed in cinnamon. That didn't stop the arguments from spilling through her mind, but a younger woman was already approaching with a small stack of plates and forks.

"Here you are, Constable." The pretty blond placed the dishes on the table in front of him and smiled at the girls. "I can make up some tea or hot cocoa if anyone would like."

"I would!" Mary glanced to her uncle. "May I?"

"Of course. Hot cocoa for all of us, please."

"Except me," Samantha inserted. "Tea is fine." Someone had to maintain some sanity.

The woman turned to go but not before a long side glance at Nathan made her attraction to him obvious. A smile curved her full lips—but the man in question did not seem to notice. His focus was on the pie as he reached for a knife. A knife that the baby in his arms was also reaching for.

Samantha cringed. "Would you like me to take Lucy?"

"Or you can cut the pie." He slid the knife across the table.

"Of course." She dragged the pie in front of her and slid the knife down the middle. Just as she was about to make the second cut, Nathan held up his hand for her to stop.

"You're doing that wrong."

"What?" How could she be cutting it wrong? How many ways were there to cut a pie?

"Too small of pieces. There are only five of us. Though I don't imagine Lucy will eat much. Why don't you cut it in quarters, and I'll share with Lucy."

"Quarters?" He had to be joking. It wasn't as though they were required to eat the whole pie. There were only four of them, and it was still morning.

"Maybe I should cut it." He raised a brow as though challenging her.

"Maybe you should." He could be the one to try scooping out a quarter of a pie without it crumbing to pieces. She slid the knife and pie across the table and took Lucy onto her lap. The baby reached for the closest fork, but Samantha snatched it from her. A spoon would be safer.

Nathan's smile was subtle as he slid the knife to make a small sliver of pie, which he easily scooped onto the first plate and set it in front of Samantha. A sixteenth. On the small side but appropriate. "That's for Lucy."

Samantha settled into her chair, trying not to cringe as his second slice took a good sixth of the pie. He plated it and set it in front of Abby. "Does that look good?"

The girl reached for her fork in response, allowing the quilt to drop from her shoulders. Samantha felt some of the tension ebb from her shoulders as she watched the girl focus on her pie.

"Mary." Nathan set a similar-sized piece in front of the oldest girl, and cut another sixth for himself, leaving just under half a pie in place, edges crumbling, juice leaking from the sides. "Have you had breakfast yet, Miss Ingles?"

"I've never been much for breakfast, I'm afraid." Her appetite was usually lacking in the morning. Though now, her stomach roiled and pinched at the aroma rising from the pie.

"Good." He pulled the last plate close and slid a fork under the corner of the remaining piece.

"You haven't cut it."

"Do I need to?" Without waiting for a reply, Nathan scooped the piece—or at least most of it—onto the plate. The huge piece of pie crumbled before it settled into place, but that didn't seem to deter him. He merely tipped the pie pan sideways and pushed the remaining fragments of apple and crust onto the pile of pie on the plate. Then placed it in front of her.

Samantha tried to gather her jaw, but all she could do was stare. Until Mary began to giggle. Samantha looked at the girl and her sparkling eyes. Even Abby's usual dour expression had given way to a hint of amusement.

"Are you sure you don't intend this for yourself, Constable?" Samantha reached to exchange plates with him, but he caught her wrist.

"Oh no. You will need to keep up your strength. This will serve as both breakfast and a treat."

She tried to push against his hold. "But I don't like eating breakfast."

He tipped his head toward the girls, eyes narrowing though the humor never left. "Are you sure you should be admitting that in present company?"

Heat rushed to her cheeks while Mary's giggling increased. After lecturing the girls every morning on the importance of breakfast, she really should watch her words. "I mean, I feel a healthier breakfast would be better."

"What could be healthier than apples? I'm surprised at you, Miss Ingles. Set a good example for the girls and eat what has been served you." He gave a firm push on the plate, bringing the pie directly back in front of her.

A strange sort of panic tinged her chest. "I can't eat this big of a piece."

"Well, it would be impolite to put it back." Nathan winked. "Besides, you don't know until you've tried."

"Is everything all right?"

Samantha jerked at the woman's voice behind her. Heat filled her, and she pulled away from Nathan's grasp.

"Of course," he boomed, his blue eyes smiling at the lady.

Samantha felt another surge of heat accompanied by a very unpleasant sensation in her stomach.

The blond didn't make any comment about the ridiculous serving sizes, or the mountain of pie heaped on Samantha's plate, while she set a steaming pot of cocoa in the center of the table along with three mugs. "I'll be right back with the tea," she said, despite her focus being completely on Nathan.

But of course he would attract the young, pretty woman who could cook apple pie. Samantha quietly picked up her fork and stabbed it into the heap of crust and fruit, though her appetite had fled.

Chapter 26

The wind had eased off the next day, so Nathan returned to take the girls, and their *nanny*, on another outing. He led the way under a green canopy, Lucy on his shoulders. The thin dirt path followed the stream along its course, steep in places. Mary passed him with a stick in hand, tapping trunks as she went. Farther behind followed Abby and Samantha. The latter had hold on the child's hand, leading her. A blanket draped over Abby's shoulders, but her eyes were a little more focused than usual as she searched the dark corners of the forest. His comment about keeping a look out for bears had probably encouraged that. But at least it gave her something else to concentrate on.

Just as the pie had.

Nathan chuckled to himself thinking of the feigned glare on Samantha's face as they had waited for her to finish her pie. She hadn't actually complained though, so he was willing to guess she'd actually enjoyed every last bite.

"How far are we going?" Samantha asked.

Nathan's gaze dropped to her ankles, tucked away in her shoes. She did appear to be favoring the one leg with a slight limp. "Is your foot hurting?"

"A little. But I don't want to disappoint the girls. Are the falls much farther?"

He turned back to his oldest niece who had paused to wait for them. "Mary, how much farther?"

The girl looked up the trail, as though trying to pull the answer from her memory. She'd been the one to tell him of the waterfall up this path.

"You know what," Samantha waved them on. "Don't worry about me. I can rest here, perhaps with Lucy, and you three can go ahead. I'm sure we'll be fine."

"But what about the bear?" Abby asked in a soft voice, drawing all attention to her. Nathan had hardly heard more than one or two words out of her up to now, and as such, even the simple question was monumentally significant.

Samantha looked at him with equal questioning in her eyes though she didn't voice it.

"I haven't heard of any reports in the area," was the best he could offer. She gave a tight smile and kept her grip on Abby's hand. "I'm sure I can make it a little farther."

No one said much as they continued up the path, the rush of the creek drawing them along over roots and around logs. The current grew more intense as they came through the forest coverings. Mary gave a happy yelp a moment before Nathan stepped past a large pine to see the unobstructed falls. White water cascading down a rocky cliff. Though not a large waterfall, the swell of the spring melt off the mountain added to its magnificence.

Samantha's breathing came heavy beside him, and he offered his free hand. She gripped it and allowed him to lead her for the final steps to the bank at the base of the waterfall before she slipped away to sink onto a log. Abby sat beside her.

"Was it worth the walk?" Nathan questioned Samantha, fighting the urge to nudge her. Instead, he lowered Lucy from his shoulders.

When Samantha gave no answer, he glanced down. She sat rigidly, her arms folded across her stomach as though she were ill, her eyes glistening. Abby had adopted a similar pose but leaned her head against Samantha as though seeking comfort.

"Are you all right?"

Samantha's jaw tightened and her head gave the tiniest shake.

"Is it your foot? Is it hurting worse?" He almost hoped for that answer, though somehow doubted it.

Instead of replying, she pushed to her feet and started back down the trail.

"Miss Ingles?" he called after her.

"I'm fine," she threw over her shoulder. "Enjoy yourselves."

"Samantha." He glanced to where Mary stood at the bank, within reach of the light mist rising from the base of the falls. Her gaze followed Samantha and then darted to him with questioning.

"Should we go after her?"

He felt they should but didn't want to steal this moment from the girls. Abby sat where Samantha had left her, eyes glued on the falls. Lucy collected pine cones from the ground.

"Is she angry again?"

That brought Nathan's head up. "Angry? Why would she be angry?"

Mary's shoulder rose an inch. "She argued with Mama when she and Papa brought us up here last time."

"Why would she argue with your mama?"

The girl bit her lip. "Said we should be in school. Mama and Papa took us up here instead."

Nathan glanced to where Samantha had disappeared into the foliage. Was that why she had fled? Anger? No, that wasn't the expression she wore. "When were you here last?"

Mary's breath trembled, and her chin quivered. "That day." He almost didn't hear her over the waterfall.

"That day?" He looked at Abby, who hadn't moved.

Tears tumbled from Mary's eyes. "Before the slide. We came up here for a picnic. Mama, Papa, and the boys. John stood here throwing stones. Athol kept trying to wade in. Abby climbed that tree almost to the top until Mama yelled at her to get down."

Nathan only glanced at the old pine before turning to the girl in question. Still no reaction. Only silence. Mary's arms flung around his torso before he saw her. He held on while she cried. His own eyes burned as he imagined that perfect last day Peter had spent with his family. Had he had any inclination that he only had one more day...

———◆◆◆———

Samantha's foot screamed at her to pause and rest, but she couldn't bring herself to stop. She weaved along the almost nonexistent path while her vision blurred, making the way more difficult to navigate. Curse these tears! What had happened to the control she'd built over the years, the ability to shove aside her feelings for logic?

Logic dictated that she was not at fault for her feelings the day before the slide. She couldn't have known what would happen. Her reasoning at the time had been perfect. The children needed to be in school, and their parents had made a habit of taking them from their studies.

Logic also suggested that even given the events of the next twelve hours, one final frolic had done little good. The children had plenty of memories with their parents, and this was only an added sorrow now—she'd seen the look on both Abby and Mary's faces.

Such logic had little effect on her current emotions.

Or the images flitting through her mind—not of the Stanfords but of her own parents.

Samantha tucked herself behind a large tree and forced her lungs to expand. She had to regain control, because this was ridiculous! She was a mature woman, and her loss had been years ago. Decades. It was time to put it all behind her, just as the girls would be required to do. That was life.

She wiped her cheeks and measured her breath. Yes, she could do this—lock away all the sentiment and pain that should have been long forgotten by now. She had to be an example to the girls over the next few days and help them prepare for their future. Nathan was correct. She knew how to do it. Teach them to focus on tasks and not feelings. Teach them that there was more to life than sentiment and loss—survival in this cold world required a heart that could be controlled.

Lucy was the best off with her understanding of loss so incomplete.

Abby seemed to have herself well in hand—at least as well as Samantha ever had. Mary on the other hand... She wore those emotions on her sleeve.

The silence of the forest surrounded Samantha, the falls too distant and even the rush of the stream muted through the thick evergreen foliage.

Samantha's pulse quickened. She stepped around the pine and started back the way she had come. Or had this been the way? The stream should be right there, shouldn't it? Maybe a few paces farther. Yes, there was a slope and rocks below—but no water. Why was there no water in the stream?

She searched the area, realization settling though her. This wasn't the stream they had followed to the falls. She had left the path at some point.

"That's fine." Her voice seemed to echo in her ears. "It can't be far." She'd simply retrace her steps. Either way, Coleman was in the valley, so as long as she made her way downward, sooner or later she'd find the town or road. It's not like she had wandered so very far.

"Everything is fine." She picked her way downward, adjusting her path so it should lead her back to the stream. Once she found the stream, it would be easy to follow it the remainder of the way to town. She shook her head and laughed out loud at how ridiculous it would be if Nathan and the girls arrived back at the boardinghouse before she did. They didn't need to know that she'd gotten sidetracked. Or lost.

"Not lost."

Just a little off course.

Samantha continued walking, making her way around the underbrush and over fallen logs. The path she had thought she was on was now nowhere to be found, and the way was increasingly difficult to pass, especially as her ankle's complaints became more piercing with each step. Finally, she sat on a log to give her foot a rest. Despite not moving overly quickly, her breath came in hasty gasps as though she had run the last mile. Somewhere in the distance a dog howled. Or was that a wolf? Hadn't she heard there were wolves in these mountains? And bears?

"You're fine," Samantha tried to reassure herself. For the little good it did. She was not fine. Not at any level. She was broken, sprained, and a wreck on so many levels. She had once prided herself on being of use to others, of putting their needs above her own, but she had nothing to give right now, only nightmares and tears and the panic rising in her chest attempting to choke out reason.

Chapter 27

"Where on earth have you been?"

Nathan led the girls into the room without acknowledging his sister-in-law's outburst. He had no energy to explain himself. Well past noon, the girls were hungry, and he wanted to report for at least a few hours of duty this afternoon. As soon as he knew— "Where is Miss Ingles?"

Maddie huffed. "She was with you. Where did you leave her?"

She hadn't returned? "I didn't leave her anywhere. She needed a few minutes by herself and walked on ahead."

Maddie's brows shot skyward. "A schoolteacher who can't even stay with her charges for a few hours without needing time for herself? Really, Nate? How is she supposed to be of any help to us?"

Nathan felt himself bristle as he handed Lucy over to Mary and lowered his voice for the little good it would do in saving the girls from hearing his growing anger. "You forget what Miss Ingles has endured along with the rest of Frank's citizens. She was trapped under a roof for hours and had her livelihood ripped away. She knew. . ." He glanced at Mary's wide eyes and lowered his voice further. "She knew plenty of the people who lost their lives. Some were her students. She has every reason to need time by herself."

He turned on his heel, before letting any more of his thoughts on the matter slip out. Maddie didn't need to know about Samantha's other losses. And he didn't want to waste another minute in his sister-in-law's presence. He brushed past Charles, who was on his way up the stairs, but didn't spare a word for him either. Maddie would no doubt expound on Nathan's outburst.

He made it down the stairs before it occurred to him that Samantha was staying in the boardinghouse and may have taken refuge in her room. Instead of returning to inquire of Charles or Maddie, Nathan made his way to the kitchen, where two women busied themselves with preparations for the next meal. The younger who had served them their pie paused and smiled at him. "You've returned, Constable. We are out of pie but have a chocolate cake."

"No, thank you. I just need to know which room Miss Ingles is staying in."

"Miss Ingles?" Her smile faltered. "Of course. Top of the stairs, second door on your right."

"Thank you." He thought of asking if she had seen Samantha's return but thought better of it. Best keep their interactions brief considering the woman's reactions to him. He offered a nod and started back up the stairs. Charles met him at the top.

"What is this about Miss Ingles not returning?"

Nathan shook his head and pushed past. "I can't be sure she hasn't returned. Merely that we did not return together."

"Did you have a falling-out?"

Nathan refused to look at his brother. "For the last time, there is nothing between Miss Ingles and me. I had the girls in hand, so she was free to take a few moments alone." He knocked on the door and waited. Footsteps within steadied the thud in his chest. Until the door opened to a stranger, a woman with blond hair tucked into a twist at the nape of her neck. Her eyes widened. "Constable." Her hand came to her mouth. "Have you brought word? Of my husband?"

"I—no. I'm sorry, I don't know who your husband is."

Her face fell along with her shoulders. "I'm sorry. I keep hoping I'll hear something."

"Your husband was at Frank?"

She nodded. "He was visiting the Grahams but had other business in the area, so he might not have stayed at the ranch."

The ranch that was right in the middle of the slide. "I'm so sorry."

She waved a hand in the air as though trying to dislodge the apology. "But if that is not why you are here, what can I help you with, Constable?"

Nathan straightened. "You have a new roommate. Samantha Ingles. I am looking for her."

"Oh? Is she in some sort of trouble?"

"I hope not."

The woman tightened the shawl around her shoulders. "I'm afraid I haven't met Miss Ingles yet. I was late getting in last night, and she was gone before I awoke this morning."

Nathan offered a quick thanks and turned away—face-to-face with his brother.

"You're worried about her?" Charles raised a brow.

"I want to make sure she made it back safely." But Nathan had no reassurance of that. Was it possible they had passed her on their return? Uneasiness moved him past his brother and back down the stairs.

"Where are you going?"

"To find her," Nathan called over his shoulder. Was it possible she had stepped off the trail? Or had she paused somewhere else in town and would return soon? Had she gotten lost, or was she simply biding her time so as not to have to face him again so soon? Nathan blew out his breath and continued toward the trailhead leading to Rainbow Falls. He needed to know Samantha was safe.

Nathan asked everyone he passed on his way to the trailhead and glanced into every shop to be certain she hadn't made it back to Coleman. Still, uncertainty reigned. There was no sign of her, but she was a grown woman. Perhaps he was overly concerned. All she needed to do was follow the stream back to town. She had wished for seclusion. If he went about his day as planned, surely she would make her way back to the boardinghouse before evening.

Yet a nagging doubt stayed with him as he made his way up the trail, watching for any sign of her passing. While he could identify the imprint of her shoes from their trek up the slope, he could see none that indicated she had returned.

"Miss Ingles?" he called out, searching the woods for any sign of the lady.

There was nothing for it. He would not rest easy until he found her.

———◆◆◆———

Samantha hugged her arms against the growing chill in the air. The sun hovered low along the rocky western peaks, but even if it hung directly above her, little warmth would penetrate the heavy branches surrounding her. She should have brought a shawl, but the day had been warm when they'd left the boardinghouse with the girls.

Hopefully Nathan had successfully returned them to town. But of course he must have. He was a Mountie and wouldn't have trouble following a simple trail.

Curse her tears! If she had simply held herself together, she would have easily found her way back as well. But, no! She had become a blubbering mess again, and now she had no idea where she was, though she should. The sun was in the west. The town had to be somewhere south of here. So why was there still no sign of it or the stream? Of course, it didn't help that without her spectacles, the world was blurry at any distance, so details were difficult to see unless she was on top of them. She would never be able to find the trail in such a state.

"Oh, God. . ." The plea slipped from her heart before her mind could consider the point of asking for help from a being she didn't know existed. But as her eyes slipped closed, the darkness pulled her back under the collapsing roof while the world roared. She had cried out to the heavens, and somehow she had survived. The roof had not crushed her. The rocks had not buried her. Rescuers had come.

Perhaps they would again.

"Please help someone find me, God."

She shook her head. The only one who knew she was out here was

Nathan. Would he see where she had left the path? Would his sense of duty send him after her—he felt little else for her, that was certain.

Shaking herself from the melancholy pulling her down, Samantha pushed to her feet yet again, ignoring the throbbing pain in her ankle. She was an intelligent woman and refused to give up. Logic, not emotion, was needed. At some point, she had lost the path and the stream. They would likely be to the west along with the setting sun. She had been trying to work her way downward but was obviously on the wrong slope. Southwest was her best bet of finding her way back to Coleman. Even if it included climbing upward again.

She turned in that direction—which looked far too much like every other one. Trees, rocks, and more trees. Again, the overwhelming sense of desperation forced her eyes upward. "Is this the right direction, God?"

What about the direction of your life?

The strange thought struck with surprising force. Would her life be any different if she had asked?

Samantha pushed away the consideration and started back up the slope, trying to keep her steps light as to not increase the pain too greatly in her foot. The past week of healing was likely undone in the last couple of hours. She should have stayed at the boardinghouse instead of following Nathan. He would have been fine without her. As would the girls. In fact, if she were to disappear in these woods, or if the rocks had crushed her a week earlier, no one would have felt her absence. Teachers were easy enough to replace. It was mothers, daughters, sisters, and friends who were wept over and missed, and she was none of those. Only the school board would have needed to be informed of her demise, and they would have simply made note of the need for a replacement and removed her file. Discarded into a dustbin or fireplace.

All memory of her existence erased and forgotten.

Her breathing slowed, but her eyes stayed clear. She couldn't be completely forgotten, could she? There were students whose lives she had impacted. Surely they would spare a thought for her once in a while. . .

Samantha hugged herself tighter, the chill sinking deeper. It wasn't the same as having family or even a close friend to mourn your loss.

Her head snapped up at the muffled sound coming from her left. An animal perhaps? Not a wolf, but a bear might make the low moan.

"Samantha."

Not a moan. A call! Someone was calling her name. Relief spilled into a franticness to be found, and she started hurrying in that direction, not caring that her path was fraught with underbrush and spiked logs. "Hello!"

"Samantha?"

Oh, how glorious her name sounded. *Her* name. A name that few had called her since childhood. Ahead, a flash of red appeared like a beacon between the trees. "Nathan." His name clogged her throat, and she chided herself for the sudden rush of emotion. "Over here!" Her lungs burned almost as badly as her foot. "I'm here!"

He made a straight path toward her, ducking under branches and leaping boulders to get to her. She planted her palm against a wide fir and filled her lungs, her gaze never deviating from the approaching figure in scarlet. Her Mountie to the rescue.

Only, he wasn't hers.

Nathan's lungs were heaving for air by the time he reached her. He dragged the hat from his head and wiped his sleeve across his brow. "What happened? Why did you leave the path?"

"I didn't mean to. I got turned around." Heat rushed to her face with likely a dose of color at the memory of her hasty departure from the waterfall. "I'm sorry."

He looked her up and down as though making certain she was indeed in one piece, and then motioned with his head back the way he'd come. "You came quite a distance."

"I thought I could find my way." She looked past him, not brave enough to hold his gaze. "The girls are safe?"

"Of course. I looked for you at the boardinghouse first."

Despite the embarrassment, she forced her gaze to meet his. "Thank you. For looking."

He merely nodded as though it were nothing, and perhaps to him it was. All in a day's work while in uniform, right? He probably rescued women on a regular basis, attractive women like the blond at the boardinghouse.

"We had best be on our way. I have wasted enough of your time." Samantha pushed forward, sidestepping him, trying not to limp as she followed the trail he had broken—rough as it was.

Nathan's steps and the crunch of breaking underbrush followed her. "It would only be a waste of time if I hadn't found you," he said. "If you were relaxing back in Coleman at some diner."

Samantha shook her head. "I am sure you had better things to do than tromping through the woods searching for a schoolteacher who should have stayed put in the first place. I shouldn't have abandoned you with the children. They were my responsibility too."

"You had your reasons." He grew closer with each step, but she couldn't quicken hers. There wasn't much of a path, and she was barely staying on her feet. "Though I admit to curiosity. Mary said you might be angry again. Like you were when they went there as a family a week ago."

Samantha stopped. Her pride and sense of self-preservation screamed at her to continue walking, or to return his questioning with a flippant answer. But that wasn't how she wanted to be remembered. "I wasn't angry. Not really." The truth settled into her stomach and soured there. "I was jealous."

Chapter 28

Nathan stepped close enough to touch her sleeve, but she didn't look back. "Jealous?" he questioned. Somehow that wasn't an emotion he would have associated with her.

Samantha shook her head and wiped one hand across her face. "I can't even explain. Far easier to deny it." She started walking again, but her limp was more evident than moments ago.

He slipped beside her and draped her arm over his shoulder. "We're not in a hurry. Take your time."

Samantha stood stiffly for several long moments before murmuring, "I can manage."

"But you don't have to. I'm here now. Lean into me." He glanced at her face as she looked up at him. "I could always carry you."

She shook her head far too quickly. "I'm tired of burdening others."

"Hardly a burden." And what was more, he felt his words. He didn't mind her closeness at all. Which was strange.

Even as she rolled her eyes at him and began to pull away.

Nathan pulled her back and swept his arm under her legs and into the air. "I mean it. You have shouldered most of the responsibility for the girls over the past week—a burden that should have been mine." One he should have focused on instead of trying to escape.

"You are calling your nieces a burden?" Samantha glanced at him out of the corner of her eye, probably just as aware as he was of how close their faces were now.

"Only in the most loving sense of the word. Not like you referred to yourself."

Her eyes closed momentarily. Allowing him free perusal of her face, from the smudge of dirt across her cheek, to the strands of hair falling free of her pins. Hardly the uptight, mousy spinster he had once judged her to be. Far from it. She was warm and alive and kind and. . .

He shook his head, clearing the thoughts. Now was neither the time nor place to contemplate the curve of her lips or the dimple in her chin. "But just for the record, you have never been a burden to me. Nor can I fathom you becoming one."

"He said while carrying her up the slope of a mountain?"

A chuckle slipped from him. "Are you writing our story?"

She stiffened in his arms. "We don't have a story. . . Do we?"

"I think everyone involved with the landslide has a story that should be told. Why not us?"

She was silent for a moment. "Because I have never been a fan of short tragedies." Even being so close, he hardly heard her words. She glanced at the ground. "Really, I can walk."

"Once we get back to the trail, maybe. The ground is too uneven here."

"Exactly. You can't see your feet and could easily trip over a root or branch and sprain *your* ankle. And then where will we be?"

"We'd make quite the pair, wouldn't we." He again chuckled, feeling much more lighthearted than he had any right to. But after so much worry for her safety, the release was freeing.

"I wish you wouldn't talk like that," she said under her breath, probably not intending to speak at all. Even while she relaxed into his hold, he could feel her withdraw, her gaze focused on the path.

"Our story doesn't have to be a tragedy," he tried. "Yes, there has been a lot of tragedy—I have felt it as keenly as anyone who has lost family and friends.

But there is a place for faith and hope as well. The girls' survival. Yours."

Samantha pressed a thin smile. "Until we all go our own ways—you back to your work, and the girls to separate homes, perhaps not to see each other for years. Is that not a tragedy for them?"

He met her gaze. Perhaps the girls being separated wouldn't be the only unfortunate farewell.

"And short is best in this case," she continued. "Better than drawing out goodbyes."

Was she still speaking of the girls? "Where will you go?"

A shrug. "Wherever I am sent to teach. Probably to Lethbridge or Calgary for the summer while I wait to see where I'm needed."

"Not back to Frank?"

She looked at him with wide eyes. "Why would they ever allow anyone back there? How could they be sure more of the mountain won't come down?"

"I guess we will find out soon enough. The government has the mountain covered with surveyors and geologists to determine how safe the town will be moving forward."

Samantha shook her head. "I couldn't imagine anyone wanting to go back there no matter what their findings. I would never be able to trust that mountain. . .never mind the memories." She sank against him, and he tightened his hold despite the burn in his arms. Thankfully they were nearing the trail, and he would soon set her down.

Except, when that time came, he found himself hesitant. He allowed her feet to touch the ground but kept his hold while she steadied herself and looked up at him. The top of her head only came to his chin, so her face tipped upward, her lips slightly pursed with questioning. Why was he looking at her mouth? He glanced into her eyes to see that they had shifted to his mouth. Was she considering the same? A simple kiss?

———◆◆———

What was wrong with her? Why couldn't she avert her gaze, or her thoughts? Instead, Samantha stared at the subtle curve of Nathan's mouth, wondering what it would feel like to truly be kissed. To be wanted. To be loved. To belong to someone. To not be alone or forgotten.

She felt her body lean forward, felt the wool of his coat against her palms, along with the rigidness of his chest. His arms encircled her, holding her in place as though she truly did belong here. With him. Was it possible he felt the same pull—or any pull?

She was only an inch or so from knowing for sure.

Samantha closed her eyes but didn't dare move. What if this moment was conjured by desires that were hers alone? He was only trying to steady her on her feet. Or was there more? Did he wish to make a fool of her, toy with her for the sake of a laugh as others had done? What a fool she was to hope. She tucked her chin and looked away before she made any more of a fool of herself.

And felt his withdrawal.

"We should probably..." Her voice was a little too high-pitched, and she paused to correct it. How embarrassing if he saw how affected she was by him. But then, that was why men took any interest in her, to toy with her, to be entertained by her reactions.

"Yes. I need to get you back to Coleman." He kept his hand on her arm. "The daylight won't last much longer this deep in the mountains."

Samantha glanced to the west, through the tops of the trees, at the top slice of the sun already tucking itself behind a mountain. Rays spread out like a fan but couldn't breach the shadows of the forest floor. A sudden chill sank through her, causing a slight shiver. She hoped it had gone undetected, but Nathan still had hold on her arm and his brow pinched with concern.

"You're cold?"

"I'm fine." Or she would be once they started moving again and she was able to put some distance between them.

He shook his head and began unbuttoning his scarlet coat.

"Honestly, I'll be fine."

Yet even as she protested, he draped the warmth over her shoulders, and she couldn't help but melt into the radiant bliss and the scent of woods, and soap, and *him*. As though that wasn't enough, he again slipped under her arm, and wrapped his arm around her back. Suddenly, she was almost too warm.

He's merely doing his duty.

That was all. She was a lady in distress, and he was a stalwart officer of the law. There was nothing else between them. There couldn't be.

"What happened after your parents were killed?"

Samantha jerked at the question.

He glanced at her out of the corner of his eye. "You don't have to speak of it, if you'd rather not."

It was one of the last topics she would choose, but the explanation was forming in her head. "Nothing. I was already attending a boarding school. My parents had left enough," and then some, "so I simply continued on that path."

"You had no other family to take you in?"

Did she have an answer for that? "None that offered." The only grandparents Samantha knew of were still in England, her father having left there as a young man set on adventure. Mother had family somewhere in Eastern Canada, but Samantha had never met them, and they had never reached out. She wasn't sure if they even knew about her.

"I don't like that the girls are being separated," Nathan said softly, "but at least they will have family, right? That will help."

Help them not become like her? "I'm sure it will," she managed.

"I just can't get rid of the guilt that I'm not doing more. I promised Mary I would do everything in my power to keep them together and make sure they have a good home. I'm pretty sure she feels I've failed them."

"I'm sure you're doing your best." Samantha wasn't sure what else to say. This conversation had never been about her, so why feel as though she had opened up to him for no reason?

"Exactly! I'm a bachelor with demanding employment. It's not like I can take them in myself." He huffed out a laugh. "Or that my brothers would even allow me to. No, Charles has everything quite in hand as always. Always his way. Who cares what I think? Why should that change?"

"I care." The words slipped out, though thankfully quietly. Hopefully, he hadn't heard them.

He had. Nathan looked down at her with surprise. Or shock—maybe that was a better word for his expression.

"About the girls," Samantha squeaked out. "And I think you know them and their needs better than someone who has only just taken notice that they exist."

He shook his head, frown deepening. "I hardly acknowledged their existence either before I showed up here a week ago. I'd only seen the older girls once before then."

She looked at him more openly. Though she hadn't met him in her time with the Stanfords, the family had not acted estranged from him. "They talked of you so frequently and with so much pride, I thought you had more of a relationship with your brother and his family."

"They talked about me?"

"The children loved to tell their classmates about their uncle, the Mountie. Your brother too. And they said you lived nearby, so I assumed. . ."

Nathan started walking, his focus on the trail. Well, his gaze was fixed on the trail, but she guessed by the stiffness in his gait that his focus was very much internal.

"It's none of my business."

"No? We've kind of placed you right in the middle of it. Only fair that you know I haven't been very close to any of my brothers or their families for years. Especially Peter. He's tried to mend things between us, but I've been slow to forgive."

Samantha couldn't help but ask. "Forgive?"

He blew out his breath. "Rosemary was my age, a couple years younger than Peter. We met in school and became friends. I thought we had something deeper than friendship and started imagining a future with her." Nathan shook his head but said nothing more.

Samantha easily pieced the rest together—and tried to tuck away the uncomfortable sensation of jealousy. Rosemary Stanford had been a beautiful woman even after giving birth to seven children—how much more so had she been as a youth with her blond tresses and blue eyes? It had likely been easy for Nathan to fall in love with her. "But Peter stole her affection instead."

"Yeah." He huffed a laugh. "What hurt the worst was everyone's reaction. The rest of the family seemed to think it a fine joke. So I struck out on my own at seventeen. Worked a few odd jobs before joining the academy. I admit I had a bit of a chip on my shoulder when it came to my siblings—guess I was tired of being overlooked and trying to prove myself to them."

Samantha would gladly steer the conversation further from Rosemary. "And your parents?"

Nathan stiffened even more.

"I'd rather not talk about them."

"Again, none of my business. I'm sorry." Samantha clamped her mouth closed, not knowing how to move beyond the awkwardness increasing with each step. Perhaps this is why she was meant to be alone. She had no experience with men and needed to put any thoughts of this one as far from her as possible. The quicker they made it back to the boardinghouse the better.

"It's not your fault," he finally murmured. "It's mine. I just. . . I was never close to my parents. Either of them." His voice came flat, emotionless.

Samantha wanted to say she was sorry, but her silence was probably preferred.

"They were too busy to worry about me, and I have my own life now." Though his tone remained flat, he couldn't hide the pain in his pinched expression.

That was something she did understand. "And here I was jealous of you and your big family," she whispered, not sure if she wanted him to hear.

"And I would have thought as an only child, you would have been your parents' only focus. While they were alive." He winced. "I'm sorry. That was thoughtless of me."

"No, you're right. And I wish that had been the case. But they had their own lives, and I was usually left behind."

"Guess there's no guarantee for family life and finding your place." He cracked a smile at her. A smile that held no humor.

Samantha returned the sad smile. Couldn't help it at this strange commonality she had not expected. "I hope that if I ever do, by some miracle, have children of my own. . ." She wet her lips, wishing she hadn't opened her mouth. What a hypocrite she was. She had no idea how to be a mother and would probably fail miserably if she ever had a child of her own.

"What?"

She sighed. "I hope I can show each of my children their worth to me, make certain that each of them feels loved."

His smile both softened and grew. "I agree."

Chapter 29

Not much else was said as they made their way down the narrow trail to Coleman. The town was bustling with the business of early evening, folks rushing home or hurrying to finish their day. Samantha ducked her head while Nathan asked a stranger for a ride in the back of his wagon the remainder of the way to the boardinghouse. Though grateful to not have to take another step, again she was a burden on those around her.

Thankfully, Nathan led her directly to her room once at the boardinghouse—the last thing she wanted was anyone else to see her in this state. He tapped on the door before opening it for her with the key provided by the landlord. The room was quiet and dark, but Nathan took a moment to light a lamp for her before stepping back into the open doorway.

"Is there anything else you need?"

"No. Thank you."

He didn't move. "I'll ask someone to bring up some dinner, so you don't have to walk downstairs again tonight."

"That would be nice." She inched toward the bed, her legs aching and ankle pulsating pain through the joint.

Nathan still didn't move.

Heat crept up Samantha's neck. "Is there something you need?"

"Um." The corner of his mouth tipped up. "My coat."

"Oh!" The heat rushed to her cheeks making her wish he had left the room dark. How stupid of her! Of course he needed his uniform. Though it felt gloriously warm around her shoulders, she yanked the coat free and held it out. "Thank you. Again."

He stepped near and took the red coat. "Of course."

"I mean, for everything. For coming back for me. For helping me. I would still be out there if not for you." Her chest tightened at the thought, and the understanding of how much she owed him, and how much she wished there was a way to repay him besides repeating such trite words. She glanced at his mouth. That would be a way to show how grateful she truly was, but she was hardly the type of woman to throw herself into a man's arms—despite being in those arms for the past hour or so. No, he would hardly appreciate a kiss from her.

Samantha jerked her gaze back to his. "Thank you."

He stiffened away, coat in hand, probably aware of the direction of her thoughts and mortified by them. *She* definitely was.

"Oh, hello!" A woman's voice penetrated Samantha's consciousness.

Nathan spun and shoved his arms back into his coat, hurrying from the room. He paused only long enough to nod at the blond woman before disappearing down the hall.

"Well," the woman said, stepping into the room. "I'm sorry if I intruded."

"What?" Samantha brushed her hands down her skirts, and then over her hair—what a disaster! All of this was a disaster. If rumor reached the school board, she would never be allowed to teach again. "Of course not. Constable Stanford was merely seeing me safely here. I had a mishap."

"I see." The woman, probably a few years younger than Samantha, smiled and closed the door. She lit a second lamp to better illuminate the small room. "You must be Miss Ingles."

"Yes." Samantha stood in place, not sure what to say or do. She couldn't remember feeling so flustered—except a few minutes ago under Nathan's scrutiny. Or in his embrace on the side of the mountain. *Oh, goodness!*

"You should probably sit down. You don't look well."

Samantha did so, sinking onto the edge of her bed. Samantha brought her foot up to remove her shoe.

"Oh dear! What did you do?"

Samantha kept her focus on the swollen ankle. It looked almost as bad as that first day but with no new abrasions. Just swelling. "It'll be fine. I just walked too far today. I should have given my foot more time to heal."

A moment of silence compelled Samantha to raise her gaze to the wide brown eyes of the woman staring at her. "Were you in the slide?" she finally asked softly.

Samantha nodded, though that was the last thing she wanted to discuss.

"I'm so sorry. I can only imagine how frightening that must have been. Just the thought of it—and of those who might still be out there." Her chin trembled, and her head gave a quick shake. "Not that anyone is still alive. I just. . ." Again, her head shook. "I shouldn't have said anything. You've been through enough. She sank to the bed across from Samantha. "Did you lose anyone?"

"Students. People I knew. Not anyone close—not like most." And that separation, that disconnect, only made her feel worse.

"You wouldn't have met. . .or heard of a Ned Morgan?" The woman shook her head, groaning. "No, of course not. He didn't spend much time in Frank. He was friends with the Grahams and hadn't planned to stay long."

"Unless he had a student in the Frank School, I wouldn't have known him. Did he. . .?" Samantha couldn't ask.

The woman's eyes misted. "I don't know. That's the worst of it. Ned is my husband. He came to Frank with a cow/calf pair he had planned to sell the Grahams. They probably invited him to stay for the night. Mrs. Graham is. . .*was* one of the sweetest hostesses. She enjoyed company and was a wonderful cook, so I know there's a chance Ned stayed the night." Her shoulders rose while her expression twisted. "Is he buried under hundreds of tons of rock with them? I don't know. I came as soon as I heard about the slide. But there's nothing. I just can't stop hoping he camped somewhere else and will show up." She wiped at tears as they escaped to her cheeks. "I'm sorry. I haven't really talked it through with anyone. I've only asked if he's been seen or if anyone knows where he might be. But it's been a week, and I. . ." She looked to Samantha with such pleading. "I'm losing hope."

Samanatha's heart broke for the woman, but it was Nathan's face she pictured when she tried to imagine the loss. She hobbled to the second bed and set her hand on Mrs. Morgan's arm. Just like comforting a child after an injury in the schoolyard. A slight pat on the arm.

Mrs. Morgan twisted and hugged Samantha while more tears fell. What now? Samantha wasn't equipped to handle such a swell of emotion. What did she have to offer this complete stranger?

She sat silently while the woman cried. Thankfully Samantha's eyes stayed dry—probably because she'd already run out of tears. By the time the woman pulled back, Samantha's brain had cleared enough to offer something that might help. "Why don't you speak with Constable Stanford about your husband?"

"I've already bothered the police. There is little they can do unless something turns up."

"Perhaps, but I think Nath—Constable Stanford would be able to give finding him, or what happened to him, a little more focus. It's worth a try."

Mrs. Morgan nodded and offered her thanks and apologies. Samantha moved back to her bed. A little distance to reset her thoughts and equilibrium. She had changed her clothes and wrapped her ankle in a fresh linen bandage Mrs. Morgan found, when a baby's wails filtered through the wall separating her room from the Stanfords. Poor Lucy.

Mrs. Stanford didn't sound much happier.

"I'll bring you some dinner," Mrs. Morgan offered before slipping out the door. Samantha didn't bother letting her know that Nathan had offered the same. It would be worked out without her. And if not, she would probably be hungry enough to eat two helpings after such an exhausting day.

But for now. . . Samantha dropped onto her side and pulled a quilt over her head. Just for a moment, she wanted to hide from it all. Hide from the feeling that she should be the one to comfort Lucy. Hide from her confusing feelings for Nathan. Oh, that she would go back to the bliss of numbness and indifference. If only she could somehow squeeze her emotions back inside and lock her heart away.

Chapter 30

MAY 9TH

Nathan leaned against a boulder the size of a house, trying not to think of the damage it had done before it finally settled halfway up the opposite slope from Turtle Mountain. The sun beat down with surprising force, and sweat ran down his back. He tugged at the collar of his scarlet coat, feeling like hands gripped his throat as he read name after name on the list held in his hands.

> *Charles Ackroyd and wife Nancy*
> *William and John Bobbles*
> *Joe Brighton*
> *Bumis (miner and unmarried)*
> *Byeskid (miner and unmarried)*
> *Alex Clark (Laborer), Wife Amillia, Children:*
> *Charles, Albert, Alfred, Ellen, Gertrude*

Nathan lowered the list to tug his notebook from his pocket. He flipped through the pages, seeking the name. Clark. There it was on his list.

Lillian Clark, the lone survivor of her family
because she spent her first night away from
home at the boardinghouse she worked at.

The poor girl had survived but buried her parents and five siblings. Was that a miracle or a tragedy...or both? Nathan tucked the book away and continued down the list of the dead—or assumed dead, as most bodies would never be recovered.

The lump in his stomach grew with each name he read.

JW Clark
Ben Cumus, wife and two children
Jack or Alfred Dawes (miner) and two friends from Wales

Nathan sighed. Two unnamed friends from across the Atlantic. Their families would probably never know what became of their sons or husbands.

T Delap (engineer and married)

But no mention if his wife had been buried with him.

A few names down he found the Grahams.

Alexander Graham and wife Maggie Graham
James Graham (rancher), wife, and sons John and Joseph

Strangely the wife hadn't been named. But that detail, along with a lot more, would probably be filled in at some point. This had to be the ranch where Ned Morgan had visited the day before the slide. But had he stayed the night to be buried with his hosts or made it out of the slide's reach?

Nathan set his jaw. He was a Mountie and was capable of tracking a man. He would continue hunting until he found Morgan—if he was alive.

Nathan read down the remainder of the list. Full families, miners, laborers, railroad workers, a couple of stable hands—line after line, near a hundred souls. Small checks marked the handful whose bodies had been accounted for.

Peter Stanford remained unmarked, while tiny marks hovered over the names of Rosemary and their boys.

That knowledge would forever haunt him.

"Constable Stanford." Constable Hardy approached over the rugged terrain. "I am headed back to Frank. Are you finished with that list?"

"Yeah."

Hardy folded the sheet and tucked it back into his uniform's breast pocket. "We've received orders to cease the search. No one would have survived half this time, and the dead. . ." He wiped his hand across his neck, "They're better left undisturbed at this point." Some of the color faded from his face, either from the unsettled sensation of ending the search, or the memories of what had already been found. "Tomorrow, they plan on lifting the evacuation order for Frank so there's not much more we can do here."

While Nathan couldn't argue with the last statement, the first clenched like a fist in his stomach. "They are going to allow folks back into Frank? How can that be safe?"

Hardy shrugged while his focus rose to the rugged scar across the side of the mountain. "We got briefed this morning. The geologists Prime Minister Laurier sent out have been all over the north peak and up and down those slopes and have no concerns about there being another slide. They figure that what came down is all that will."

"They figure?" Nathan couldn't help the edge to his voice. How could anyone take chances with lives at stake?

Hardy gave an impatient glare. "That is my wording, not theirs. They have deemed it safe, and we will announce the end of the evacuation order in the morning."

"Do you really think anyone will want to come back?" Samantha had already made her thoughts clear on the matter. She wanted to go as far away from Frank and Turtle Mountain as possible. She wasn't the only one.

"Folks are hardy, and most of the town still has business and homes here. Never mind the mine. They have been discussing reopening it."

They—whoever *they* were—were crazy. But that was none of Nathan's affair, and he had no interest in it. "What about me? We'll be pulling out right away?" He pushed away from the gargantuan boulder and followed Constable Hardy down the slope.

"Yes, the company will return to Fort MacLeod on Monday." He glanced at Nathan. "Do you need more time to get your nieces settled?"

His brain shouted yes, but what point was there in putting off the inevitable? Charles had everything in hand, and they had Miss Ingles. Within a few days, the girls would all be on their way to their new homes. The fact was, Nathan had sworn his duty elsewhere and had told Constable Hardy he was fit for duty. How could he rescind that now?

Nathan forced his shoulders to straighten, and he tugged his hat lower on his brow. "No, sir. I have no further business here." It was all he could do to push aside Mary's pleading gaze...or the need in Samantha's.

He tried not to think about that as he took his leave and rode toward Coleman. He could no longer avoid what awaited him there, pausing briefly at a small shop in Blairmore that had been able to repair Samantha's spectacles. Almost as good as new.

All Nathan had to do was report that he needed to get back to his duties elsewhere and turn everything here over to Charles—who had already happily taken control. Nathan groaned. Who was he kidding? He had to explain to Mary why he would be gone and say goodbye to Samantha. Which really shouldn't be so hard after purposefully avoiding them both for most of two days.

"Whoa." Nathan reined in his horse and swung to the ground. The sun's rays had lost their power, but still he felt overheated and more winded than he had any right to be.

"Keep it simple," he reminded himself. When breaking bad news to someone, like a death or an arrest, short and to the point was the most merciful. Short and to the point.

"I need to report back to my superiors at Fort MacLeod on Monday." That was simple enough. "I'm sorry I can't keep my promise to keep you and your sisters together and make sure you have a happy home." Far too complicated and the words would cling to the back of his throat like they did now. It wasn't like he hadn't tried. It wasn't like he had any control over the situation.

Nathan forced his lungs to expand as he started toward the boardinghouse. No wonder he had avoided this place the past two days. He itched to walk away now, go find something to drink with a little more potency than his usual coffee—something he hadn't considered doing for almost thirteen years. He'd been young and stupid then, and on the run from feelings he didn't quite understand. He'd gotten brain-numbing drunk and woke up with a splitting headache—reality still staring him in the face, only this time with an empty wallet. There was no point to drinking, and he'd never gone there since.

Yet, here he was again, considering drowning himself.

"Nate?" a man boomed from behind him. "Well, I'll be!"

Nathan jerked his head to where a young man stood just outside the doorway of the boardinghouse.

"I never would have recognized you without the uniform." The man lunged forward to throw a hug around Nathan's shoulders.

In truth Nathan never would have recognized his little brother either, after so many years. He'd grown a good foot since Nathan had left, and his usual auburn mass of curls had been trimmed and was mostly contained under his hat.

"Wilfred?"

"Got here as soon as I could after getting word from Charles." The grin had slipped from his face. "Haven't made it as far as the slide yet, but I saw photos in the paper. Can't believe it."

The door swung open again, and Charles stepped out. He frowned at Nathan. "There you are. We were stepping out to find a quieter place to talk. You might as well come along. The women folk are dealing with the children."

Nathan glanced at Will. "Your whole family came?"

"No, no, just me. Laura is at home still recovering. Our baby's barely a month old. That's why I can't stay long. Need to be on the train first thing Monday. There is only so much my Laura can take of her mother." He shrugged. "Though it was nice she could come and take care of things while I'm away. I must admit an extra pair of hands around the house will do a world of good with Laura not up and about much yet, and the two little ones acting like whirlwinds of disaster. Mary appears to be a levelheaded girl and is good with her sisters."

The sisters she would soon be ripped from, so she could chase after

Will's "whirlwinds" and help maintain a house.

"Hopefully we won't have to stay much longer either." Charles started down the street. "Maddie is restless to get home and get the baby into a proper routine. While she appreciates Miss Ingles' assistance with the child, no one can calm a child quite like Mrs. Davidson, our nanny. That and dealing with Abigail has Maddie at the end of her rope." He stepped off the boardwalk and led them across the road to the Coleman Hotel. "You saw her, Will. Stubbornly unresponsive. Brent will have his hands full."

Nathan kept pace though his boots felt as though they had been dipped in lead.

"They haven't arrived yet?" Will asked.

"Tomorrow, according to our last correspondence. Had to take care of some business before leaving Calgary."

"Brent's in Calgary now?" That surprised Nathan. He hadn't realized his brother had moved from Saskatoon. With Nathan's last posting in the bustling town, was it possible they had crossed paths?

"Where have you been?" Charles rolled his eyes. "Brent moved out three years ago. Bought a small mill right off that river that runs through the town. Seems to be doing well for himself." He motioned his brothers into the hotel and made his way to what could be deemed a dining room, though somewhat rough around the edges. They found a table, and Nathan pulled up an extra chair. Charles focused on Will while setting his hat on the table. "As you see, Nate hasn't changed much. Still lost in his own world."

Will looked from one brother to the other. "Not the way I remember it. But we're a bit closer in age. You were the one off and about doing your own thing."

"Yeah, Charles, maybe you're the one who wasn't paying attention. And stop calling me Nate. I hate it."

Charles raised a brow. "But it's your name. It's what we've always called you."

"When I was two feet shorter than you. I go by Nathan now. Or Constable Stanford," Nathan spat out, "if that's too hard to remember."

Charles's eyes widened. "Who put a burr under your saddle?"

"You did." Nathan shoved back from the table, unable to suppress the frustration heating his chest, feeding a deeper anger. "You show up here and take control without any consideration for those girls and what is best for them."

Charles groaned and leaned back in his chair. "This again? Of course we're doing what's best for the girls. We're giving them homes. And what makes you an expert on them or what they need? You know nothing about children, and it's not like you have anything to offer."

"Sure I do. I mean, maybe I don't know much about children, but I know enough." They needed to be seen and loved and not taken for granted. How could he abandon Peter's girls? "And maybe I can offer them something."

"Like what?" Charles burst out. "We've been over this already. You're hardly in a position to provide them with a home, never mind a family."

"I could." The words slipped out on their own, but Nathan couldn't stop now. He was done being pushed around and told what to do. He owed Peter. And he'd promised Mary. "Just because I'm a Mountie doesn't mean I can't provide a home and family. Plenty of constables have wives and kids."

"Yes, Nate. *Wives.* But you don't have one of those, do you?"

"Maybe not yet, but I can get one." What was he saying? His brain was churning so quickly, it was hard to keep up with what came out of his own mouth. A face came to mind, looking up at him with such need. He'd wanted to kiss her. "Samantha. Samantha and I can marry."

"Miss Ingles?" Laughter erupted from Charles. "You have to be joking." Was he? "No."

"Who?" Will questioned, leaning into the table.

Charles shook his head, still scoffing. "Miss Ingles, the mousy school-marm who's helping Maddie with the girls."

Nathan shoved to his feet, sending the chair toppling. It banged against the floor. "Don't talk about her like that. There is nothing wrong with her, and she would make a fine mother for the girls. At least then they could stay together."

Charles moaned. "Do you hear yourself, Nate—or Nathan, or *whoever* you are now? You are willing to give up your freedom and tie yourself to that schoolmarm for the sake of those girls? They will be fine. They will have good homes. Don't make this about *you*."

Nathan pointed a finger at him, fighting the urge to lash out with a fist instead. "This has nothing to do with me." He turned and strode from the room, letting the door slam behind him. He made it halfway back to the boardinghouse where he had left Rover tied before he felt his thoughts settle into place. Was he willing to marry a woman who was still very much a mystery to him, and who he hadn't even *liked* until a couple of days ago? Was he willing to tie himself to her and three young girls—an instant family and so much responsibility? What had happened to riding away in another day and not looking back?

Chapter 31

Alone at last. Well, alone with the girls, at least. No more Mrs. Stanford peering over her shoulder and critiquing everything she did. Yes, Samantha had little experience with babies, but it wasn't as though she didn't spend most of her days with children in the schoolhouse.

Samantha sank into a rocking chair and braced her sore foot on a stool. Lucy cuddled into her chest, thumb in her mouth, eyes blinking slowly. Her freshly washed hair smelled of lavender and sunshine, and Samantha couldn't resist breathing deeply as she pressed her lips to the silky head while letting her gaze wander to where Mary read *The Princess and the Goblin* to Abby. The middle girl sat quietly, only half mindful of her sister's story. Even Mary seemed distant today—ever since yet another uncle showed up, the one who would take her away.

A sigh slipped painfully from Samantha's chest. Why had she stayed and allowed herself to grow more attached to these children? While she had been fond of students in the past—usually bright ones who excelled and listened well—she'd never felt this depth of...what was she supposed to call it? Affection? Care? *Love?*

Samantha shook the latter word from her head as a knock sounded on the door. Lucy jerked at the sound but settled again almost immediately, her eyes closing fully. Samantha looked at Mary, who nodded before the request was even made. The girls set the book aside and moved across the room—as though a villain, or goblin, lurked on the other side of the door. Mary's feet dragged and her frown deepened. Until the door opened to reveal a tall figure in a scarlet coat. Mary threw herself into his arms. And clung tight.

Nathan returned the embrace with as much fervor, lifting the girl off her feet. His eyes squeezed closed as though in pain.

"Don't let him take me away," Mary squeaked. "I don't want to go."

"I know," Nathan mumbled. He glanced at Abby with a grimace in place. Then he met Samantha's gaze. Her face immediately warmed for no reason. Or perhaps because she hadn't seen him since he'd walked her off the mountain. What must he think of her?

"I saw Maddie taking tea in the dining room, so I wanted a minute to talk to you."

"You did?" Samantha tried not to consider what he might have to say. Or, what she *wanted* him to say.

Nathan nodded, his jaw setting. Then he seemed to remember something and jerked to pull something out of his pocket. "Your spectacles. I'm sorry it took so long to get them fixed." He stepped across the room, hand extended. Then, realizing her hands were busy, he pulled the cloth wrapping them and crouched to place them on her nose. She blinked as his face became even clearer.

"Thank you," she said breathlessly. Perhaps it was the weight of the child against her chest that made it hard to fill her lungs.

"Maybe that was why you lost the trail."

She had definitely struggled to see clearly that day but wouldn't confess the main reason.

"Samantha. . ." Nathan rocked back on his heels and jerked to his feet. Then he turned to the older two girls who watched on. "Mary, would you mind taking Lucy for a moment? I need to speak with Miss Ingles."

The girl stepped in as directed, though her eyes seemed to continue their plea for her uncle not to leave.

"Just for a moment," he repeated and then offered a hand to Samantha. Her ankle pinched in protest, but the pain was tolerable now. He led her as far as the hallway before closing the door behind them. "I need to ask you a favor."

"A favor?"

"For the sake of the girls. I know I have already asked so much already, and you have your own life and plans to consider, but I can't allow the girls to be separated—to be. . .*farmed out.* I'm so tired of Charles thinking he knows best and can push me around." Nathan huffed out a breath.

"You want more help with the girls?"

"I am in no position to raise them alone." He pulled the flat-brimmed Stetson from his head. "But with you at my side. . ."

"You want me to help you?" Samantha didn't have the strength to ask how long the arrangement would last, or how it would work with his bachelor status. Even if she went along with his plan until the fall, what would that do for her reputation and her suitability to teach? Teachers were held to very high standards. She would be risking everything, even if she had separate accommodations. Working as a nanny for a bachelor. It was out of the question on every level.

And yet she longed to agree.

"I need you, Samantha. It's the only way I'd be able to keep them."

Oh, how she loved hearing him say her name, and oh, to be able to say yes! But the end would still be the same. She would still have to say goodbye when other, more suitable arrangements were made. But by then, how much more would leaving them hurt?

"Please, consider it."

His pleading only made the answer more obvious. She was already too attached, not just to the girls but to this man. She could not allow herself to fall for him, she could not bear to stand aside while he figured out how to make do without her, as he would have to. He'd probably seek a wife, someone younger and prettier and sweeter tempered—someone more like Rosemary Stanford, his first love. The thought of it pierced Samantha to the core. "I can't."

Nathan opened his mouth, but she wouldn't let him speak.

"I'm a teacher. That has always been my dream and my life. I can't give it up. I want what is best for the girls, and it hurts my heart that they can't stay together, or with you, but I'm not the answer to your problem." *As much as I wish I could be.*

Because she knew that in a matter of days, her dream had changed and her heart yearned for more than a superficial relationship with children where she came and went from their lives in rhythm with the Canadian snow. She wanted to be *central* to their lives and be able to offer them her whole heart. To be a mother. "I'm sorry."

Nathan stepped back, nodding slowly. His face, a mask. "I'll figure out something else."

"I'm sure you will." Samantha forced what probably looked nothing like a smile and fled back into the room. It took everything in her not to turn back and tell him she'd changed her mind.

———— •◆• ————

"Fool." Nathan swallowed the urge to curse as he sagged against the wall. How had he thought proposing a good idea? Of course she wouldn't give up her teaching for him, a man she hardly knew. Despite some attraction to him—he'd seen it in her eyes on more than one occasion. *That* was hardly worth basing a relationship on. He had the girls to think of and fight for, but they were hardly Samantha's concern—hardly a reason to tie herself to him "till death do you part."

But now what? He'd failed Mary and Abby and even Lucy, though she was the least likely to hold it against him. So much for being a hero in scarlet riding in to save the day.

Footsteps on the stairs pulled Nathan upright, and he started in the opposite direction despite it being a dead end. He wasn't in the mood to face anyone—even a stranger.

"Nathan," Will called. His footsteps followed. Escape was futile.

"What?" Nathan held his expression stoic, not wanting his little brother to see how affected the conversation with Samantha had left him.

"Are you serious about taking on Peter's daughters? All of them?"

He had been, but it seemed impossible now. "They need each other. They've already lost enough."

Will released a breath and nodded. "You're probably right, even if Charles doesn't see it that way. Here I thought I was coming to the rescue and doing the right thing, but now you have me doubting myself and this whole plan. But can you take them? I don't know who else would consider it. With the new baby and two young'uns already pushing us to our limits, Laura and I can't take on more. Brent might be able to, but Charles doesn't think he'd consider it. And no one else had volunteered. So that leaves you."

"So I'll figure it out." Nathan snapped back, more defensive than he should be. Will wasn't the enemy.

Instead of replying, Will nodded thoughtfully.

Nathan felt himself deflate. Who was he kidding? Charles was right, as always, curse the man. Nathan still had nothing to offer the girls but false hope. The best thing he could do was accept defeat—and help Mary accept reality.

"What do you plan to do?"

"I don't know." The most honest answer yet.

"Has your schoolteacher agreed to marry you?" Will prodded gently. "Charles said you haven't known each other very long."

"Charles—" Nathan bit his tongue and planted his hat on his head. The brother in question appeared at the top of the stairs with his wife at his side. Thankfully, Will waved them away, and they returned into their room without comment.

"Charles is trying to do what he feels is in the girls' best interest. But I would support you if you did have a home for the girls."

The truth hung in the air between them.

"I. . ." Nathan shook his head. "I don't. I don't have anything but this uniform. How pathetic is that?" He strode away. He owed Mary an explanation, but he didn't have one for her right now. All he had was failure. And an ache radiating out from his center. As Nathan mounted his horse, Samantha's rejection weaseled its way into his thoughts. He'd never asked anyone to marry him before, and admittedly, he had done a horrible job of it, but she didn't seem the type who wanted sentiment and promises of love. And how could he promise that? Would they have grown to love each other given time together?

Nathan allowed his eyelids to slide closed and pictured Samantha's tear-stained face and pursed lips. And the determined wrinkle of her nose when she argued with him, her brown eyes sparking with fire and determination.

No. Falling in love with her wouldn't have been a problem.

Chapter 32

MAY 10TH

A sunny Sunday, just as it should be. Yet no amount of warmth could penetrate the chill that gripped Samantha. Despite the return of her spectacles, the world was a blur as the small group made their way to the small church nestled in the heart of the mountain valley community. Thankfully the church was a short walk from the boardinghouse, as Samantha's foot already protested the abuse. "One more day."

"What was that?" Will Stanford asked from behind her. She liked the younger Stanford well enough, but in too many ways he reminded her of his brother who she had not seen since his offer of employment the day before.

"Nothing. Nothing important." She glanced down at Abby and squeezed the girl's hand. Any sign of breaking through her walls had faded over the last couple of days with Nathan's absence and the shifting of her world. Despite the "lost in her own world" look she wore, Abby was old enough and intelligent enough to know what changes were coming and how they would affect her. Was it any wonder the girl had crawled deeper inside herself?

Samantha knew well where that path led.

"My brother speaks highly of you, Miss Ingles."

She startled at the sound of Will's voice beside her and looked up to see him watching her closely.

"You look surprised." His eyes narrowed.

"Maybe a little." She managed to lift one shoulder. "We have had our differences."

"I imagine so. Nathan's always had very set ideas."

"As have I." She found greater fault with her own. Maybe she should reconsider. For the sake of the girls. Just for the summer, which would give him time to make other arrangements for their care. Would that be so hard?

The answer was a very clear yes.

Her emotions were already frazzled.

But the girls. They would be able to stay together. Wouldn't that be worth the sacrifice?

"He needs a strong-willed woman. But mostly, someone who will really see him."

"I. . ." She had no answer for that. Was Will suggesting something more should develop between his brother and her? He obviously hadn't been paying much attention. "I hope he finds that someday." Someday soon.

Will started to say something more, but they were already entering the church and the narrow door forced them into single file. Will stepped aside and allowed her to lead Abby inside the small shiplap building. Whitewashed walls brightened the otherwise dimly lit room that hosted a dozen or so benches. Extra chairs had been lined against the walls to provide more seating.

Charles, carrying Lucy, and Maddie led the way to a pew near the front. Mary dropped into the seat beside her aunt, her gaze downcast, looking very much like her younger sister. Samantha had no choice but to sit next, with Abby separating her from Will. She glanced back at the door, where folks of every age entered to find seating. No sign of a scarlet coat.

Disappointment and relief battled as she focused forward, but not before catching sight of Mrs. Morgan out of the corner of her eye. Samantha had been so busy with the girls they hadn't spoken much more, but her heart bled a little every time she thought of the woman's plight and how hard not knowing must be.

The meeting began with a somber hymn and prayer. Then the pastor stood and cleared his voice. "Before we begin, I feel we should pause and send up a silent prayer for those who have lost lives and loved ones in the recent disaster at Frank." He flattened a paper over his open Bible. "I was given a list of names—some of the known victims."

Then he began to read. Name after name, men, women and children. Some of which Samantha recognized. Her eyes watered. A weight leaned against her side, and she shifted to wrap her arm around Mary. She offered the same to Abby and was surprised when the girl sank against her. For a moment, more than just her arms were full, so much so, that her heart ached. How could she abandon these children?

"We have also been asked to announce," the pastor said finally, "that our neighbors and friends who have joined us from Frank are allowed to return to their homes. The evacuation order had been lifted, and the mountain has been deemed safe."

Samantha's chest tightened. How could that be? How could they possibly allow anyone back in that town after such a short time? The thought of Turtle Mountain looming over her, miles of rock laid out across the valley. . . Never. She couldn't return to Frank, even if that was the only teaching position offered her.

"I wish we could just go home," Mary whispered.

Samantha tightened her hold. There was no home for them to return to.

The pastor continued, digging into his Bible, but Samantha hardly heard the sermon of lost sheep and coins, not with names of the dead sifting through her head, and the girls sidled up next to her. She felt a heavy gaze and glanced to see Will watching. She focused forward again, pretended that she was interested in what the pastor was saying about God seeking and finding. And something about joy.

Samantha couldn't remember the last time she'd felt something akin to joy or happiness. Other than that ridiculous moment when Nathan had loaded her plate with pie and the girls had suddenly been children again. There had been something in that moment she wished she could feel again.

"'Be still, and know that I am God', the psalmist wrote."

Samantha's head snapped up at the pastor's words. He continued, but her mind clung to the simple phrase: *Be still.* For a moment she was under the roof again, fighting panic as those same words had seeped into her heart. *Be still.*

And know that I am God.

She hadn't understood that part.

Another prayer ended the meeting, and Samantha moved to follow the flow from the church. A glimpse of a red coat pulled her head around to the back of the room. But no. It was an older constable, not Nathan. She allowed Mary to keep her hand and lead her into the brilliance of noonday, where folks paused to visit and discuss the newest developments at Frank. Samantha was halfway across the yard before she caught sight of the Mountie again. A younger constable stood at his side in conversation.

Nathan had come.

He stepped to the side and motioned to a young couple she had never seen before, but it didn't take too much effort to see the familiarity between the man and Nathan. The other brother, the one who would steal Abby away.

"It's for the best," Samantha whispered. "For the best."

"No." Mary pulled away, taking Abby's hand and leading her in the direction of the boardinghouse. Samantha followed. Safer than facing Nathan again so soon.

The girls darted up the stairs and into the room, slamming the door behind them. Samantha gently pushed it open. "Mary."

The girl set her jaw and glared.

"It won't be so bad. You'll see. You have cousins and family who will love you and take care of you."

"They aren't my family. I don't even know them." She folded her arms and set her jaw. "Mama would want me to stay with Abby and Lucy, to take care of them."

There was no argument for that. "I'm sorry." For how could she not feel some responsibility? If only there were a way to accept Nathan's proposal without risking her heart, reputation, and career. Just for the summer. Four months. Couldn't she do that for them? Samantha released the breath she had been holding. Maybe she would talk to Nathan again, maybe they could find a way to keep the sisters together. That is what their parents would want. Samantha could almost hear Rosemary begging from beyond the grave. She loved her daughters so much.

Samantha wished she could reassure Mary, but before she could find the words, the room was swarmed by aunts and uncles. A brief introduction was made to the newly arrived couple while Samantha inched her way to the door. She'd hoped to see Nathan, but there was no sign of him. Just as well. She needed time to think and plan before speaking with him again. Yet time was short. One more day, and the girls would find their world ripped apart yet again.

———◆◆———

Nathan tossed his hat aside and then pulled at the buttons on the collar of his coat, very aware of the extra weight in the breast pocket. He sank onto the edge of the cot and fished out the notebook. Miracles indeed. He tapped the book against his knee. He should be in Coleman discussing things with his brothers, trying to work out a compromise. Instead, he hid himself away, running from what he couldn't control.

"What now, God?"

Silence was the only answer, yet it seemed to fill his ears, pulsating with the beat of his heart.

"What do I do?"

Nathan felt like a boy again, with so little say in his world—so much he wanted, but ignored by anyone who could give it to him. There was nothing he could do. Even now as a man and as an officer of the law—powerless over anything that really mattered.

He stood just as Peter had, in the open, with no strength against the slide of rocks crashing down.

Warmth clouded his vision.

"It's in Your hands, God. I've got nothing."

Chapter 33

~⌒~

The sun was barely glowing through the curtains. Samantha sat on the edge of her bed, watching as her roommate packed her small carpet bag. "It's time I go home." Mrs. Morgan had quietly announced. "I can't stay here forever, hoping against hope."

Samantha had wanted to argue. Her husband had not been named yesterday among the dead, so it was possible he was alive. But reality sat heavier. Most of the dead would never be found. So nothing was said.

Mrs. Morgan offered a tight smile as she latched her bag. "I'm not saying I've lost hope. Just that life has to continue too." She slipped from the room, abandoning Samantha to her thoughts.

Life has to continue.

Samantha's hands trembled while she dressed. Would she even have a chance to speak with Nathan? Surely he would come to say goodbye to the girls. Surely it wouldn't be too late.

Foot wrapped, spectacles in place, and spine straight, Samantha opened her door and stepped into the hallway just as Charles burst out of his room, nought on but his pants. His head whipped back and forth before settling on her. He shoved an arm into his shirt. "Where are the girls?"

"What—what do you mean?"

"The girls are gone. All three." He swore under his breath and spun back into his room. The door slammed.

Samantha stared, while voices raised from within the Stanfords' room, increasing in pitch and volume. The girls were missing? How? Why? Panic climbed Samantha's throat, and she hurried down the stairs. Someone would have seen them. Maybe they had gotten hungry and hadn't wanted to wait for Maddie to wake? But even while Samantha tried to excuse their disappearance, the answer settled heavily onto her chest. Mary had taken matters into her own hands to keep her sisters close. They had run away.

Thunder on the stairs preceded Charles rushing past and into the dining room, the kitchen, and then back into the foyer. He shoved through the door to the outside without a word to her. Samantha followed onto the boardwalk. Where would they have gone? They wouldn't take the train—it wouldn't arrive for hours, and they would be found by then. Mary was smarter than that. Would she try to find Nathan? He'd be coming here to say goodbye, so what would the point be? No, she'd be trying to make it on their own. Somewhere. Somehow.

Oh, those poor girls. How desperate Mary must have felt to do something so drastic and dangerous as running away with her two little sisters.

Only a few minutes passed before Charles returned with two of his brothers on his heels. Sharp voices cracked back and forth between them like the snap of a whip as they rushed past her again, back inside the boardinghouse. Only Will spared her a glance, but he said nothing until he reappeared a couple of minutes later.

"Do you have any idea where they might have gone?"

Samantha shook her head. "All I know is Mary was understandably upset yesterday about the thought of being separated from her sisters. What other choice was given her?"

Charles appeared behind him. "So this is all *our* fault? More likely Nate put the idea in her mind. It's just like the harebrained things he tried as a kid."

"Nathan would never risk anything happening to those girls," Samantha snapped. "He loves them."

Charles shook his head. "He just doesn't like being told what to do." He looked her up and down. "His desperation was a little too evident this time."

Will tugged his older brother away. "That is uncalled for, Charles. And we're wasting time. I propose we all take a different road out of town and see if we can catch up with them or find someone who's seen them."

The third brother appeared. Brent appeared closest to Nathan's age, but with a reddish hue to his hair. "I'll drop by the livery to see about a horse and then take the road west out of town." He moved as though to leave, then glanced back at Samantha. "You're Nate's schoolteacher?" He laughed as he hurried away.

"Don't pay any attention to either of these fools," Will said before turning to Charles. "We'll also need horses, so I'll catch up with Brent and be back here when we've got them. Best talk to some of the folks around town to see if anyone saw which way the girls went."

Soon Samantha was alone again, though she felt like she'd been trampled. Was any relationship with her so horrible? The brothers' words rang with mocking and left a sting. She would have thought she'd be used to it by now.

No more waiting and dwelling on what she couldn't control. Samantha made her way to the livery, hoping the men would be done with their business before she arrived. She'd rent a buggy or wagon and figure out where to go from there. *Anything* was better than sitting here and helplessly waiting.

The three Stanford brothers were mounted but appeared to be having one last discussion outside the livery, so Samantha hung back at the corner of the hotel. As soon as they took their leave, headed in three directions, she stepped out from her hiding spot. A man built like a boxer looked over as she approached. After a cursory glance, he turned back inside the livery.

"Wait," she called, hastening.

He looked back and pushed his sweat-stained bowler hat back from his brow.

"I need a buggy, just for the morning."

He scrubbed his fingers through a full beard. "Want a horse with that?" he asked in a flat voice. His eyes crinkled with mirth.

"Of course."

"You know how to drive one?"

"I have in the past." Once. For a few minutes.

"I don't have any buggies available today, and my last wagon needs work. If you come back around noon, I might have it ready."

"I need something now. Anything."

Again, his fingers combed through his beard, a grizzled brown and gray thing. "I have a gelding that would probably be gentle enough for you."

"A horse? Ride a horse?" She'd only ridden once, and it had been years ago.

"Like I said, that's all I have available this morning. But don't worry. He's an old gentle soul. Won't give you any trouble."

Indecision bound Samantha's hands into fists, and she forced them to relax. *Breathe.* "All right."

He smiled and turned inside the stables. She remained in place, trying not to fidget or retreat back to the boardinghouse to wait. She had to focus on the problem at hand. Where would Mary have taken her sisters? If the train was her plan, she would hide for a time before attempting to board. The trail to the falls would provide a temporary hiding place, but hopefully they would be wary after Samantha lost her way.

"I wish we could just go home," Mary had said.

Of course. Frank. The evacuation order had been lifted. Folks were allowed to return to their homes. Mary had heard the announcement at church.

Only, their home didn't exist anymore.

"Here you go, ma'am." The man led out a mammoth-like horse—or mule, judging from the ears.

Samantha shuffled back a step. "Oh."

"Like I said, he's a gentle soul and won't give you any trouble."

This animal was also the only way she would make it back to Frank. She breathed deeply—a horrible decision so close to the stable—and signed the paper extended to her before handing over the required deposit. The man tucked both into his coat pocket and stepped to offer Samantha a hand—more like a shove—into the saddle.

"There you are, ma'am. I hope you have a pleasant ride. I'll see you this afternoon."

Samantha managed a nod while she gathered the reins and pulled the animal's head around. A good thing the Stanford men were well on their way, as they would surely have more reason to mock now.

<hr>

"What do you mean the girls are *gone*?" Nathan bit out. He was halfway to Coleman to say goodbye, but seeing Charles cantering toward Frank had pulled him up short.

"I woke up this morning, and they were nowhere to be seen. How am I to know what happened?"

"Because you pushed them too far." Nathan encouraged his horse past, Coleman still his destination.

"Where are you going?" his brother shouted at him, but he didn't pause. With his brothers already searching the roads, the best use of his time was starting his investigation at the origin. Hopefully Mary had left clues behind.

As Red Rover raced down the road, all Nathan could think of was how this was all his fault. He should have spoken with Mary sooner, should have found a way to keep his promise to her. He'd failed her, Abby, and Lucy. He'd find them and figure out a way to set things right. Somehow.

The sight of a mule trotting down the road toward him, a woman holding on for dear life, slowed him, and he pulled Rover to a walk. "Samantha?"

Her face was flushed, and her eyes widened. She pulled back on the reins and jostled to a stop. "Nathan. Constable." Her words were breathy. "The girls are missing."

"I heard. I'm on my way back to Coleman to see what I can find."

She shook her head. "I don't think there is anything there. I'm sure

Mary took matters into her own hands. And how can we blame her? You were right. I should have accepted, and then this wouldn't have happened. It's my fault."

"No," Nathan shook his head, while trying to push down the hurt—why should it hurt? He'd proposed for the sake of the girls, so why should he be disappointed that they were the only reason she regretted turning him down? "They aren't your responsibility."

"Yet I feel so responsible." She pushed her spectacles higher on her pert nose. They acted as perfect frames for her large eyes.

"It's my fault more than anyone's, but it hardly matters right now. We need to find them before anything happens to them."

"What do you think could happen?"

That wasn't a question he wanted to answer. While he still believed most people were decent folks, he'd been in law enforcement too long to shrug off the possibilities. Never mind the weather. Even into May as they were, in the Canadian Rockies temperatures could still drop below freezing at night. Did they even have food or funds? "Let's just find them."

Samantha nodded and kicked her mule toward Blairmore and Frank. Nathan sat in indecision. He wanted to start at the boardinghouse in Coleman and make sure they hadn't just slipped out for a walk or to hide nearby, but Samantha seemed so certain in her direction, and she'd spent the most time with the girls. The only thing she looked nervous about was staying on the mule, and he would never forgive himself if anything happened to her.

Nathan reined his horse to keep pace beside her. "So where do you think Mary went and why?"

"I think she's trying to go home."

"They don't have a home."

Samantha looked at him out of the corner of her eye. "Not much of one. But. . .that's where I would have gone. If I could have."

He remained quiet, hoping she would expound. The thud of the horse's hooves against the well-packed road counted out the minutes.

"When my parents died, that's what I wanted more than anything. I wanted to go home, even though I hadn't been there in months. I wanted to curl up in my old bed and hide under my blankets, pretend everything could go back to the way it had been when I was younger."

"So you think Mary is making her way back to their cottage? Or what is left of it?"

"I think she will want to say goodbye to her life there, while she plans what to do next." Samantha sighed. "I could be wrong. Maybe she's just trying to put as much distance as possible between them and Coleman. Or maybe they slipped out to have a little bit longer together and say goodbye. She's been so withdrawn the past couple days, I don't know."

"I guess we won't know until we find them. But with Maddie waiting back at the boardinghouse in case they return and every other road being searched, we might as well follow your hunch. If they aren't there, we'll figure out the next step."

Samantha nodded before turning her full focus to the road and the beast that carried her. Her knuckles were white from her grip on the reins. She was a force to be reckoned with, this woman. And with each mile, despite being at her side, he mourned the loss of her.

Chapter 34

As Turtle Mountain came into view, Samantha's breath caught. The gaping scar disfigured its entire face. Below, the valley stretched out with a jagged blanket of pale stone. She couldn't help but recoil, the motion drawing her mount to a halt. Somehow it looked even wider and broader and more horrible than she remembered. Especially now with names etched in the rock by her mind's eye.

"It's safe," Nathan encouraged. "They wouldn't have lifted the evacuation otherwise." Yet even his voice carried doubt. "Let's find those girls."

Yes. The girls. They had to find the girls. Samantha forced the mule forward, grateful she didn't have to find strength in her own legs. The town of Frank opened up before her, the school perched so happily beside the church and overlooking the valley as though nothing had happened. Only, they remained empty. No children ran around the schoolyard or hurried across the field so as not to be late for class.

Dominion Avenue had little more activity. Despite permission to return, it seemed the only people interested were those with businesses to salvage. All the houses, hotels, and most of the shops gave the impression of a ghost town—perhaps the best description for what remained of Frank.

"It's still early. More will return," Nathan said.

"I don't know why anyone would want to," Samantha whispered. The thought of living under the shadow of the scarred mountain—with no way to wipe away the memory of those who had been killed—would be like living in a cemetery. Urgency grew to find the girls, so they wouldn't have to face this place alone.

Down Dominion Avenue past the bank and hotels, mercantile, and boardinghouse, to where Manitoba Avenue came into view. Samantha jerked the mule to a stop and slid to the ground. Her legs wobbled and her ankle protested, but she continued on foot, trusting that Nathan would manage the mule. She didn't have the strength nor confidence to deal with him now that she was on the ground. The crunch of a single pair of boots came alongside her, and she glanced to see that Nathan had tied both animals and left them behind.

"Are you all right?" he prodded.

"No." Not even a little. She was better equipped to deal with all this two weeks ago before she'd allowed her defenses to fall. Now it was like seeing the damage and desolation for the first time, and her heart thudded painfully against her ribs.

I can't do this.

Warmth slipped across her shoulders as Nathan's hand braced her. She wasn't alone. For the first time in as long as she could remember, she didn't have to face this alone.

You were not alone.

The water had receded, though Gold Stream still ran off course. The rocks heaped around the cottages—or what remained of them—had dried, caked dirt covering them, a reminder of the mud that night.

"Mary!" Nathan called. "Abby!"

Samantha pulled away to begin her climb over the rubble. Boards, limbs of trees, and cedar shakes from the roofs were littered among the limestones. The Stanford cottage, or at least the roof and attic, had been ripped from the rest of the house but had somehow stayed afloat on the river of rock.

You were not alone.

Be still, and know that I am God.

The thought followed her toward what could have easily been her end. Looking at it now, in the light of day, how could she question that God had some hand in preserving her life? She blinked hard and pressed forward. Now was not the time for breaking down into a pile of mush on the side of the slide. She kept walking, the uneven terrain forcing her to slow and pick her way closer, if only to spare her ankle from more serious injury.

"I don't think they're here," Nathan said from behind her. "There's nothing left for them here."

There was nothing left for her either, yet she felt the draw. . .to confront what had happened that night, to see where she had been pinned. She scaled the roof toward the gaping hole someone had ripped open. Nathan met her there and offered her a hand, as though already knowing her intent. He lowered her gently into the attic.

"Oh, God," she whispered, gratitude mingled with a dozen other emotions spanning the full spectrum. Awe. Fear. Lingering terror. Joy. And overwhelming sadness. She allowed herself to feel it all, both high and low as she took in what remained. The slivers of light through the cracked roof. The mangled bed frame. The mattress that had covered her, both holding her in place and saving her life. Broken glass from the frame that had held her parents' photo. A porcelain pitcher and basin spreading white shards across the floor, the small table they had sat on reduced to splinters.

Hushed voices trickled through the cracks in the thin wall as they had so often in the past.

Samantha's head snapped up, and Nathan met her gaze. She moved first, dropping down to crawl under a beam that had given way. The second bedroom had little more head room and less light, but enough to make out the three girls huddled together on what had been their bed. Relief stole Samantha's strength, but she managed to cross the floor and gather Abby and Lucy into her arms. She reached out to brush tangled hair back from Mary's tear-stained face, then pressed a kiss to her head. "Thank goodness, we found you. I've been worried sick."

"I'm sorry. But I won't let them take Abby and Lucy from me." Her eyes shifted to where Nathan crouched and her jaw set.

Samantha sank to the floor, and Abby climbed onto her lap to bury her face in Samantha's shoulder while she cried. Samantha couldn't help her own tears from falling while she swayed with the trembling child. Lucy cuddled in, watching on with interest, innocently unaware of what had happened here or why her sisters were upset.

"Mary," Nathan started, working his way to them. "I'm sorry. I tried." He opened his arms to her, but she remained in place, shaking her head.

"I won't go back. I won't let you take us back."

"Sweetheart...I can't let you stay here. You need a home. Your sisters need homes. There is only so much I can do. My hands are tied."

Guilt crept through Samantha. "Nathan." She waited until he looked at her, though she'd rather he didn't. She must look a sight with fresh tears on her face and her hair windblown from the ride here. But their agreement had nothing to do with attraction. "I accept. I'll help you with the girls, if you can convince your brothers to leave them with you."

Before Nathan could speak, Mary threw herself around his neck. "Oh, please, please keep us."

He looked helplessly at Samantha and her heart bled a little. "Are you sure?" he asked.

She managed to nod. It would only be for the summer. Surely she could keep herself together for that long. For Mary. For Abby who continued to cling to her. Yes. She could do it for the girls. It wasn't as though Nathan would always be around. His work would keep him busy, as would finding her replacement. All she had to do was manage not to fall completely in love, a slippery slope she already teetered on.

———◆◆———

Nathan wasn't sure whether to feel relief or panic as Samantha agreed to be his wife—for the sake of the girls. The victory was diminished by the understanding he would always be secondary. Even if she did eventually feel anything for him, the girls would always be the reason she'd consented. Her affection for them was evident in everything she did.

He *shouldn't* feel jealous, but there it was. Even now, she seemed to go out of her way to avoid him. She walked with Abby tucked against her side, Mary gripping her other hand. He followed with Lucy in his arms as they made their way toward the Frank Hotel. He hoped to find breakfast for the girls and figure out what to do from there. He would need to track down his brothers and convince them to leave the girls in his care.

A battle had been won, but the war still raged.

And if the war was won, he would spend the rest of his life as he had as a child—feeling unimportant and overlooked, but this time by his wife.

The hotel was open but so much quieter than two weeks earlier. Again, they were greeted by the raised brows of the proprietor. "We didn't expect anyone today, Constable. At least not so early. I'm afraid we planned on spending the day dusting and restocking the kitchen."

"We don't require a room, just a place to sit for a bit."

Samantha stepped beside him. "And something for the children to eat if you have anything available."

"Of course." The man waved them toward the dining room before disappearing into the kitchen.

Samantha situated the girls around a table and pulled a chair close to Abby so she could drape an arm across her shoulders—Abby, whose now dry eyes seemed so much more vibrant and aware of the world than he had seen them yet. It was as though the tears had cleared away the fog she had been hiding behind. Perhaps that was why Samantha's had seemed so dull when they had first met. He couldn't reconcile the vibrant woman across from him with the uptight schoolmarm of two weeks ago.

"Would you like me to wait with the girls while you speak with your brothers?"

Samantha's question focused Nathan's wandering thoughts. "Yes. My brothers." Probably an argument best not held in the presence of children. Though he wasn't sure he should leave Mary out of the discussion. "Let me think about it."

Samantha nodded and again turned her full attention to the girls. Making sure they were comfortable, fussing over their dresses and the fact that Abby's buttons didn't line up properly. Was this how their marriage would be? One of strict convenience and not affection? He wasn't sure he could do it. He hadn't acknowledged as much, even to himself, but he wanted to be loved. Really *loved*. To be seen for who he was and loved for who he was.

"My wife will bring out some flapjacks in a few minutes." The proprietor set a pot of coffee on the table along with two cups. "She has sausages as well, though they will take a little longer to prepare."

"Of course. Thank you." Nathan poured a steaming cup of the dark liquid and breathed deeply. He wouldn't think of the future Mrs. Stanford. It would just distract him from the tasks at hand. He took a sip and felt the scald on his tongue. "You're right. I'll return your mule and track down my brothers. We'll bring a wagon for you and then settle everything in Coleman." None of them wanted to linger under the mountain longer than needed.

"Very well." Samantha still didn't look at him, and he struggled not to swear under his breath. Instead, he took his leave, but paused on the street, then fished his notebook out of his pocket.

> *Samantha has agreed to marry me. I will count this*
> *a miracle if only for the sake of the girls. Who knows,*
> *perhaps someday she will come to love me too.*

He groaned, wishing for an eraser. All he could do was scratch a line through it, then another and another. He shoved the notebook in his pocket and hurried to where the animals waited at the end of Dominion Avenue. He had his boot in the first stirrup when he heard Charles's call.

"Anything?"

Nathan bit back a curse. He wasn't in the right frame of mind for an argument. He'd hoped for a hard ride to clear his head. Swinging up on his horse, he faced his older brother. "Yeah. We found them."

Charles cocked his head, his eyes falling on the mule. "We?"

"Miss Ingles knew where they would be."

Charles scoffed. "She lied to us this morning, sending us on a wild goose chase?"

"She didn't lie. She had a hunch. She knows the girls." And would be exactly what they needed in a mother. He had no choice but to press forward. "She has them at the hotel eating breakfast."

Charles glanced up and down the street. "Which hotel? I don't trust her with them."

"Don't trust her? She's the best thing for those girls. They need her. So let them be. They have been through enough and can use a few minutes of peace." As could he, though he wouldn't hold his breath.

"There isn't time for that. The train will be leaving Coleman just after noon. We need to get them back and arrange everything." He grumbled something under his breath about hoping that Brent had had the sense to turn back already.

"You still think you can pack them up like cattle and haul them off with no concern for what they have been though and what they want? They need each other."

Charles swore. "Give it up, Nate. This is hard enough for everyone already."

"If it's too inconvenient for you, you give it up. Leave without Lucy."

"That's not happening. Maddie's already attached to the baby. She has her heart set on it."

"This isn't about Maddie. This is about what is best for the girls. What Peter and Rosemary would have wanted for them."

"It's not about you either." Charles threw up his hands, startling his horse to shift under him. "Peter would want them to have homes."

"A home. He would want them together."

"We've been through this. Will even told me about your attempt to woo the schoolmarm. He said she declined your proposal, so you are hardly in the position to argue."

"She said yes." Nathan cut in. "She said she'd marry me."

Charles sank back. "What?"

"Samantha has agreed to marry me. I want the girls—all three of them. I will do whatever it takes to raise them like Peter and Rosemary would want. Because you're right. It's not about you or me. This is about Peter and Rosemary and their daughters. If you're willing to take their daughters and give them a home *together*, then maybe we have something to talk about."

Charles stared. "You're serious. You're willing to sacrifice your freedom and career."

"Yes." He just didn't want to consider how much it truly would cost him.

Chapter 35

Samantha didn't feel like she could take a full breath until they had reached Blairmore, with Turtle Mountain no longer in sight. Though Nathan had intended her to ride on the seat of the wagon next to him, Samantha opted to stay in the back with the girls. Abby was still clingy, though a little more talkative now, commenting on the river and a herd of mountain sheep they spotted on a nearby slope. Mary had taken her place as the somber one, no doubt braced to face her aunts and uncles who would be livid from her disappearance that morning and held her future in their hands.

Nathan hadn't said much on the matter. Only that no one was boarding a train today, and conversations were needed before they proceeded. Samantha would gladly tuck herself away with the girls and not face the Stanford brothers or their oh-so-perfect wives.

They arrived in Coleman far too quickly for Samantha's liking and pulled up to the boardinghouse. Nathan was there to assist Samantha down from the back of the wagon and then unload the girls. Charles and Brent appeared in the doorway, with Will farther behind them.

"Why don't you take the girls into the dining room?" Nathan suggested.

Samantha took Abby's hand. "I wonder if they have any fresh apple pie."

Nathan's hand braced her elbow while he leaned in close. "I knew you'd want more."

She couldn't help the twitch of a smile but made no reply—not under the scrutiny of his brothers. The brothers shifted out of the way as Nathan led her in and directed her to the right, where a large man with heavy beard blocked the way, too busy in his discussion with the pretty blond.

"But do you know where she went?" The man sounded almost frantic.

"It would hardly be couth to interrogate our guests when they leave," the woman protested. "I'm sorry, Mr. Morgan."

"Morgan?" Samantha and Nathan said in unison. They glanced at each other.

"Are you Ned Morgan?" Nathan questioned.

Samantha almost laughed at the look of uncertainty on the man's expression as he eyed Nathan's red uniform. "Yes."

Nathan smiled, the first real one Samantha had seen in days.

"You're alive," Samantha breathed, hitching Lucy higher on her hip. "You didn't stay the night of the slide at the Graham Ranch?"

Morgan's brows arched in surprise. "No. I considered it but felt uneasy about staying out there. I had some horses back in Frank, so I figured I should head back there. Spent the night camped just north of Frank."

And just out of the path of the slide. "Your wife was so worried when you didn't return after the slide, she came looking for you."

"So you *did* meet my wife? She would have found me faster if she'd stayed home. I hung out near Frank to help with rescues until everyone was evacuated, then figured I should head home. Course, she wasn't there by then, and seems we've been just missing each other since."

Samantha felt a laugh bubble in her chest. "She'll be so happy and so relieved."

Ned Morgan speared her with a look. "Then you know where she's headed?"

"Home. She said it was time to go home."

Ned's shoulders sagged as though released from supporting a huge weight. "Yes, it is. Thank you, ma'am." He tipped his hat and slipped past them.

Samantha led the girls into the dining room, very aware of Nathan following, notebook in hand. He paused at a table and pulled a pencil from his pocket to scribble something down.

"What are you writing?"

He finished before answering. The book snapped closed. "Miracles."

"Miracles?"

Nathan shrugged as though it were nothing unusual. "They've been hard to ignore."

She stared at him. "What are you talking about? You mean like Mr. Morgan being alive? That's a miracle?" She shook her head, but could it be so simple?

"I think his wife would say so."

Samantha opened her mouth but closed it just as quickly. She didn't want to discuss God or faith with his brothers flanking him. She got the girls situated at a table, very aware of the eyes on her.

Charles spoke first. "I'd like to know how Miss Ingles really feels about this arrangement you've roped her into. She doesn't strike me as the kind who's made marriage a priority."

Marriage? The word pinged around in her brain but wasn't quite vocalized.

"Or maybe that's the only reason she'd set her sights on Nate here?" The other brother suggested. "Desperate to leave spinsterhood behind?"

Samantha twisted to face them. "Excuse me?" This had nothing to do with marriage. Why would they mock her like this? She was so tired of men like them.

"Shut up, Brent." Nathan grabbed his shoulder to tug him away. "She's the one who deserves better than me." He glanced back at her. There was something hard in his gaze.

"How dare you?" Samantha had heard enough. Felt enough. She refused to be mocked—especially by Nathan. It cut far too deeply. She gently pushed Lucy into his arms and stalked past, unable to meet his gaze as her face flamed. She heard someone's surprised laughter. Had that been Nathan too? She couldn't bear to know the truth. She ran up the stairs, cursing her sore foot as she went. If only the thing would finish healing and leave her in peace!

The door to her room closed behind her with a bang, and her breath came in jagged spurts. She couldn't do it, couldn't face him again, knowing how he truly felt about her. Not even as a friend. He was just like so many other men, who found sport in mocking the homely spinster, or mousy schoolmarm. She'd heard it all, but it had never hurt so much. The worst part was that the girls would suffer because of it.

◆◆◆

Nathan jostled Lucy, everything in him wanting to grip Brent by the collar and shove him into the closest wall. "How haven't you learned to keep your mouth shut?" Remarks like that had been bad enough when they'd been kids, but in Samantha's presence they were purely cruel.

"Sorry," Brent jerked away. "I was joking. I meant it more against you than her. Though, really, Nate, she's not the kind of woman I pictured you with."

"What, someone who is intelligent and good? Who's dedicated her life to bettering others?" Nathan handed Lucy off to Charles, done wasting his breath on his brothers. He needed to find Samantha and set things to rights. It was her reaction to him that clenched his stomach. He'd hurt her, and he wasn't sure how.

Maddie and Beth stood at the top of the stairs, intrigue in their eyes as he walked past. When he took no pause to answer their questions, they headed downstairs. Good, they could interrogate their husbands and leave him be. He paused in front of Samantha's door and tapped lightly.

No answer.

"Samantha, please. We need to talk." He needed to apologize for his family and his own part in it. Whatever it took. For the girls. He knocked a little harder.

"Go away." He couldn't tell if it was the muffle of the door or if she was crying.

"I can't do that. Please open the door."

Silence. He leaned his head against the door. Strange how a day ago, he wasn't certain of marrying her, and now his greatest fear was losing her. He fell forward as the door swung open, and he stumbled into the room.

Samantha gasped and lunged out of the way.

"Sorry. I. . ." Nathan's words died. Her cheeks were dry, but her eyes wore a sheen of moisture and her nose was tinged with red. "Samantha."

"I believe it would be more appropriate if you called me *Miss Ingles*. I have given it some thought, and I will still agree to nanny for the sake of the girls. But we will keep it professional. You are the employer, and you will find someone to replace me as soon as possible."

"Replace you? I don't want anyone else." Nathan tried to sort through what she was saying. "And I don't want a nanny for the girls. I meant my proposal."

"You proposed I help you with the girls as a nanny. So I don't understand why you and your brothers felt the need to tease—"

"I proposed marriage, Samantha. And I am just as angry at my brothers. Their behavior is unacceptable, and I would gladly pummel them if it didn't go against this uniform and my duty to the law."

Her brow crinkled. "Why are you still mocking me? I thought you were different. I know I'm not pretty or gentle or anything that a man would want in a wife." A tear trickled down her cheek. "But. . ." She shook her head and turned away. "Please just go."

His boots remained rooted in place though he couldn't understand what had gone so horribly wrong. "I would never mock you, Samantha. Please believe me. I care for you, I really do. I guess I could have been clearer when we talked about the girls, but I wasn't asking you to work for me. I—I did. . . I *do* want you to be my wife."

"What?" Her hands pressed to her cheeks.

"I don't want this to be the end of our story."

"Why? Seems somewhat appropriate." She left off there, but he could hear what she left unsaid.

"Short and tragic? You said you don't like those stories."

"The mountain has already crumbled. People have died. It is a tragedy."

Nathan shook his head, while pulling the notebook from his pocket. "Yes, it started that way, and there is nothing we can do to change that. I lost my brother and buried his wife and sons along with so many others. But that isn't the whole story of Frank, and you know it."

"I have a hard time believing in miracles. I just want to be left alone. I'm so confused."

Again, he'd been dismissed. And he had little left to argue. Nathan walked past her and set the notebook on the small table between the beds. He turned back to her and stopped. He touched her shoulder. Brushed a strand of hair from her cheek along with a trail of moisture. "I do believe in miracles." He couldn't help his gaze from falling to her mouth. Couldn't help brushing his own lips against hers. Just once. A last attempt to tell her he was sorry. Only this felt nothing like an apology, and it was far too difficult to pull away.

Nathan made it to the hall and pulled the door closed behind him, leaving her in peace as she'd requested. He filled his lungs. Somehow the air still smelled like her. All he could do was hold on to the hope she would find a way to forgive him for every misunderstanding, all of his mistakes. And for his family.

Because he really, *really* didn't want that to be their last kiss.

Chapter 36

If only Samantha could trust him. Her heart hammered in her chest at a truly unhealthy rate. It would not surprise her if she keeled over right where she stood. He'd kissed her. Not more than a breath of a kiss, but it had reached every fiber of her, right to her toes. How was that possible?

He couldn't have meant it. Not the kiss. Not the proposal. Well, perhaps the proposal—he wanted the girls to have a home together. But not the kiss. They hardly knew each other. *And*, he hadn't cared a whit about her half of that time. If anything, he'd disliked her.

Samantha eyed the notebook he'd left on the table. Miracles, he'd said? She sat on the edge of the bed and flipped through the pages. Most were blank. Several had information jotted down that seemed disconnected from anything—random names and dates. Probably notes for who knew what.

Then she found it, nestled in the heart of the book. A list.

> *Miracles of Frank:*
> *Abby and Mary were saved, protected by the way*
> *the roof was ripped from the rest of the house.*

Her heart squeezed at how closely the girls had come to dying, and she with them.

*Baby Lucy was thrown from the house (onto a bale
of straw according to the accounts). How could that
be possible if not for God's intervention? And where
did the straw even come from, if not from God?*

That did seem difficult to argue with. Some figured the straw had
been carried from the livery a half mile away. If the baby landed on the
rock, her poor little body would have been broken.

*Seventeen miners trapped but alive were able to dig themselves
to safety just before they lost needed air and strength.
    Lillian Clark, the lone survivor of her family
because she spent her first night away from
home at the boardinghouse she worked at.*

Yes, but the rest of her family had been killed. How could one balance
tragedy with miracle? Was God's hand in it all?

*The Chestnut brothers had to spend an extra
night at a hotel instead of moving into their
cottage which was destroyed by the slide.*

A miracle for them, but what of the three men who had remained in
the cottage when it was destroyed? Samantha groaned. This was getting
her nowhere. She snapped the book closed and stood to pace the floor.
The book stared up at her from the edge of the bed, begging not to be
ignored. *Fine!* She'd read a little bit further.

*The railway work crew that survived because they arrived in
Frank a day late. A hundred and twenty-eight men spared.
They waited that night in railway cars near Morrissey,
BC, but the freight train that was supposed to transport
them forgot to pick them up. They arrived late on the 30ᵗʰ.*

Samantha hadn't heard of that account. A frustrating mistake that
saved lives?

*Sid Choquette and the others on the engine at the mine
that night being able to race the slide to safety, and then for*

*Sid to be able to cross over a mile of rock, even while more
fell, to flag down the Spokane Flyer before it hit the slide.
How many people were spared because the train did not
arrive any earlier and Sid was able to make it to them?*

Samantha closed her eyes, for a moment picturing Nathan that rainy morning when he'd told her about Sid and the passenger train. How had so much changed between them in such a short time? But was it enough? She forced her eyes open and focused on the black ink spilling across the page with such wonders. But were these miracles? Had God truly interceded?

*The Ennis family. The whole family somehow survived
despite their house being in the way of the slide. Their
home was heaped upon by rocks, but despite injuries, all
family members are recovering. Including baby Gladys
who was thrown into mud and was assumed dead.*

*Three-year-old Fernie Watkins was found
lying in the rocks unharmed. Her family survived
despite their house being destroyed.*

*The Bansemer family, their house was moved by the slide,
pushed from its foundation, and the whole family survived.*

He had underlined *pushed from its foundation* several times as though even he struggled to believe the account. Her chest tightened. These were people she knew, children she had taught. And she'd seen their cottages. How easy it would have been for more to have died.

*Decades of buried grief were finally released. Maybe Miss Ingles
really is what Mary and Abby need. Who would have thought?*

Samantha rolled her bottom lip through her teeth. He saw that as a miracle?

*Miss Ingles has agreed to stay with the girls.
They have a little more time before their world
is upended again. Perhaps a little miracle.*

Apple Pie.

Abby's voice and Mary's laughter.

More tears rolled down her cheeks. Oh that they would leave her vision clear to continue reading.

> *Perfect days and memories made. I wonder if Peter*
> *sensed he was almost out of time with his family.*

Samantha couldn't regret her own memories made with Nathan and the girls. She couldn't help but treasure some of the simplest moments— like ones with apple pie.

> *Finding Samantha on the mountain. I may*
> *have found a little bit of myself there too.*

Her breathing slowed. What did he mean by that? Could he be truly earnest in his words to her a few minutes ago? And in that kiss? Dare she believe? In *miracles?*

> *God not only preserved Samantha's life but allowed*
> *her to stay and help me with the girls. They have*
> *needed her more than I was ready to admit.*

There was a scribbled-out sentence next, and Samantha skipped down the page.

> *Ned Morgan, assumed dead in the slide,*
> *will soon be reunited with his wife.*

Samantha laid the book on her lap, though the words remained clear in her thoughts. Yes, horrible things had happened in the Crowsnest Valley, but most folks in Frank remained unharmed, and far more than should have been, including herself.

She looked back at the scratched-out sentence, making out all the words she could until she finally pieced the lines together. . .

She needed a pencil. A brief search brought one to her hand, and she added lines of her own.

> *The Thornley siblings choose to spend the evening in the Frank*
> *hotel, safe from harm when the rocks crushed the shoe shop.*
> *Lester Johnson survived the destruction of his home,*
> *pinned under the floor, though he doesn't remember*

how he came to be there. He was able to find an escape
through the rocks and despite injury, made it to help.

She continued writing, filling two more pages. Miracles she could no longer refute, from a God she could no longer ignore. If only He could clear away the confusion and fear still clenching her chest at the thought of moving forward.

———◆••———

The dining room door was open, and he could see his brothers and their wives seated with the girls at a table, extra chairs pulled in close, but he couldn't bring himself to face them yet. He escaped outside and started to walk, though hardly caring about direction. All he could think about was what a mess he had made of things, the image of Samantha's tears like a punch to the gut, even while the memory of their brief kiss stirred his soul, waking him to possibilities. Possibilities like walking back upstairs and kissing her properly.

"Fool."

He probably shouldn't have kissed her at all. She probably wouldn't want anything to do with him now after his blotched proposal. Looking back, he could kick himself. He never had voiced the part about marriage, had he? No wonder she'd assumed he merely wished to hire her to help with the girls.

"Idiot."

Nathan found himself alongside the Old Man River and sank to a rock near the bank. A shadow appeared beside him, and a moment later Will sat beside him, stretching out his legs and crossing his ankles. "Brent and Charles plan to make their apologies to Miss Ingles."

"Good." Though Nathan doubted it would do much good to mend the damage done.

"It was you they were trying to get at."

"Of course." His brothers had always taken pleasure in needling him on everything from looks as an awkward youth to the fact his best friend had chosen his brother over him. Was it any wonder he had wanted to leave home as soon as he was able? At least in the past, their teasing had only affected *him*—not someone he cared about.

"I talked to them about the girls, told them I agreed with you. We should stop thinking about what's most convenient for us but what is best for the girls. We owe that to Peter."

Nathan managed a nod. Good, one of them was more able to give the girls a home and family. His promise to Mary would be satisfied, and he could continue on as a bachelor, his focus where it should be—maintaining the law in the Alberta district of the Northwest Territories.

"Do you think Miss Ingles will still have you?"

Nathan pulled his hat from his head and dropped it to the ground beside him. This rock was growing more and more uncomfortable by the minute. "The truth of it? I don't think she ever wanted me." Had anyone ever? He'd always been just one more mouth to feed, one more child to discipline. Even now, he was just another constable on the force—one more uniform to order around.

Maybe he was wrong about wanting what was best for the girls. Maybe he had just liked the idea of meaning something more to someone. Mary had looked to him as though he were the only one who she could truly depend on. Or at least she had, until Samantha had stood at his side, and then she'd looked to both of them—but that had been okay.

Nathan shook his head and tried to shift the direction of his thoughts. "So what have they decided? I'm sure Charles has it all planned again by now."

"Nope." Will twitched a smile. "He's at a loss of how to proceed without you. Both he and Brent have agreed to not fight you so long as you marry."

A surge of triumph died a quick death. "So they ruin my chances of marrying Samantha and then agree to it?" He had some choice words for his brothers—ones that were better swallowed. "Great."

"So what are you sitting sulking for? Go win her back. Convince her you love her." He gave Nathan a slap on the back before pushing to his feet. "I'm sure she'll come around. I hear women can't resist a man in a uniform." He picked up Nathan's flat-brimmed Stetson and pushed it back in his hand. "If that is what you want."

"What I want?"

"Charles and Brent are idiots, but I've seen the way you look at her."

"We haven't known each other that long." A couple of highly stressful weeks. Hardly the best circumstances for forming a lasting relationship.

"But you have known each other in extremities, and obviously at your worst." Will gave a smile and started away. "Love is a choice."

Nathan sat for a while longer, watching the water flow past him, hastening downstream toward Frank, unaware of the direction it would take or the obstacles it would have to work around.

Chapter 37

Samantha would have been content to remain in her room for the rest of the day and avoid facing anyone but for the gnawing need to speak with Nathan, to resolve their misunderstanding and plans for the girls once and for all.

She splashed cold water over her face, until there was no sign of tears, then set about doing her hair—first, in her usual tight bun, before catching her reflection in the mirror. The uptight schoolmarm had returned. Samantha pulled the pins and let her long locks fall down her back. But that wasn't quite right either—too informal for the discussion that would need to be had. Plus, it looked like she was trying too hard to garner Nathan's attention. His brothers would see right through her.

Samantha pulled up the sides of her hair and twisted them into a soft bun, while allowing the back to flow. Probably still too relaxed, but she was done overthinking it. She wet her lips and pinched her cheeks, then pulled her spectacles from her nose. The world blurred. While it might improve her appearance, she needed to see Nathan's reactions. The spectacles had to stay.

"What am I doing?" she pressed her hands over her stomach but couldn't stay the fluttering within. No, not fluttering. She was nauseous with nerves. And a sip of tepid water did nothing for it.

Better to just get this over with. She picked up Nathan's notebook and headed down the stairs. The dining room was loud with chatter, and she peeked through the door, catching Charles's eye. He shifted in his seat, while everyone else continued their conversation. Nathan's scarlet coat was nowhere to be seen, so at least she didn't have to confront his family. Yet.

Samantha turned away before anyone else could notice her and pulled the door open to escape outside, stepping into a solid wall. His hands kept her from crashing into his chest or stumbling backward.

"Samantha."

She looked up with hopes of seeing Nathan, but it was his younger brother standing there. She pulled back. "I'm so sorry!"

"Think nothing of it." He released her arms. "You seem in a hurry."

"Yes, I was hoping to find Nathan." At a loss of what to say, she held up the notebook. "I need to return this to him."

"Of course." The corners of his mouth turned upward. "Why don't I take you to him?"

She shook her head. The last thing their conversation needed was an audience. "If you just point me in the right direction."

"It might be a bit of a walk," Will protested. "He headed to the Blairmore cemetery."

"Oh." That would be too far for her to walk.

"I'll be right back."

Before she could say anything more, he started off at a jog toward the livery. Samantha blew out her breath, tempted to retreat to her room. But no, there were things needing to be said. Will returned surprisingly quickly with a small buggy and the mule she had ridden that morning. The mule looked much more comfortable in his current position, though he gave her a sidelong glance as Will helped her up on the seat. She clenched the book, trying to sort through her jumbled thoughts and rehearse what she would say to Nathan.

"What's the book?" Will asked as the buggy jostled toward Blairmore.

"Just some thoughts Nathan wrote down. About the slide."

He nodded. "Losing Peter has been really hard on him."

"I'm sure it's been difficult for all of you."

"Yeah, but it's different for Nate. I was quite a bit younger, and tagged along, but didn't have the same relationship. They were best friends. And then there was Rosemary. I think her death has hit him doubly hard."

"He told me they were close friends." *With a hope of something more*, wasn't that how he worded it? A lie. He'd loved her. Of course her death would be difficult even so many years later. All this time, Samantha had pictured him mourning mainly for his brother, but maybe that wasn't the case.

Be still.

It was hard to heed the thought as Will continued talking, sharing stories from their childhood, his focus on Nathan and Peter, but Rosemary was there as well, lurking in the sidelines and slowly inserting herself between the two brothers.

Samantha didn't realize how truly affected she was until they reached the small cemetery, and she saw Nathan standing over Rosemary Stanford's grave, wiping tears from his eyes. The image burned into her, and she felt her own tears swell.

"I can't do it." She couldn't spend her life competing with the memory of that woman. She would never be as beautiful, as kind, as good a homemaker, or mother. If she accepted Nathan's proposal, Samantha would always live in Rosemary's shadow, trying to raise her daughters, trying to win Nathan's heart away from a ghost.

"Can't what?" Will asked.

As though she would tell him the truth. "I can't impose. Nathan needs time to say goodbye properly. It's better we leave." Now, before he noticed them. "Please."

Will stared at her for a moment longer before nodding and directing the buggy past. They looped through town, before heading back to Coleman. Silence hung uncomfortably between them. In the distance a train sounded its whistle.

"That can't be right. The train was supposed to be through here over an hour ago."

Will nodded. "Fellow at livery was talking about that. Seems there were some delays and it's running late."

Samantha leaned forward in her seat, a quick calculation sending a shiver through her. They were close enough—she'd have time to grab her things and make it to the station. No awkward or long goodbyes. No holding on to unrealistic hopes or allowing herself to rethink her decision. Another miracle perhaps?

———◆•◆———

"She's gone?" Nathan couldn't help but repeat himself, couldn't really believe it to be true. His throat felt like it was swelling, making it hard to swallow as he clutched his notebook that Will had handed him with the news. "What did she say?"

"Not much. Just asked me to say goodbye to the girls for her, tell them she was sorry she didn't have time to say it herself. Then she asked me to give you this book and tell you thank you."

"Thank you?" For what? For putting his heart out on a limb again only to have it fall out from under him? For making a fool of himself in front of her and his brothers? Oh, what a fool he was! He clung to the anger as it was more welcome than the hurt and loneliness swelling beneath it.

"She didn't elaborate, and her request caught me off guard. One moment we're on our way to find you because she had something to say, and next thing I know she's asking me to drive her to the station."

Nathan's head came up, and he shoved the notebook into his pocket. "You were bringing her to find me?"

"Made it as far as the cemetery, but then she changed her mind. Said she didn't want to bother you." Will shrugged, though he appeared contrite. "Maybe she'd always been planning to say goodbye."

"It would have been nice to hear it in person." He let the air from his lungs and felt his shoulders slump as well. Samantha was gone. He wasn't sure what to do with that, or the fact everything was slipping out of his control. Her retreat was an obvious answer to his proposal, which meant he had nothing to offer the girls—he had failed Mary and her sisters yet again. They would be separated, and there was nothing he could do about it. Samantha could have at least said goodbye in person.

"I'm sorry, Nate. I know you were trying to make things work."

"Yeah, well..." There was nothing for it now. He needed to face Mary and Abby and let them know he couldn't keep them. Charles would be happy about it—no one challenging his perfect plan. He wasn't sure which bothered him the most.

"Everyone already knows," Will supplied as they approached the boardinghouse. "Figured I could spare you having to tell everyone."

"Thanks." That was a bit of a relief, but still his feet dragged. "Don't suppose I can ride off and leave you to break the news?"

Will slowed. "Like you did last time?" His tone bordered on accusatory.

Nathan looked at his little brother, remembering him as he had been, an eleven-year-old boy who had once tailed Nathan and Peter around wherever he could despite the gaps in their ages. The only reason Will had earned a goodbye was because he'd seen Nathan sneaking out and had wanted to go too. Instead, Nathan had given him instructions on what to tell the family when they realized he was gone.

"Those girls, Mary especially, deserve more from you."

"I know." It wasn't just about him this time. Looking at the hurt in his brother's eyes, he realized that maybe it hadn't been back then either. He'd left and hardly looked back, leaving others to miss him and worry about him. "I'm sorry."

Will paused and faced him. Then nodded. "I have a lot going on right now with the new baby, but maybe later in the summer I could come out for a few days and visit. If Laura's up to the trip, I'd love for her to meet you."

"I'd like that. Or I could come out to see you at some point. Might be easier than making the trip with the babies." His chest felt strangely lighter as his brother's face brightened.

"That'd be great."

The next thought returned the frown to Nathan's face. "I should probably come visit Mary anyway."

Will nodded, his own expression falling. "I wish it could be different."

Nathan clapped him on the shoulder and started walking again. "You've done what you can." They both had. All he could do now was say goodbye and pray the girls would adjust well to their new homes.

Chapter 38

JUNE 1ST

Nathan climbed the steep stairs to the southwest lookout tower of Fort MacLeod as he had often done over the past couple of weeks. Somewhere to be alone as he looked to the west and the distant mountains. The view still left him feeling gutted, but for some reason he kept returning.

Leaning against the thick log wall, Nathan drew his hat from his head. He'd received word from Will earlier that week. Mary was faring as well as could be expected. She was a wonderful help with the toddlers but still cried herself to sleep. His other brothers had not been so quick to reply to Nathan's letter asking about each of the girls. He could only pray all was well with them.

Footsteps up the stairs made Nathan cringe. He straightened away from the wall and shoved his hat back on his head.

"I thought I saw you headed this way," Constable Hardy said. "You've been quite elusive since we've returned."

"Just busy." And ready to make himself scarce once again.

"Eating your meals by yourself? Begging every assignment that comes up?" Hardy frowned. "Are you sure you're ready to be back here?"

"Of course." Mostly because there was nowhere else for him to be.

"Inspector Primrose had already approved a leave of absence if you require it."

Nathan stiffened at the thought of losing his uniform and the distractions provided while on duty. "I'm fine where I am."

Hardy nodded, though didn't appear convinced. "We heard more news out of Frank."

Nathan's head came up.

"They've opened the mine again and have been busy clearing out the old shafts. Found one of the mine's mules, alive."

"Alive? In the back of the mine?" How was that possible?

"He somehow survived the past month eating his bridle and gnawing on wood from the sounds of it. They got him out and have been feeding him. Charlie. Guess that's his name."

"That's incredible." The poor animal. To survive so long in the back of a mine. Nothing short of a miracle. As soon as Constable Hardy started back down the stairs, Nathan reached for his notebook. He'd used it over the past couple of weeks, but this was the first time turning back to his list of miracles since Will had returned it to him. He stared at the gentle flow of handwriting that continued where his blockier style left off.

> *The Thornley siblings choose to spend the evening in the Frank hotel, safe from harm when the rocks crushed the shoe shop.*

Samantha. She must have added to his list. He hadn't even heard about the Thornleys. Or Lester Johnson. . .

> *Survived the destruction of his home, pinned under the floor, though he doesn't remember how he came to be there. He was able to find an escape through the rocks and despite injury, made it to help.*

He continued reading, his heart beating harder with each line.

> *Clothes for the girls and myself supplied by Miss Thornley.*
> *A place to stay and a purpose while*
> *I figured out what to do next.*

The photo of my parents recovered from
what remained of the cottage.

Strong arms offering support when I needed it most. I
never realized how much it helps to have someone at your
side, hearing your pain and offering comfort. That day in
the woods was the first time I wasn't left to cry alone.

Nathan clenched his jaw against a sudden surge of emotion as he remembered holding Samantha for the first time while her tears warmed his shoulder. He continued down the list, each line just making him miss her more. Toward the end he found the lone sentence—

A proposal of marriage from a man I could very easily love.

He stared at the words, hope battling against reality. Why then, *why* had she left him?

Nathan read the list again, searching for some clue as to why she would leave without even saying goodbye. Nothing. Frustration surged, and he snapped the book closed. He couldn't live like this, not knowing, not when everything he read pointed to her sharing at least some of his affection. Nathan paced the small tower, thoughts churning, heart pounding. If he went after her, it would no longer be about the girls and providing a home for them. It would be simply her and him and whatever future they built for themselves.

A future? A real marriage? Was it worth the risk of more rejection?

Nathan looked again to the mountains in the west, and his breath slowed at the thought of Peter on the top of the mine, probably enjoying a sandwich Rosemary had prepared for him while he visited with his friends, laughing about his kids' antics. Life was a risk, with no guarantee of how much of it you'd get.

Don't waste it.

He could almost hear Peter and Rosemary chiding him, encouraging him not to linger in this rut of his own making but to pursue what really mattered. Like picnics in the mountains and apple pie.

———— ◆◆ ————

JUNE 10ᵀᴴ

Samantha set the novel aside and stretched her neck, stiff from hours of reading. She reached for her tea but then thought better of it. Though half a cup remained, it was no doubt cold after being forgotten for the past hour. Probably well past time to step out of the house to stretch her legs. She quite enjoyed the bustling activity of Calgary in the spring, and a walk along the river with some breadcrumbs for the geese might be exactly what she needed.

After donning her fitted forest green jacket and pinning her hat in place, Samantha paused in front of the hall mirror. It was strange to hardly recognize herself yet spark memories of her mother. The plainly dressed schoolmarm was almost entirely absent now, replaced by a fashionable society miss.

She startled at a sudden knocking at the front door. Mrs. Nash's footsteps came from the kitchen, but Samantha waved her housekeeper back. She was capable of answering the door. With one final glance to make sure she was presentable, Samantha pulled open the door. A sharp intake of breath sent her into a coughing fit.

"Are you all right?" Nathan hurried to pat her back.

"Fine," she gasped and tried to clear her throat. "I just breathed wrong."

"Breathed wrong?" He stepped back, and a smile pulled at his lips. "You haven't been sick or an—"

"No, no. I'm as healthy as can be." She dared to meet his gaze, very aware of her pounding heart. *Be still.* "Just surprised."

He shrugged, his brown tweed coat tightening across his shoulders, his blue eyes searching hers. "Mounties are known for finding who they're looking for."

"I guess I didn't expect you to be looking for *me*." Not now that she served no purpose for him. The girls would all be settled in their new homes. None of them needed her anymore. She bit the inside of her cheek to keep her emotions checked.

"I didn't expect you to disappear without so much as a goodbye."

It had seemed like such a good idea until the train had pulled away from Coleman, but she was left with hours—weeks—of questioning her hasty decision. Regret still kept her awake long after she tucked herself into bed each night.

"I want to know why."

"Why?" Samantha's heart thudded painfully as all the reasons awakened in her mind. Dare she be so honest with him? She glanced back into the house where Mrs. Nash looked on like a protective watchdog, then back at Nathan. "Why don't we walk? I was just about to step out."

"Of course. I wouldn't want to disturb your employer."

Samantha couldn't help the chuckle that bubbled up. "I am not currently employed. In fact, I've decided to take some time away from teaching." Time to pause and rediscover herself and what she wanted from life.

He motioned toward the elegant, two-story brick home. "Who have you been staying with?"

"No one. This is my house." Though it still seemed strange to admit to it. "My parents purchased the property before their deaths but had never lived here. I'm not sure they actually planned to settle in Calgary, as my mother was not fond of prairie winters, but I like it. For now, it fits my needs."

Nathan looked back at the house and then studied her openly. "It's only been a couple of weeks, but you seem a completely different person."

Samantha couldn't help but straighten her spectacles. "We hardly know each other. I hardly know myself." She steeled herself to broach the subject that lingered between them like a sore thumb. "How could we possibly build a marriage on two weeks of acquaintanceship?"

"That is why you left?" He seemed strangely encouraged.

"One of the reasons." She felt her chest deflate. "As much as I care for those girls, we would be committing to a lifetime, even though they would only need us for a few years of that. Mary is almost thirteen. In another five or six years, she would be gone from our home, but you would be stuck with me for the next fifty."

"It might not have been so horrible."

"Or it might have been torture for you. You should be with a woman you are at least attracted to, but preferably someone you can love." Someone more like Rosemary, but Samantha could never voice that out loud.

Nathan faced her fully. "I am attracted to you. And I believe I could come to love you if you give me a chance."

She stared, though her pesky thoughts seemed determined to dwell on their brief kiss a month earlier.

"When you talk about our hypothetical future, you only mention *my* potential misery. What about you? Would you also be miserable?"

No. . .and yes. She started walking again. "What happened at Frank, with the slide, with coming so close to death and then watching the girls face something so similar to my own past. . . I'm not who I was April twenty-eighth. A little over a month has passed, and I am still trying to figure out who I am now and what I want." She'd finally allowed herself to access the inheritance her parents had left, including this house. There were decisions with the estate she had put off making for more than a decade, avoiding them even after she had come of age.

"What do you want, Samantha?"

She looked up at him, her heart in her throat. *That* was what she wanted—her name on someone's lips. "I want to matter to someone."

Nathan stood silent, staring at her, his eyes glistening. Time seemed to pause, though she was aware the world continued without them. "You do," Nathan whispered hoarsely. "You do matter. To me."

A tear trickled down her cheek.

"I think I already love you."

More tears. Goodness, he needed to stop talking or she would soon be a blubbering mess. She pressed her hands to her wet cheeks and tried to blink away the growing pressure behind her eyes.

"Give me a chance." Nathan took her hand, intertwining his fingers with hers. "Give me time. Let me court you properly, and write you letters when I'm away, and maybe win your heart."

"You still want me? Even after I ruined your chances of keeping the girls together?" This made no sense. Dare she trust it? "You don't need me anymore."

Nathan stepped close and looked at her with such intensity it stole her breath. "I think maybe I do," he murmured. He leaned down and brushed his mouth over hers, then paused, still touching. His palm warmed her cheek, and he leaned in and deepened the kiss—adding fervor to each caress and prodding her to reply until she could not help but do so. Agony mingled with bliss when he finally drew away enough to whisper, "I do."

Chapter 39

"Are you ready?"

Nathan squeezed his wife's hand and offered a nod, though he wasn't sure he was. Even after weeks of discussion, letters exchanged, and half a day on the train. Thankfully, Samantha didn't hesitate to knock on the door of the small house.

Only a moment passed before it was flung open. "You're here!" Will boomed.

Nathan allowed his brother to throw a hug around his shoulders and returned the embrace.

"Congratulations on the wedding. I wish we could have been there."

Guilt wormed its way into Nathan's gut. He hadn't even considered inviting any of his family until after the event. "Thanks." He glanced around the dimly lit room before focusing again on his brother. "Did you tell her?"

"I didn't. I thought I would leave that for you." His smile softened, and he beckoned them through the sitting room, down a hall and out into a backyard where they were met by children's laughter. "It's been far too warm in the house, so they spend most afternoons out here in the shade."

A pretty brunette rocked on a porch swing, infant in arms. The child wore nothing but a diaper, with a light linen blanket tucked around him. Several feet away Mary sat on the lush grass, flanked by two small girls as she fashioned dresses out of scraps of cloth for two dolls. She glanced up and froze, her eyes pinging between Nathan and Samantha.

"This is your Uncle Nathan and Aunt Samantha," Will announced to his children. The small girls popped up and ran to their father so he could scoop them up to finish the introductions. "And these angels are Ginger and Rachel." He stepped back to include his wife. "I don't believe you have met Laura yet. And the youngest is George."

Nathan allowed his wife to return pleasantries with his sister-in-law, while he returned his focus to Mary. She sat watching him, her expression reserved but for the slight widening of her eyes. She ran her bottom lip between her teeth. Nathan stepped to her and crouched low. "No hello?"

She shook her head. "Why. . . Why are you here?"

"To see you. To see how you enjoy living here."

Mary shrugged and looked back to the pale blue cloth she held. "It's all right."

"Would you prefer to stay here?"

Her gaze shot up. "Do I have a choice?"

He nodded.

Before Nathan could say anything more, she threw her arms around his neck. "You'll take me with you?"

He nodded again. "If that is what you want. We can't guarantee that Abby or Lucy will be able to join us, but we will do what we can. At least we can visit them. Would you like that?"

She nodded enthusiastically. "Yes, yes, yes."

"Then go pack your things." Samantha encouraged from behind him.

Laura stood to join them. "No need. I saw to that first thing this morning while she was watching the girls for me." The young woman smiled warmly, and Mary released Nathan to embrace her aunt. "We will miss you, Mary."

Mary glanced back at Nathan. "We can come and visit sometimes, can't we?"

"Of course," Samantha answered. "Of course."

The next two hours were spent sharing stories and plans. They ate an early dinner, and then Will arranged a wagon and gave them a ride back to the train station in the nearby town. They would spend the night in Calgary and then start their journey eastward in the morning.

<hr>

AUGUST 12TH

"You may speak with her if you like, not that she'll say anything in return." Both frustration and resignation tinged Beth Stanford's voice as she led the way into a small but comely parlor. "The other children have gone down to the swimming hole for the afternoon, but Abigail prefers to sit here and look at books."

Samantha's heart ached for the girl who sat alone with a picture book, a blanket draped over her legs despite the warmth of the day. Her pale face rose as they entered, revealing dark rings under her large eyes.

"I can't decide if it's worth sending her to school with the other children next month," Beth continued. "Brent doesn't have an opinion. He's working all day and leaves all of this to me."

Samantha would leave Nathan to discuss a change in arrangements with his brother and sister-in-law. Abby needed her. Samantha didn't bother with a chair, and instead lowered to the floor beside the child. Mary followed suit so they formed a tight circle. Tight enough for Mary to pull her sister into an embrace. Samantha allowed them their time but couldn't hold back from smoothing a hand across the child's ashen cheek just as a tear tumbled free.

"Oh, Abby," Samantha encircled both girls with her arms and pressed her forehead to theirs while they cried.

"It's okay, Abby, we won't leave you here," Mary whispered in her sister's ear. "We don't have to be apart anymore."

Samantha glanced at Nathan, and he nodded. He took Beth by the elbow and led her from the room. They would speak to Brent and make things right, make it so they could keep Mary's promise. Abby belonged with them.

———◆◆◆———

AUGUST 15TH

Home. Never mind that over a decade had passed since Nathan had last laid eyes on the family farm, or that trees had grown, buildings had received new coats of paint and repairs. It still seemed familiar in a way he hadn't expected.

Nathan drove the buggy down the long lane leading to the house he had grown up in. A second, much larger one, had been constructed nearby, probably for Charles and his family. Two men appeared to be working on a threshing machine, but neither was his brother. On the cusp of harvest, Charles was likely very busy. It appeared he had done a lot to grow farm operations and move the business into the new century. Good for him.

"Here we are," Nathan announced, though their arrival was obvious enough.

Samantha squeezed his hand and held on until he met her gaze. Her subtle smile infused him with much-needed confidence. With the girls following closely, Nathan started in the direction of the older house. His mother answered the door, though for a moment he hardly recognized her. Her once dark hair was now streaked with gray, and deep wrinkles fanned out from her eyes. She stared for a moment before a smile stretched across her face and she threw her arms around Nathan's neck.

"Oh, Nate, you're home!" She pulled back enough to plant a kiss on each of his cheeks. "Look at you! Charles told us all about you. A Mounted Policeman! We couldn't be prouder." She went on for another minute or two before she seemed to notice Samantha and the girls. He made the introductions, and she continued to gush, embracing each in turn. All Nathan could do was watch, feeling as though in a dream. What had happened to the busy woman he'd known, who was too distracted to notice her child's need?

He was unprepared for Charles's sudden appearance, like a storm rushing into the kitchen where they sat enjoying freshly baked bread and tea.

"It *is* you." Charles glared at Nathan.

Nathan stood and tugged his jacket straight. "You never replied to my letters."

"Because I have nothing to say to you."

"Charlie!" their mother's voice snapped, reminding Nathan of the woman who had raised him. "That is no way to welcome your brother."

"No, it's all right." Nathan pasted on a smile. "He's just not used to other people having an opinion that differs from his." He bit his tongue on any further comments. Aggravating his brother would not help anything.

"The girls were perfectly fine where they were. Just because you finally convinced someone to marry you, doesn't give you a right to them."

Nathan took a breath and checked his temper. "Why don't we step outside a minute." He didn't wait for Charles, but gave his wife a quick kiss on the lips and headed out the door. Charles followed just as expected. "I'm not here to steal Lucy," Nathan said as soon as they'd cleared earshot of those in the kitchen.

"You expect me to believe that after you've obviously pushed Will and Brent into giving up the other girls?"

Nathan faced his brother. "They gave Abby and Mary the choice. I only gave them the option. They need each other. They're sisters."

Charles laughed. "You're one to talk. You left home as soon as you were able and never looked back. You didn't care that your family—especially Mother—was worried sick not hearing from you for years at a time, not knowing if you were alive or dead. At least it was easier to track you after you joined the North-West Mounted Police. A nice letter to the superintendent and we were usually informed where you were posted."

Nathan swallowed hard. "You looked for me?" He'd been so certain they'd been unaffected by his absence.

"Yes." Charles shook his head. "Not that it ever mattered to you."

"It would have. If I'd known."

His brother did not appear convinced. "I don't know what your game is now, why you suddenly care about anyone else in this family, why you think you know what's best for those girls, but Lucy and the other girls are not playthings or pawns for you to prove something by. Peter would want them to have good homes."

"That's all I want for them too." Nathan took a breath, feeling his anger slip away. "And if Lucy is happy and thriving here, I won't say anything more about it. We will let the girls spend time with her and try to visit often enough that they can know her, and that is all."

Charles narrowed a look at him.

"And for the record, I didn't think it would matter."

"What?"

"Disappearing." Nathan swallowed hard but forced the words. "I didn't think anyone would be affected by my absence, that anyone would care." Instead of going back into the house, he started out across the yard toward the creek that ran through the property. He needed a few minutes by himself, a little time to rewrite his understanding of the past.

Chapter 40

~⌒

Samantha ran her hand across Nathan's shoulders, offering what comfort she could while he propped the worn Bible on his knee. *Died April 29ᵗʰ, 1903.* He wrote the words after Peter and Rosemary's names, and then after each of the boys' birth dates. Samantha's eyes watered, and she allowed the tears to roll down her cheeks as her husband closed the worn Bible. Its cover bore scars from that day.

Nathan stood from the bench someone had placed in the heart of the small cemetery and tucked the Bible into his satchel. It rested beside the notebook they continued to fill. Endless miracles, if one was only willing to see them.

Samantha moved into his arms. Looming shadows stretched across the valley as the sun slipped toward the mountain peaks to the west of the small cemetery. A cool breeze swept from the snow-crested peaks of Turtle Mountain and its confederates, but Samantha found warmth in her husband's embrace. He squeezed her shoulders and pressed a kiss to her hairline, before calling to the girls.

"It's time to go."

Mary repositioned the flowers they had brought for her mother's grave, leaning them against the granite headstone that had replaced the simple wood cross before taking Lucy's hand. She led the two-year-old toward the buggy waiting for them.

"Time to go," Samantha whispered. She drew away from Nathan to wrap an arm around Abby's shoulders. The child stood at the foot of her brothers' graves, eyes still glistening from the tears she had shed upon their arrival.

"Do you think they are happy in heaven together?" she whispered.

"I'm sure of it." A surety that had increased exponentially over the past year.

Abby managed a tremulous smile and leaned into Samantha's embrace before they continued to the buggy. Samantha lifted Lucy and set her on her lap. How grateful she was that Charles and Maddie had agreed to allow the baby to join her sisters—Samantha couldn't imagine their lives without the little angel. Samantha had been surprised how open Maddie had been to give over guardianship of the girl and had been the one to convince her husband. Maybe it had been how eagerly the toddler had responded to her sisters, or how passionately Mary had pleaded her case. The sisters were finally reunited and could spend their childhood together. Another miracle.

Nathan directed the horses toward Frank. They only had an hour or so before needing to be at the train station to catch the Spokane Flyer to Fort MacLeod. From there they would begin the next chapter of their lives as they accompanied Nathan to his new posting in Rowley, a small rural community in central Alberta—far from the mountains and any chance of landslides.

As the buggy rolled through Frank, Samantha took in what remained of the once-bustling town. Yes, some had returned to their homes and businesses, but the town and everyone who lived there were forever changed. As was she. The schoolhouse sat as it always had beside the church, seemingly untouched by the heaps of limestone acting as backdrop. Yet it was silent. No children playing in the yard. No bell's chime releasing them to their homes at the end of the day.

It was strange to think about what her life would still be like if the mountain had never crumbled into this valley. Everything would have stayed exactly the same as it had been a year ago. She would have never met Nathan and never dealt with the buried pain from her past. She would never have experienced the joy of motherhood or the wonder of new life growing within her. The babe inside shifted, and she couldn't help but smile. While she would never wish for the landslide and the terror it had brought, Samantha was grateful for the good that God had brought about from something so horrible.

Maybe that was the real story of miracles and more proof of God's hand in their lives. If not for the bad, how would they recognize or appreciate the good? Samantha reached out and took her husband's hand, holding tight. Whatever else came, she hoped they could always see God's intervention on their behalf, no matter how slight it might seem.

Samantha filled her lungs with the cool spring air and thanked God for that simple but wonderful miracle.

Historical Note

Around 4:10 a.m. on April 29ᵗʰ, 1903, approximately 110 million metric tons of limestone broke from the side of Turtle Mountain and crashed down into the Crowsnest Valley, burying ranches, camps, an active coal mine, and part of the town of Frank. What has come to be known as Frank Slide was the deadliest landslide in North American recorded history, claiming the lives of more than seventy people.

I first visited Frank Slide as a child, as it is located only an hour's drive from my home. All I remember from that experience was the heaps of rocks and boulders and the story of the mine horse named Charlie (who unfortunately did die shortly after his rescue, due to being overfed). When driving through the Crowsnest Pass as an adult, I began to appreciate the terror of that night and the horrible loss of life. Not until expanding my research while writing this story did the miracles of Frank shine through everything horrible that happened.

A couple of quick notes where history differed from the book: the Mounted Police did not arrive until the next day (the 30ᵗʰ), but I have them a little quicker on their feet so Nathan could participate with the rescue party seeking the trapped miners. Also, the first recorded use of the term "Mountie" was not for a few more years, so it might not have been in use at this time.

The most important thing to note when reading this book is that other than Samantha, every other character who survived the slide is based on a real person and their experience.

The three sisters (Rosemary, Abigail, and Lucy Stanford) are based on actual sisters: Rosemary, Jessie, and Marion Lietch and their miraculous survival—which includes baby Marion landing safely on hay when thrown from the house. Their parents and four brothers were killed, but the girls were saved and raised by different relatives. Unfortunately, they were not reunited for about forty years.

Here are some of the other stories of Frank and names you will now recognize:

Seventeen miners were trapped inside the mine, and they soon realized clearing the entrance would take too long. One of the men suggested they dig upward instead, following a line of coal to the surface. Coal was softer than limestone, and they were able to break through to fresh air before running out of oxygen—after thirteen hours of being trapped.

Lillian Clark was the lone survivor of her family because she spent her first night away from home at the boardinghouse she worked at.

Charles and Robert Chestnut had to spend an extra night at a hotel instead of moving into their cabin, which was destroyed by the slide. The three Welshmen who were staying at the cabin were killed.

A hundred and twenty-eight men of a railway work crew survived because they arrived in Frank one day late—after the camp they would have been staying at was buried with the foreman. They waited the night of the 28th in railway cars near Morrissey, BC, but the freight train that was supposed to transport them forgot to pick them up. They arrived late on the 30th, after the danger, but in time to help with the rescue efforts.

An engineer and two brakemen, including Sid Choquette, were up at the mine as the slide started. At the first sound of tumbling rock, the engineer hollered for his brakemen to leap aboard, and they literally raced the slide to safety. Sid and the other brakeman were able to cross over a mile of shot rock, while more rock fell. Sid arrived in time to flag down the Spokane Flyer before it hit the slide—and was rewarded twenty-five dollars for his heroism!

The entire Ennis family somehow survived despite their house being directly in the path of the slide. Their home was heaped upon by rocks, but despite injuries, all family members recovered, including fifteen-month-old Gladys who was thrown into mud and was assumed dead but was found and able to be revived.

Three-year-old Fernie Watkins was found lying in the rocks unharmed. Her family survived despite their house being destroyed. Her father was one of the miners who dug his way to safety. Her mother had rock fragments embedded in her skin that had to be removed by Dr. Malcolmson.

The Bansemer family's house was moved by the slide, pushed entirely from its foundation, with them inside it. The whole family survived.

Ned Morgan (I have no idea if he was married or not!) had been at

James Graham's ranch earlier the evening before but had felt uneasy about staying the night and returned to Frank for his horses.

Ellen Thornley had been staying with her brother at his shoe shop, but John convinced her that they should spend her last evening at the Frank Hotel, where they were safe from harm when the slide crushed the shoe shop.

Lester Johnson really did survive the destruction of his home, pinned under the floor, though he didn't remember how he came to be there. He was able to find an escape through the rocks and, despite injury, made it to help. His mother and stepfather, Nancy and Charles Ackroyd, were killed.

Having little personal information about the survivors, I did take some liberties with their personalities and backstories to enhance Samantha and Nathan's story, but the important part was that they survived. . .and that was a miracle.

To keep from freezing in the great white north, Angela K Couch cuddles under quilts with her laptop. Winning short story contests, being a semi-finalist in ACFW's Genesis Contest, and a finalist in the 2016 International Digital Awards also helped warm her up. As a passionate believer in Christ, her faith permeates the stories she tells. Her martial arts training, experience with horses, and appreciation for good romance sneak in as well. When not writing, she stays fit (and toasty warm) by chasing after five munchkins.

A Day to Remember

A series of exciting novels featuring historic North American disasters that changed landscapes and multiple lives. Whether by nature or by man, each of these disasters altered history and was a day to remember.

When the Flames Ravaged
By Rhonda Dragomir
July 6, 1944

World War II Gold Star widow Evelyn Halstead is taken in by her brother and soothed by the love of his wife and children. Evelyn refuses to cower in grief, so on a sweltering July day in 1944, the family attends the Ringling Brothers and Barnum & Bailey Circus in Hartford. When a blaze ignites the big top, Evelyn fears she will lose all that remains of her life, while Hank Webb, who hides from his murky past behind grease paint as Fraidy Freddie the clown, steps out of the shadows to help save lives and return hope to Evelyn.

Paperback / 978–1–63609–786–2

When Hope Sank
By Denise Weimer
April 27, 1865

The Civil War has taken everything from Lily Livingston, leaving her to work for her uncle at a squalid inn along the Arkansas riverfront that is overrun by spies and bushwhackers. Her only hope of escape is a marriage promise she is uncertain will be fulfilled. When on April 27, 1865, the steamboat Sultana, overloaded with soldiers, explodes and sinks, Lily does all she can to help the victims, including Lieutenant Cade Palmer. But what would the wounded surgeon think of her if he knew she could have prevented the disaster—and may have knowledge of another in the making?

Paperback / 978–1–63609–829–6